Susan was born in 1969 in South London. She has had a varied career, including packing pies, working for an insurance company and many years with the Royal Mail. She married and had two children. She divorced when her children were young, and for many years she was a single parent.

She decided she wanted to carve herself a new career so she studied for a BSc (Hons) in Social Science. She then completed her PGCE and became a teacher. She met and married Caroline, and a few years later they started fostering. They live in a small village in Kent. Susan discovered that her passion is writing and this is her first published novel.

Enjoy :)

(June 19)

Susan

Dedication

I would like to dedicate this book to Caroline who is not just my wife, but also my life.

Susan Ash

WHO AM I?

AUSTIN MACAULEY PUBLISHERS™

LONDON • CAMBRIDGE • NEW YORK • SHARJAH

A CIP catalogue record for this title is available from the British Library.

ISBN 9781788486200 (Paperback)
ISBN 9781788486217 (Hardback)
ISBN 9781788486224 (E-Book)

www.austinmacauley.com

First Published (2018)
Austin Macauley Publishers Ltd™
25 Canada Square
Canary Wharf
London
E14 5LQ

Acknowledgements

I would like to thank Caroline for putting up with me and helping me throughout the process of writing this book. I would also like to thank her twin, Lissie, for the late night phone calls, encouragement and comments.

Lastly, I would like to thank Chris who, at the time of writing this, was my Supporting Social Worker. He sat through hours and hours of my moaning. I wouldn't be the woman I am today without him. How do I know this? Well, he told me so!

Chapter 1

Some might think that it's a bit cold for a run, but I love it!

Out early, before it's busy, it sets me up for a day sitting in lectures. Today is a long day at Uni and it's also my nephew, Little Harry's, fifth birthday. We all call him Little Harry, as my dad is known as Big Harry. My sister, Jess, is having a party for him this evening, so it will be great catching up with everyone and actually seeing Little Harry on his birthday.

Running gives me time with my thoughts, which I don't get very often. I seem to be always reading, writing an essay or sitting in a lecture these days. But out here on the beach it's just me and my thoughts... oh... except for the odd few people around who are generally friendly and exchange a hello or a nod. The exception to this is the lady who runs with her Labrador. This dog always wants to say hello and nearly trips me up and the lady always gets really embarrassed.

So, let's think about today... home, shower and then bus into Uni. Dad's going to pick me up and we'll go to the party together... I must remember to take the card and the present with me. Ah... here comes Labrador Lady. She doesn't jump up at me this morning, she's already knocking someone else over, in a friendly way! Oh, I must remember to call my driving instructor to cancel tonight's lesson... which should be fine, as I've already pre-warned her that I might be cancelling.

What's the time now? 7.30a.m.... OK, if I get a move on, I'll have time to make my healthy-ish lunch before I go...

which is a good idea as I'm sure that there'll be lots of sausage rolls and crisps at the party this evening.

"Morning, lovely day again!"

Oh, I must remember that I need to take a blouse with me to change into tonight. On days like these, I always think it would be really nice if I had a dog who could run with me… it would have to be quite a big dog, I couldn't be doing with a little dog getting under my feet and tripping me up.

"Morning, how are you?"

"Good, yes I'm good thanks, you?"

Maybe a Doberman… It would definitely need to be a dog with short hair or it would get very dirty down here at the beach… and I couldn't be bathing it every day… Ah, nearly home already… the run seemed to go really quickly this time… seven thousand steps on my Fitbit though, that's not a bad start to the day!

"Morning!"

That's good, I managed to get everything done (I think) and I'm on the bus… good start to the morning!

Morning lectures went well, it's lunchtime already… I think I'll sit out in the sunshine to eat my lunch today. Cassie and Louise have already bagged a bench and they're calling me over. Cassie is telling Louise all about the holiday that she wants us to go on. She wants to go skiing. Louise is telling her that it's nearly summer and we should be planning a beach holiday and planning the winter holiday after that. After finishing my lunch, I excuse myself and call my sister. I know she will be stressing about tonight and the party.

"Hi Jess, it's Sam. How are you? Is everything sorted for tonight?"

"Ice? Really! I'm coming on the bus! Oh no, it's OK, Dad's picking me up, so it's fine. I'll ask him to stop at the shop and I'll grab you some."

"OK, alright. See you tonight!"

"Sorry ladies, I say rejoining the conversation, I needed to call Jess as I knew she would be stressing… so, are we skiing or swimming in the Med? I vote for both!"

Only five minutes till the next lecture… it's all getting a bit serious now. We've not got long left until the end of term. We're all hoping to be teachers! I've wanted to be a teacher for as long as I can remember. My dad's a teacher. Geography. He loves it! He's nearly sixty now, though, so he'll probably retire soon. I want to teach Art and Design, although lately I've had a few doubts about teaching and have been looking into Social Work. I know I definitely want to do something that I feel will make a difference. Still, I don't have to decide just now. My final exams are coming up very soon. Once I've sat them, I can choose my path, Teaching or Social Work.

Where's Dad? It's not like him to be late… he's the best dad in the world and he would do anything for Jess and me. I know it's been really hard for him since my mum died, fourteen years ago. I was only ten and Jess was fourteen. It was a really hard time for us all. It was Valentine's Day and we were in the car with Mum while Dad was at work. A lorry came out of nowhere and crashed into us. They said that my mum died instantly. Jess suffered two broken legs and to this day she still has a limp. We both had cuts and bruises but other than that, I guess we were quite lucky. The driver of the lorry had apparently suffered from a heart attack at the wheel. It was a very tragic accident and a day that Jess and I will never forget, and often re-live.

Poor Dad was left to look after Jess and me and although we were quite well-behaved, I realise now just how hard it was for him. I really appreciate all he did for us. It really couldn't have been easy for him at times. It was Dad that had to explain to us all about lady's issues and talk to us about the birds and bees, and many other subjects. He did all of this on his own. Both he and Mum were only children. He did brilliantly and never thought about any other options. We are his girls and he will take care of us. That's why he's my hero!

I remember a time, a year or so after Mum died, when I was in a singing show at school. Of course, my dad and Jess were in the audience, supporting me as always. It was coming up to my song, I just stood there and cried. All my friends had their mum and dad in the audience. Why wasn't my mum there? Why had she been taken? Why MY mum? My dad was suddenly beside me, hugging me and wiping away my tears, telling me that everything would be fine and that he knew I would sing amazingly and make him, Jess and my mum very proud. He put a necklace around my neck. It was my mum's.

"I can't have this! What if I lose it?" I remember looking down to the floor.

My dad held me tight and said that he knew my mum would want me to wear it and look after it the best I could. He said he knew I'd look after it and if by some accident I did happen to lose it, that it would not be the end of the world. I looked into his tearful eyes and promised that I would do my best to look after it. I said that I would always treasure it.

And to this day I've treasured it. It is gold with a beautiful heart-shaped locket that contains two tiny faded photos, one of Mum and Dad and the other of Jess and me. Before any big event, or if I'm scared or if I just need support, I find myself twiddling the necklace between my thumb and forefinger. I often remember that moment I shared with Dad. It just reminds me of how wonderful he is. Saying that he would have understood if I had lost it was just so typical of him. He never put pressure on me or Jess. He always did what was best for us.

I could hear a car tooting its horn. Ah, of course! It's Dad, come to pick me up. It snapped me out of my daydream. I stopped fiddling with my necklace and jumped into his car.

"Hi, Dad!"

"Hello Sam, really sorry I'm late. Jess asked me to pick up Little Harry's cake."

"It's OK, you're only a few minutes late. What's the cake?"

"Have a look… it's… is it the Hulk?"

Opening up the box, I laugh.

"No, it's Iron Man... and it's a pretty cool cake. I think he'll love it! You have done good, you are such a cool Grandad!"

Dad asked his normal question, "So, how was your day?"

"Yeah, not bad. I'm looking forward to seeing Jess and the boys tonight."

"And don't forget Matthew!" he says.

"Oh yes, him too!"

We all love Matthew. He adores Jess and the boys. They are the centre of his world. We could not have picked anyone better for Jess. Matthew and Jess have been married for nine years, which seems a long time as they're only 27. They were childhood sweethearts and are inseparable. They have Little Harry, who is five today, and John, who is seven. They're all very happy, which is lovely to see. I've not had time to have a relationship, really. I'm always studying, which everyone constantly reminds me of...

"Met anyone yet?"

"Ever going to get married?"

"Are you going to have kids?"

I just smile and say... "Maybe one day!"

These conversations always make me think about the start of that film, I can't remember its title... "You have no messages."

Who knows, maybe one day when I'm ready? Fate... I'm a big believer in Fate... when the time is right and all that.

"Sam, are you listening to me?"

"Sorry, what did you say?"

"Don't worry, we're at the shop now. What do you need?"

"I'll run in and grab the ice."

"We're nearly there now, Sam, and I'm really looking forward to seeing them all," he says, driving into their street.

"Oh look, there's little Harry… he's running down the driveway!"

"Can you manage the cake and your bag and I'll get the present out of the boot?" he says, pulling up on the driveway.

"Of course I can!"

Little Harry loved his party and his present; it was lovely catching up with everyone. I'm not sure that Dad was meant to be quite so competitive at Musical Statues. I don't think anyone has told him that he's nearly sixty… however, it was lovely watching him have so much fun with his grandsons. It's lucky for him that it's Friday and he can have a lay in tomorrow morning.

This weekend, I plan to lock myself away in my room and revise for my final exams next week. Then I can work out which direction I want my life to go in. My coursework is all handed in, so at least I don't have to worry about that… which is a huge weight off my mind!

"Are you going to get in the car?"

"Sorry Dad, miles away. Yes, let's go home."

As I got into the car, Dad said how proud of all of us he is, and that he knew Mum would be smiling down on us. As he said this, I went to touch my necklace for reassurance, but it had gone!

I don't believe it! The hardest week of my life, educationally, is about to start and I have lost my necklace! Not just any necklace, but my anchor, my comfort blanket… I feel lost! I'll have to re-trace my steps. When did I last have it? As I got into the car after Uni? If so, it must be in the car or at Jess's house, or… oh no… in the shop where I bought the ice?

I can't tell Dad, I need to check everywhere first. I'll have a shower and re-trace my steps in my head.

"Are you OK Sam? You've been very quiet since we got home."

"I'm fine. Just tired and I want to jump into the shower!"

OMG! What a relief!

As I took my top and bra off, my necklace fell to the floor. The catch must have come undone sometime during the day. I got out of the shower and made Dad and myself mugs of steaming hot chocolate. We cuddled up on the sofa and watched the news.

"Are you sure you're OK?"

"I am now!" I twiddled my necklace.

My plan is to finish my drink and go to bed. I want to go for a long run along the beach tomorrow morning, to clear the cobwebs so that I'm ready to settle down and revise.

7a.m.… did I really set my alarm on a Saturday morning? Yes, I did! So I jumped out of bed, eager and wide-eyed… OK, I'm lying… I stumbled out of bed, saying "Why did I do this?"

Off I set, down to the beach. There's a really nice breeze this morning.

"Morning… quieter today, isn't it!"

Always is on a Saturday, and even quieter on a Sunday… so maybe I should run tomorrow morning as well? Let's see how the revision goes today and whether I need a battery re-charge in the morning.

"Morning!"

I have exams on Monday, Wednesday and Friday, so at least they're nicely spread out.

"Hi, yes… very nice morning!"

If I can get the revision done for Monday and Wednesday's exams today, I'll be happy. It would be nice to revise for all three, but… uh oh… here comes Labrador Lady…

"Morning… oops she nearly got me again!"

"Sorry, she's a crazy dog… her name's Rosie!"

"Bye, Rosie… see you next time!"

If I get the revision done for the first two exams, then I'll still have Wednesday evening and Thursday to revise for the final exam. I'll be OK, I think, touching my necklace, just to make sure that all is well in the world… it is.

I walk into the kitchen, "Morning, how are you feeling this morning? A bit achy after all your party antics?"

"No, I'm fine, my princess. I'm planning to cook us a nice breakfast while you're in the shower, then I'll leave you in peace to get on with your studying."

"Thanks, Dad!"

I wonder where he's going on a Saturday morning… he never goes out this early on a Saturday… maybe he's just going out for my sake… or maybe he's meeting someone? Ooh… How would I feel about that? We always say that he should go on dates and meet someone special, but if he actually did, how would I feel? I want him to be happy… of course I do, however…

"Are you ever going to get out of that shower… breakfast is nearly ready!"

"OK, on my way!"

I think I'd like Dad to meet someone, just not this week… there's far too much going on this week already.

"Thanks Dad, that was delicious! Now, I need to get my head down and do some work. Where are you going? Anywhere exciting?"

"If putting Year 11's coursework onto display boards for the external examiners is exciting, then yes!"

Erm… no, not exactly. Now I feel bad for not wanting him to be meeting someone today.

"Sam!"

"Yes, Dad?"

"I said, I'll probably be out all day. Shall I bring a take-away in with me tonight?"

"Yes please!"

Before I knew it, I hear him pulling up on the driveway, so I look out of my window. He has what looks like a Chinese take-away. I can't stop yet, I think. However, when I look at the clock, I can't believe it…7p.m. already.

"Sam!"

"Hi,"

"Have you had a good day?"

"Yes" I can't believe how late it is and how much work I've done today!

"Want to watch some TV, Dad? I think I've earned a little break!"

"I was hoping you'd say that! Shall we watch a film?"

So, he dished up the Chinese food and we watched a film. Well, I say we watched a film… I'm not sure which one of us fell asleep first… the music of the closing credits woke me up. I woke him and we had a cup of hot chocolate and then went to bed.

Sunday, for me, was spent revising. Dad went over to Jess's for Sunday Roast.

Oh God… it's here! Monday morning and exam number one. I had a nice run along the beach, saw the normal crowd and even managed to avoid Rosie knocking me over.

I don't know what I would do without my dad. He dropped me off this morning because he knew how nervous I was. I think he was talking to me in the car, but I can't be certain of that. As I got out of the car, he wished me luck and told me how proud of me he is. I think the exam went very well.

Tuesday went by in a bit of a haze.

Wednesday's exam was difficult.

One exam left to go, however, I do have all day Thursday to revise for it. Run first thing… didn't see Rosie this morning. Hope everything is OK with her and her owner. I don't have time to think about that right now, though. I have one day left. One exam left… it feels exciting but scary.

I also have a driving lesson tomorrow night. I feel that I am now in a position to be able to book my driving test. My instructor has been saying that I have been ready for a few weeks now, but I wasn't ready for that extra pressure, especially during exam time.

Friday morning is finally here. Dad dropped me at Uni and gave me a big hug and told me to knock 'em dead! Oh God… what if the examiner IS dead? Oh no, no, no… he didn't mean that! I am so stressed I can't even make sense of his little joke.

"Sam!"

"Sorry, I was miles away, thanks, and see you tonight!"

OMG!!!! Exams all finished!! Uni finished!

Well, it's finished until I decide whether I want to be a teacher or a social worker, but I'm not deciding that tonight.

Tonight, I have a driving lesson and then I'm meeting up with Cassie, Louise and Christopher for a very well-earned drink. I wonder if Cassie and Louise have decided on a sun holiday or a snow holiday? And I wonder if they've roped Christopher in yet? All four of us have completed our course together. Three years ago, we all met at our Induction and we've been inseparable ever since.

Who is that banging on the door? I look out of my bedroom window and see the car with the big board on top, with a red L plate and NEW ROADS written on it. I look at the clock and I can't believe it. I must have dozed off, it's 7p.m. already. I run down the stairs.

"I'm so sorry, Nicole! It has been a really tough week!"

"It's OK," she says and smiles at me. I get into the car and I tell her all about my week, and she tells me about hers. As I'm driving along, she tells me the story of how she was nearly smashed into by a lorry yesterday. It was the lorry driver's fault, not the learner driver who was having a lesson with her at the time.

I think I must have turned a little pale. I was waiting at traffic lights. I could tell she was talking to me, so I let go of my necklace.

"Sorry, Nicole, what were you saying?" I looked at her, a bit dazed.

She said, "The lights have gone green and the car behind is tooting!"

She told me to pull over and then asked me what was wrong. I reminded her of the car crash where my mum had died and how hearing her tell that story took me straight back to that traumatic day.

"I am so sorry! I didn't think!" she said, putting her hand on my knee. The touch of her hand made me feel… well I don't know what it made me feel, I can't explain it.

"I'm a bit shaken" I tell her, "It's been a really tough week and then hearing you talk about that lorry…"

"Oh I'm so sorry." She slid her hand back off my knee. "I just didn't think about what I was saying to you. Jump out of the car and let me drive you back home. We won't count this as a lesson."

I think I told her it was OK, I think she was talking to me on the way home. My head was spinning.

"I'm sorry… I'm sorry!"

I know I'd said that a few times. I'm not really sure why, but I can't be sure what she was saying to me, so 'sorry' seemed to be an appropriate response at the time. I went indoors, burst into tears and told Dad what had happened. He hugged me and no words were needed. Later he asked me if I thought I should stay in tonight.

"No, I'll be OK in a minute!" I had earned this drink tonight and I was going to enjoy it. Plus, I need to know what decisions had been made regarding our holidays.

A great night was had by all. Cassie was a bit the worse for wear, or should I say a bit MORE worse for wear than Louise,

Christopher and me. In the end, we decided to flip a coin about the holiday, but as it turned out, none of us could flip a coin and then find it again. So, we decided that we would meet up again sometime during the week, when we were sober, to discuss it. Louise got herself a date with the man from the kebab shop, which I am sure she will cancel first thing in the morning. Christopher finally asked Cassie out and although she didn't actually say yes… she didn't actually say no either. They all tried setting me up with the barman. I was very drunk.

"I have to sort my life out," I told my friends. They all fell about laughing and asked me what I need to sort out.

"Oh, never mind… you're all drunk!" I said evasively.

I remember saying that a few times and to be honest, it got to the point that I didn't know what I was talking about, or what any of us were talking about. We all had another shot and then just one more… and then another. By the end of the night, Cassie agreed that, when they were both sober, she would go out on a date with Christopher. Louise was already regretting saying that she would go on a date with Mr Kebab. And me? Well, I was the most confused one of all. I found myself leaning against the lamp post, twiddling my necklace and thinking about how I had felt in the car earlier, when Nicole had touched my knee… why? I don't know.

Chapter 2

What's that noise? Oh… it's the phone!

"Dad, Dad, is that the phone?"

It's… it's… I can't find my watch. What's the time?

"Sam, it's 4a.m. It's not your mates messing around is it?"

"Of course not!" God, I hope not… it would not go down well if it is.

"Shall I get it?"

"No… you stay there, I'll get it."

"OK."

Please, please, please don't let it be my mates… I got home just after midnight AND I woke him up then. He is NOT going to be happy!

"Sam, Sam… can you hear me? Get up, get ready… quickly!"

Its 4a.m. What… 4a.m.! That is 4 o'clock in the morning! Are you kidding me?

"What is it, Dad?"

"It's John! He's been taken to hospital in an ambulance! Come on we have to…"

"Stop shouting… I'm here! I'm dressed! Let's go!"

Two minutes later, and both dressed, we jump into the car, I ask:

"What's happened to John?"

"I'm not sure. Let's get to the hospital and see what's going on!"

Oh God… I was so drunk such a short while ago, but now I feel stone cold sober.

"Can you drive faster?"

Please… please… let John be OK!

"What has happened… what do you know?"

"Not much, Sam, all I know is that John is in an ambulance on the way to hospital and he is in a lot of pain."

He is only seven, oh… please let him be OK. I can't imagine how we would all cope if something happened to him. Why do bad things always happen to good people?

"Sam, let's go!"

Oh… we are here already! We run into the A&E department and talk to the receptionist.

"My nephew, John, has been brought in by ambulance. Where is he? How is he? He's only seven. What's happening?"

I realise that I'm shouting at the poor woman behind the desk. I only notice this because of the way that she's staring back at me.

"Oh, I'm sorry, I'm so worried about my nephew, John. He was brought in by ambulance. Can you help me, please?" I say in a better tone and at normal volume.

At that point, a nurse walks up to Dad and me and asks us to follow him. We follow him through the double doors and there was my sister, standing in a corridor, in tears.

"Dad, Sam! Sorry it's the middle of the night. Sorry, I…"

"Stop!" I said. "What's happening? What's wrong? Where is John? How is he?"

"Sam, let Jess tell us what is happening!" said Dad.

"OK, sorry, Jess."

"Well, we've just been told that John has appendicitis… apparently it's hard to diagnose in children, but they have rushed him into theatre, because they said that if they don't move quickly it could rupture and cause... erm... peri... perit... peritonitis, I think it was."

"OK," I say, holding my sister's hand. She's clearly distressed, as anyone would expect a mother to be in this kind of situation.

"He had stomach pains." Matthew continued. "He said his belly button was hurting. The doctor didn't pick up on it straight away. We thought it was just too much party food. The doctor also said that children don't normally suffer from this before the age of ten... I ... we..."

"It's OK, Matthew, you weren't to know," Dad tried to reassure him.

We sat there for what felt like a lifetime. In fact, it was only just over an hour. Little Harry was asleep on a couch in the corner of the room.

I can't cope with this... we are all so helpless... there's just nothing that we can do... why is it taking so long? I'm supposed to be doing my Driving Theory Test today... I can easily cancel that... Oh, here comes a doctor! Please, please, please, let it be good news! Please let John be OK!

"The operation went well," the doctor was telling us.

Thank God for that! If he... Oh, that does not even bear thinking about.

"Sam! Sam, did you hear that?"

"Sorry, Jess, he said it went well, didn't he?"

"Yes, he did. You've gone very white. Sit down here for a minute"

"I'm OK," I hear myself saying as my legs give way under me. Luckily the chair is right behind me.

"I'm OK, how's John?"

"The doctor says it all went very well and that he's now in recovery, he'll then be taken down to the Children's ward. He said that parents can stay overnight, but we have Little Harry."

Dad tells her not to give it a second thought, we will take him home with us, so that Matthew and Jess can go and be with John. We all exchange hugs and I make Jess promise to give John a big hug from us and tell him that we love him.

"Of course I will!" She says. "And I will call you later on with an update."

I can hear her talking to Dad, but I realise that I'm just standing there, staring at Little Harry who is fast asleep. He's so perfect… both of my nephews are… I could not bear it if anything or anyone hurt them… unconditional love is such a powerful thing and you can never explain it until you feel it… and I'm definitely feeling it right now.

"Sam, you grab the bag and the car key and I will carry Harry!"

"OK, Dad."

We all say our goodbyes and we head off home.

My theory test is not until 4p.m, so maybe, if John is OK, I might be able to see him during visiting time and still sit my test. I have entered for my driving test and it's only a month away, so I really have to pass the theory test tomorrow.

"Are you alright, Sam?"

"I'm OK, let's just get home and get some sleep!"

I awake to the delicious smell of pancakes wafting up the stairs, Little Harry's favourite, smothered in chocolate spread… Oh no… John… how's John?

"Dad, Dad!"

"Morning! I have spoken to Jess and she said he is doing well! Come and have a pancake!"

Phew, what time is it…? Half past nine… wow! Mind you, I didn't get a lot of sleep last night, what with one thing and another! I think I will…but before I have time to formulate that idea there is a bang on my door. It flies open and in runs Little Harry.

"Wake up, Aunty Sam! Get up! We're having pancakes!" he shouts, as he jumps on me.

"Oh, good morning, little man!" I say.

"Auntie Sam, I'm not little, I'm five now!"

"Oh yes, so you are! Right, let's go and eat pancakes!"

We all eat our breakfast, get washed and dressed and head off to the hospital.

John is sore and sleepy. Sleepy is probably a good thing, as he didn't get much sleep last night, either and his little body now needs to recover. Matthew has gone home to shower and to get some clean clothes for himself and Jess, as well as a few bits and pieces for John. The doctor says that he will be kept in hospital for three or four days. We sit with Jess and John for a few hours and then Dad says that he will drop me off for my test… Oh my God! My theory test! It had completely slipped my mind! Have I practiced enough… Should I be practicing now? Have I got time?

"Sam," Jess is saying, "You forgot, didn't you!"

"No… no… well… yes."

"It's OK, though, you'll be fine!" Dad says, "And we are lucky enough to be having Little Harry again tonight, he wants to watch the Bee Movie and eat popcorn and he wants his Auntie Sam there too!"

"OK, let's go then!"

One question wrong… and I really should have got it right, but at least I've passed… and I can now sit my practical test. That is a scary thought! I've not run for a few days, I'm really missing that and I've mislaid my Fitbit, which is really annoying.

"Auntie Sam!" I look up and see Little Harry waving from the back of Dad's car. "I've been calling you, Auntie Sam!"

"Sorry Harry, I was in a world of my own!"

"Well…?" Dad says.

"I passed!"

"Oh good, because Harry and I have been shopping and we have got some goodies to eat while we are watching the film."

"And we've got hot dogs!" An excited little voice added.

"What are we waiting for? Let's get home and get our pyjamas on and have a fun evening."

I look at Dad and he smiles and tells me that John is doing really well.

"Great," I say and let go of my necklace.

"I am very proud of you," he says.

"Are you proud of me too?" Little Harry says,

"Of course I am. I told you… I think you've been a very brave boy… we've all been so worried about your brother, but he's getting better now and will be home in a few days.

Shall I ring Nicole and say that I have passed my Theory test? No, my next lesson is in two days' time and I will just tell her then.

Little Harry had a nice lay-in the morning after our video night. We all visited John at the hospital. Little Harry went home with Matthew afterwards and the nurse told us that John should be going home tomorrow, so all is going to plan… and hopefully I can run tomorrow morning. Dad and I both had an early night and I set my alarm for my run.

It's raining in the morning, but not too heavy, so I still go down to the beach to run my normal route. It's not cold and the gentle rain on my face is really quite nice.

"Morning!"

I will go to the hospital just after lunch and hopefully…

"Yes, I'm fine thanks! You? Good! Nice to see you!"

Hopefully John will be coming home today… I have my driving lesson today.

"Morning!"

I can tell Nicole that I passed my theory… still not seen Rosie. That's really unusual. I've not seen them for a few mornings now.

"Morning, yes the rain is definitely getting harder, I was just thinking that!" Just as well I am nearly home.

Dad and I go to the hospital to visit John. I can't believe how much better he looks.

"Jess, are you OK? The last few days have been really tough on you."

"I know, but I'm really looking forward to getting home and getting into my own bed!"

It's funny how we all like our own bed… and our own routines… I think I'm just going to have time for some dinner before my lesson… Nicole is late, which is not like her. It made me realise how much I was looking forward to tonight's lesson. Ah, here she is!

The lesson went very well, I was like an excited kid in a sweet shop, telling her how I passed my theory test. As I was about to get out of the car, Nicole leant over, just slightly and put her hand on my hand and said how pleased she was that I had passed. Why has she left her hand on my hand and why am I getting this feeling again? She broke the silence, saying, "Just a month to go!"

My heart sank a little… just four more lessons, probably. Why am I feeling like this and why is her hand still on mine? It feels like electricity is running between us. I blush a little. That evening I spent a long time thinking about that moment. How can a woman have that effect on me? Am I imagining it? Did she feel it too?

All is good in the world! John is home and well. Christopher and Cassie are getting on like a house on fire, and Louise did actually go out with Mr Kebab. But she won't be repeating the experience. I am meeting up with her later, she's going to come for a run with me. Dad is under lots of pressure as it is nearly exam time for his Year 11s and for some of the brighter Year 10s.

Louise and I are going to the running track. She has only run a few times, so doesn't want to go somewhere and not be able to get back. I told her she will be fine.

"How are you?" I ask.

"Good thanks! Mr Kebab was a mistake, but we had an OK night. How about you?"

"I'm good. We had a scare with John and he had to have emergency surgery to have his appendix taken out, so that was very worrying, but he is fine and back home again now."

"And you passed your theory test and you have your driving test very soon, I hear!"

"How do you know that? Oh Dad, I bet!"

"Yes, it's lovely, he is so proud of you!"

And did he tell you that Nicole put her hand on my knee and at the next lesson she touched my hand with hers and it felt... Well, it felt...

"Sam, what is wrong?"

"Sorry, what?"

"You seem very distant, Sam, not your normal self. What is it? Just everything happening all at once? Your exams, John, your theory test, your driving test coming up?"

My driving instructor turning me on... Oh God! Turning me on... it can't be that, I'm not gay... am I? No! I am twenty-four and I would know by now if I was gay... wouldn't I?

"Sam! Stop! Sit on this bench and talk to me!"

"I can't," I say, fiddling with my necklace. What can I say to her...? I might know now why I have not had a boyfriend. It's because I am gay... No, no... I can't be... I just don't know what this is. Why she makes me feel this way. How can she make me feel this way, I will have to cancel my lessons with her… find another instructor… but I like how she makes me feel… I…

"Sam, what is it?"

"Oh Louise, I'm just really tired. Like you say, it's been one thing after another, I feel like my feet have not touched the ground."

Yes, not touched the ground… she touched my knee though… held my hand for too long… why…? Why did she do that…? Does she know what she did? Did she do it on purpose…? Does she know how she is making me feel…? I didn't even know how she was making me feel until now… does she know? What happens now?

"Sam, shall we go and get something to eat and discuss holidays? We need to book one soon, or it won't happen and we'll all drift apart!"

"OK," I say, not thinking about holidays, but thinking about how her touch made me feel… this can't be happening to me! I am not gay!

Louise called Christopher, who was with Cassie, so we all met at Costa's. I had a lovely hot chocolate. We all decided that we wanted to go to a music festival and camp there for the weekend… camp! I've never camped, but Louise and Christopher do lots of camping and they both convinced Cassie and me that it would be a very good and cheap break; we all have very little money so we all agreed.

Dad was shattered, he had fallen asleep on the sofa. I'd been there an hour, watching television quietly beside him, when he suddenly jumped up and asked me why I had turned the TV channel over. He was convinced that I had only just come in!

"Have you eaten?"

"No, not yet. Have you?"

"You stay there, Dad. I'll cook. Is pasta OK with you?

"Dad… Dad!" Oh bless him, he's asleep again!

Oh no, don't leave me alone with my thoughts again. Her hand is sliding over towards my knee. Only when I imagine it… her hand does not stop at my knee… it slides up slowly… very slowly… and then…

"Sam! Do you need a hand?"

"No, thanks!"

Yes, I do! But not yours! Oh, stop it, I am not gay… what is happening to me? Why does she make me feel this way? Is she single? Is she gay? Does she know what she's doing to me? Oh God, it's the same questions going around and around in my head… and the same thoughts running through my mind. Oh God, the thoughts! Why am I feeling so aroused… what's happening to me?

We sat and ate dinner together and I told him of the plans we had all made to go camping. He was really pleased that we were going to do something fun after all our hard work. He was so pleased and happy that I thought for a moment that I would tell him all about Nicole. Tell him how I feel and how I don't understand it all… or not? No… I can't tell him! I'm really struggling with all this and I'm finding it very hard to sleep at night… How did it happen? Why did it happen? What does it all mean?

I'm going for a run in the morning, I need to clear my head. The day after that is Friday, another driving lesson… yes, definitely running in the morning. I'm still not sleeping very well, this is ridiculous! I've never, ever had trouble sleeping.

Running shoes on… I'm free… well, I say free, but my thoughts are still running round my head.

"Morning!"

Oh, stop and talk to me, then I might stop thinking for a while… where's Rosie when you need her? Yes, where is Rosie? They haven't been around for a while now.

"Morning! Yes, much nicer weather today, thankfully!"

By the time I get home, Dad has already left for work. He has left a note on the fridge.

Sam... I will be a bit late home tonight, please feel free to cook us a lovely dinner!

I will be home around 6 xxxx

I'm going to relax in a nice hot bubble bath, but the phone rings just before I am about to get in. It is Nicole... oh, what is she going to say? Don't cancel, please don't cancel! Wow, these thoughts really shock me!

"Sorry, yes I'm here!"

"Just letting you know that I will be 15 minutes late. Is that OK with you?"

"That's fine," I hear myself saying, as I let go of my necklace. "Thanks for ringing!"

She is saying bye, I think, as I put the phone down. My heart is racing... how am I going to get through this lesson? Should I cancel...? Right... bath... get into the bath and go from there! Yes, that's a good plan; that is what I'll do.

After my bath, I phone Jess.

"Are you OK, sis?" she asks.

No, I want to scream; no I'm not. Have you ever been turned on by a woman touching your knee and holding your hand? Have you tried everything to get her out of your head? Have you wondered how you will get through an hour in her presence without wanting her to touch you?

"Yes, I am fine. How is John?"

"He is doing really well. Do you want to come over tonight?"

Oh, I don't know... do I want to go over, after a whole hour's driving lesson with Nicole... how will I feel after? Maybe I should cancel?

"Erm, I am meant to be having a driving lesson. I could cancel, I guess?"

"No… you won't cancel! Your driving test is very soon. You need to concentrate and do exactly what your driving instructor tells you! She's the expert!"

Do what she tells me? If only you knew. Should I do everything that she tells me? Is this very wrong? Is this all in my head?

"Why don't you come over after your lesson tonight, then you can tell me all about it?"

"Erm… OK, but I better go and start cooking Dad's dinner. He will be home soon. I'll be over to you around 8ish, is that OK?"

"Yes, that is fine! It's the weekend, after all!"

Dad and I enjoyed a nice dinner of gammon risotto. He had some marking to do.

"Nicole has just pulled up!

Oh God, I think. I check my hair and spray some perfume… perfume? Why have I done that?

"Sam!"

"Coming!"

Why did I spray perfume? I get in the car and I can't look at her… can't look at her? What's that about? This is torture, I don't know what to do… I'm so nervous.

"Nice perfume! Chanel No. 5, isn't it?"

"Yes," I mumble.

"My favourite!" she says and smiles at me.

Oh, that's it now… I can't look at her!

Chapter 3

"How has your week been?"

"Like no other," I mumble.

"Pardon?"

"Oh, really strange," I say. "Very busy, lots going on. My nephew has been in hospital. He had to have his appendix out."

"Poor thing! How old is he?"

"He's only seven. The doctor said that it's really young to have appendicitis, but he is fine now."

Unlike me, I am anything but fine… I am dying inside… I want her to touch my knee again… hold my hand… do something, anything, so that I know this is real. Why does she make me feel this way…? What are you doing…? Does she even know what she's doing to me?

"Sam, let's drive to the old unused car park!"

"Why?"

"So we can practice your reverse parking. It's normally quite quiet there."

Do I say something… do I do something… do what? What am I thinking? Shall I say that I feel ill and I need to go home? Yes, I will say that I need to go home. That is the best idea.

"That's OK," she says.

Can she hear my thoughts? Does she know I want to go home? She can't! Can she?

"What? What's OK?" I ask.

"Oh, there's just one other learner driver here, so plenty of room for us. I want you to drive over to the back corner and reverse into that space. Only three lessons left now until your test. You need to perfect this."

Perfect... I can't think about perfect. I can't think about anything except...

"This space?"

"Yes, that's fine!"

OK, I really need to concentrate on my reversing. Stop the car, put the handbrake on... handbrake, that's what I need, put the brakes on. Just think about reversing the car... come on... I can do this! OK, I look in my mirror.

"Don't forget to look over your shoulder!" she is saying.

Oh yeah, so many things to remember!

As I look over my left shoulder, she is looking over her right shoulder, as if to show me what she meant. Our cheeks are close together, which means that our lips are close together. Should I just lean over a bit more and kiss her...? No, STOP, I tell myself. But I can't! I have that feeling again! We look into each other's eyes. The feeling is overwhelming! What should I do?

"You've stalled!"

"What?"

"You have stalled the car... put the handbrake on. Re-start the engine and then start again." She is saying in a calm voice.

Start again... Oh, I can't do this... I want to kiss her... no... I want her to kiss me... no, I don't... I'm not gay! Right, put the bloody handbrake on! Get a grip! I stall the car again. I try to put the car into neutral, but I'm getting really flustered. She puts her hand on mine to help me put it into neutral. I freeze.

"Sam, what's wrong? You're all over the place today, do you want to go home?"

"Yes… no… I don't know!"

Right, handbrake on. Start again. Please look over your shoulder when I do. I want to feel your breath on my cheek again. I want to feel much more than your breath…

"Oh God!" I mutter.

"Pardon?"

"Oh, oh… nothing."

As I put the car into reverse, we both look over our shoulders. I am staring straight into her blue eyes. She has amazing eyes. I freeze. I am scared. No, no… not scared… I am excited. I want to kiss her, but does she want to kiss me? As I am sitting there with all this running through my mind, I feel her soft lips touch mine… *Pull away, pull away*, my brain is screaming! Sod off, every other part of my body is saying. I'm thinking… no, I'm not thinking at all… this feels good. This feels so much better than good! I don't know what's happening… who am I right now? I don't know… I don't care! This feels amazing. I want more! I want her! She just bit my lip… I'm sure she did! Yes, there it is again! Not a nasty bite, just a little nibble and it's driving me crazy. I hear myself groan… that is a first for me! Oh yes please, Nicole… kiss me!

As I am thinking this, her tongue gently pushes into my mouth… Oh yes! I want this!

My tongue finds hers. Oh, it is electric… I could not fight this, even if I wanted to… she pulls her tongue out. Oh no… not yet… don't make it end yet… please! She nibbles my lip again and before I know it her tongue is back in my mouth. I don't want this kiss to ever end… She pulls away… NO, I scream in my head, don't stop! … I feel her hands on my face, stroking my cheeks.

"I really, really like your perfume!" she whispers.

"The other car…" I say.

"It went ages ago. Do you think you could please reverse this car into the space now… and then maybe you can kiss me again?"

Me, kiss her… did I kiss her? Did I? I don't care right now, I just know that I have to reverse into this space, then we can kiss again. I reverse the car perfectly this time and then turn towards her. She has a big smile on her face. She unclips her seatbelt and leans over towards me. She whispers,

"Can I kiss you, please?"

Before I could answer, her tongue was playing with mine and my seatbelt was sliding across my chest, closely followed by her hand. Her fingers were undoing my blouse. I guess the little groan I let out told her it was fine to carry on. Oh God… don't let this end! I have never felt like this… It is amazing! Oh, her hand is sliding into my bra… don't stop, please don't stop! My hands were gently pulling her hair as our tongues danced around together. Her hand was inside my bra. This is amazing… I want this! I can be gay… Oh she is doing something to my nipple. I think she is squeezing it… yes… yes… that is what she's doing. My brain just can't keep up. Her tongue, her fingers, oh I just don't know what to concentrate on. She pulls her mouth away from mine.

No, no don't stop! My brain is saying… until I feel her tongue on my nipple… oh, fuck… she's nibbling my nipple… oh, God… I'm not sure I can take much more of this.

"Are you OK?" she mumbles.

"Yes…" is all I can manage.

Then she kisses me again and her hand is in my bra once more. She gently bites my neck… that's it! I'm in heaven… who knew that I could feel like this?

She is doing my top back up and pulling away from me. Confused, I say,

"Have I done something wrong?"

"No, another car has just come into the car park. We should make a move."

She touches my hand and asks, "Was that OK? Are you OK?"

"Hi Sam. How was your driving lesson?"

"Erm… it was different!" I say to Jess an hour or so later.

Amazing… unbelievable, hot… electric and I want more… I want so much more.

"Good different, or bad different?"

"Good!" I say.

"Excellent, well, the boys are asleep and Matthew is out with his friends. Let me grab a bottle of wine from the fridge and you can tell me all about it. I haven't seen you smile like this in ages… it's really nice!"

Nice, oh no… nice does not cover it. And no, I won't be sharing what happened tonight with you… with anyone. I have to understand it myself first. What if it was a mistake, what if Nicole regrets it…? Oh God… what have I done? It was amazing though… I'm still… still… what? I don't know, but I want to do it all again… I have to… please don't regret it, Nicole! I really hope she enjoyed it… Oh, how will I face her again?

"So, tell me about your lesson?"

"No, I've got more exciting things to tell you first."

Of course, I haven't really, that is my secret. Mine and Nicole's… it needs to be my secret.

"I'm going to a music festival with Cassie, Christopher and Louise and we are going to camp for the weekend."

"You, camp, really?" she laughs.

I can think of other things I'd like to do more, if I'm honest.

"Yes… me camping, with my friends. What's so funny about that?"

"You have never camped before!"

37

"There's always a first time for everything!"

And I know that is true after what happened tonight… I definitely know that is true!

"How is John doing?" I ask.

"He's almost back to normal now. It's amazing how kids bounce back, isn't it? Are you sure you don't want to stay over tonight?"

"No, honestly, Dad is cool with picking me up at 11. It has been crazy the last week or two and I'm going to have a nice lie-in in the morning."

"Evening, Sam, have fun?"

"Hiya Dad, yes, we had a really good night, thanks for picking me up."

I'm sitting in the car playing with my necklace. Do I really have to wait a whole week before I can see her again? I don't know if I can manage that.

"Sam, are you getting out of the car?"

"Yes… do you fancy a hot chocolate?"

"Oh yes, why not, it's nearly the weekend… let's live a little!"

"You are such a devil, Dad!" I hear myself saying but, actually wondering who has been a devil tonight. Then I think, maybe it's him that I get it from. We have our hot chocolate, a quick chat and then go to bed.

I'm meeting Louise this morning. We are going to discuss our camping weekend and work out what I have to take. Or should I say… she is going to tell me what I need to take! I have never camped before, so I'm a complete novice, but she's a veteran camper! It's only four weeks until we go and just three weeks until my driving test. Just three weeks! If I pass I won't see Nicole again! Oh… I can't wait to see her on Friday, but I'm also terrified.

"Sam, Sam! I'm over here!" shouts Louise, as she rises out of her seat a little.

"Hi" I smile, "It's good to see you. How are things?"

"I'm really good thanks, it's been so nice to relax a bit now that Uni is over." She says with a huge smile on her face.

"Yes, it's really nice that the reading, essays and studying have stopped, yet my feet don't seem to have touched the ground much since we finished."

"Yes, I know exactly what you mean, but at least we can plan for the festival, it's only four weeks away. I can't wait!"

We have a good catch up and a nice hot chocolate. Am I drinking too much hot chocolate these days? I will have to run a bit further to burn off all these extra calories. We get lots sorted for our trip. I have a list of items to get, but apparently the most important thing is an air bed, so that I am not sleeping on the cold, hard ground. Also, I need layers of clothing… must wear layers, apparently! If you get cold when camping it can be hard to get warmed up again… and that won't be fun for anyone, or so I've been told. Have I really agreed to go camping? Am I mad? Actually though, I think it will be fun! I might even get up on stage and have a sing. I'd better go and do some shopping and tick off some of the items on my list. Wow, this camping shop is massive! Camping International. If I like this camping business, then I think I will be spending a few hours browsing around in here!

I'm looking forward to a nice run in the morning and then I promised Dad that I would do the shopping as he is so busy at school. I plan on doing lots more cooking; I really enjoy it, but I just haven't had enough time recently. I wonder if she's thinking about me, like I am thinking about her… oh, I do hope so. Will we kiss again on Friday? I really hope we do, in fact I hope we do more… is she single? I never thought about that before… what if she isn't? Oh it's not worth thinking about that… but I can't help it… what if she's married… what if she has a girlfriend… what if she kisses all her students and I mean nothing to her? So many thoughts running around my head as I let go of my necklace, so that I can turn the bath taps on. I am going to soak in a lovely hot bubble bath and think about how amazing it was to feel another woman's mouth on my lips, my neck and my nipples. I'm not so sure now about a hot bubble bath, maybe it should be a cold shower! Dad is out tonight, so I'm going to have pasta for dinner, watch a bit of television, and then have an early night.

Is that really my alarm clock? I'm going to make Dad's sandwiches, so that they are ready for him before I go out for my run. It's quite nice out here this morning… just me and my thoughts… Nicole? No, I really must start giving some thought to what I want to do next… do I want to be a teacher, or a Social Worker, or something completely different, like… I don't know… um… a driving instructor?

"Morning, I'm fine, thanks… you?"

No, not a driving instructor… think about something else, Sam!

"Hello, not seen you for a while… Oh really! Are you OK now though? Oh good!"

What do I need at the supermarket? I want to cook something nice for dinner tonight. We really must invite Jess and gang around soon, it's been ages since they came for dinner. Lasagna and garlic bread! That's what I'll make tonight. We both love that. I can't get my head around the fact that I like a woman… I mean really like a woman… when did that happen? Why have I never felt like this before? What do I do now?

"Morning!"

How did it happen, and why? I'm 24, and I have never really had a boyfriend, but I have never liked a woman… does this make me gay? I don't understand… why now? But I can't deny how she made me feel.

"Hiya, how are you?"

How she is STILL making me feel. I can feel the excitement running through my body, just thinking about her… does that make me gay, though? It's just her… just one woman… no other woman has had this effect on me.

"That was a lovely surprise, and a lovely dinner. Thanks Sam!"

"No problem, Dad."

I plan on making lots more nice dinners for us… he looked after me for long enough… loved me… would he still love me if he knew that I had kissed a woman… and wanted to do a lot more with that woman, I wonder?

"Sam!"

"Sorry, in a world of my own… what did you say?"

"I was just asking what your plans are for tomorrow."

"Do you know what, for the first time in as long as I can remember, I don't have plans so I'm not even going to set my alarm clock!"

"Good for you! Night."

"Night, sweet dreams!" I shout up the stairs after him.

I need to have a look at the camping list that Louise helped me to create. I've got most of it, but just need a few more bits and pieces. Where is it…? Ah ha… here it is! And all I need is a mug for coffee… a head torch which Louise says is essential for going to the toilet at night, and some matches to light the fire and the stove. It's strange, because although I feel a bit nervous, I am also very excited!

This seems to be a recurring theme in my life at the moment. I know it's early days, and I don't know how she feels… bloody hell, I can't even work out what I'm feeling, never mind her. But who can I talk to… Louise? Dad? Jess? Cassie and Christopher? Who can I talk to… do I want to talk? I don't know yet… I just don't know… I hope I can get some sleep tonight. I just go to bed early and try to predict how Friday will go. Will there be a repeat performance? Will she pretend it never happened, or will she want to kiss me again and let her tongue dance with mine?

It's Thursday night… that means that tomorrow is Friday, and that means I will see her. She will come to my house and pick me up… I will be amazed if I get any sleep. I'm going for a run in the morning. I wonder if I will see Rosie. I'm not sure if I can remember when I last saw them. I hope they are both OK. I must call my camping buddies and see how all the preparations are going.

So… my run was very nice. I met lots of people, some nodded, some spoke and others didn't acknowledge me at all. It's all fine, you soon learn who wants to talk.

Dad is at Jess's for dinner tonight. My mind is doing somersaults. Not long till she gets here now. I have time to get ready, have something to eat… just something small… not sure that I can actually eat at all… my stomach is full of butterflies. Once I'm ready, I spray on a little bit of Chanel No 5. I remember her saying that she really, really liked my perfume. I spray a little bit more on, just for luck. Should I chicken out and tell her that I am not well? No, I couldn't… even if I tried. I walk out of the front door and over to her car, looking at her to see if her facial expression will give anything away… our eyes meet, and…

Chapter 4

My mobile phone starts to ring… really? Now? Why? I look at it and it's my dad calling. I put it back into the pocket of my jeans, still ringing, and manage to slide into the driver's seat without looking at Nicole.

"Afternoon, Sam!"

My heart melts.

"You have been a naughty girl on two counts" she says gently.

"Have I?" I stutter, "Why?"

"Well, not only did you just ignore that phone call, but I do believe that you are wearing Chanel No 5 again, and you know what effect that has on me!"

I can't look at her. I think my face has turned into one huge smile. I can breathe again. I put my seatbelt on, and as I do this, she puts her hand on mine and says,

"Relax, it's all good!"

I look at her and she says,

"Hello."

Hello, and I melt… I get it now… It's from that film… "You had me at Hello." She has me at hello… I have so many questions for her. Where do I start… this is mad… What is she doing to me?

"Let's get going! You need to concentrate today, you only have two weeks left until your test."

What test? Oh, my driving test… but there's so much more you can teach me. So much more I want to learn from you.

"Nicole," I almost whisper, "I need to talk to you."

"And you can, after your driving lesson. Let's concentrate on that, then I have an hour spare before my next lesson. We can park up and you can ask me whatever you want to… deal?"

Bloody hell, now I have that TV show in my head… *Deal or No Deal*!

"Deal!" I say.

But how am I meant to get through the next hour… what questions should I ask… what do I need to know? Are there questions I shouldn't ask? Right, get through this lesson, Sam and we'll take it from there… first, I must lower my heart rate. How do I do that? I am glad she can't see how fast my heart is beating… glad she can't see what she is doing to me… how she is making me feel… or can she…? OK, pull yourself together… it's just an hour… but she's sitting next to me… I want to steal a kiss… touch her… feel her touching me… this is not helping my heart rate… concentrate… just drive, Sam!

"Sam, are you ready?"

Ready… are you joking? I am ready… but not to drive. I take a deep breath and force myself to say,

"Yes… Let's go!"

Somehow, I get through the next hour. I'm not sure I could say where I drove, or what manoeuvres I carried out, but apparently I did it and here we are in the car park of a country park. I don't know where exactly, but somehow we got here. I followed all her directions and here we are.

"You can turn the engine off now. What did you want to ask me?"

We both take our seatbelts off… my head is screaming… Kiss me! Don't talk, just kiss me…

But what actually comes out is,

"Are you married? Oh I'm so sorry… I don't know where that came from. It's just a question that keeps running around my head. I don't know what's happening here… I couldn't bear it if you were married!"

Oh shit, I just said that out loud… did I really say that out loud? I can't look at her.

"No, I'm not married, and what do you mean… 'What's happening here?'"

"I've never done anything like this before."

Oh God, why did I say that… she is going to think I am crazy now… kiss her before she can answer… do something, anything… open the car door… run! Hold on, I don't even know where I am, where would I run to? Anywhere!

"Haven't done what?" She is asking, "What do you mean? You haven't kissed a woman before, or you haven't kissed in a parked car?"

"Neither," I say and tears start to run down my face.

"Oh Sam, I am so sorry, I thought you wanted this as much as I do!"

I turn and look into her beautiful, concerned eyes.

"I do, more than I have ever wanted anything."

I lean in to kiss her, but she pulls back… Oh no… she doesn't want to kiss me…Oh God, I have really messed this all up.

"Nicole, I can't get you out of my head. I want you to kiss me. I want that more than anything."

Am I really being so forward and honest? What is happening to me?

She looked at me straight in the eyes, and said, "I'm sorry, I didn't know, you are… "

Oh no….what is she going to say… do I want to hear what she is going to say…? I am, what?

"Amazing, stunning, and I thought you were gay. I felt electricity between us and I assumed you felt the same way."

I did… I did… I do.

"I do… I really do, I have never felt this way before about anyone, man or woman, and now I'm getting it all wrong, I'm saying all the wrong things."

Oh God, I am making this so much worse… stop talking… Oh ground, open up and swallow me, please… hold on, what is she doing… she's kissing my tears… it's OK… I haven't scared her off… please say I haven't scared her off.

"Sam, I'm sorry."

She's saying sorry… why is she sorry? On no… is this goodbye? Does sorry actually mean no more kisses?

"Sorry? Why are you sorry?" I whisper.

She is still kissing my face though, that must be a good sign… it must be… or…

"I'm sorry, because I thought it was what you wanted." She whispers back to me.

It IS what I want, my heart is screaming. I hold her face and look into her eyes. I start to play with her hair, and then gently pull it.

"It's what I want more than anything in the world, now kiss me like you kissed me last week. I… "

I don't get a chance to finish that sentence, because her mouth is covering mine… I can't breathe… it's amazing… she is amazing. I hear her let out a little groan, oh God, this is making me horny. I am going to explode.

She pulls away.

"Was that OK?"

"OK, you had me at 'hello'" is all that I can say.

"Let's go for a walk," she says.

"OK," I replied, thinking that I'll do exactly what she tells me now… we stare into each other's eyes, I want to rip her clothes off... I want to explore her... I want her to explore me... but I don't know what to do... oh God... what do I do?

"Come on!" she's saying, already out of the car... I'm still in my seat, do I want to do this? Oh yes! I get out of the car, hand her the car keys and we walk off up a country path... I just follow her, my heart is beating so fast... I hope I don't pass out... can she hear my heartbeat? My heart feels like it's going to jump out of my chest... I hope she can't tell how nervous and excited I am.

"Sam, are you OK?" she says, looking at me, "We don't have to go for a walk."

I'm scared... I want to run... I could run... but I want her more than I want to run away from her... I need her.

"I'm fine!" I hear myself telling her.

Fine? Fine...? Fine is actually the last thing that I am... Where are we? ... Are there people around? I've not even noticed if there are people around... what if people see me? What if people see us? *Chill out*, I tell myself; I'm walking, just walking... but I want to do so much more...

"Are you sure you are OK? I thought we could talk. It's nice and quiet here... OK, let me start... I am single, and I really fancy you. I just assumed that you had had a gay relationship before. If you are not ready for that then I will understand."

Oh God... now it's my turn... what do I say...? *Don't fuck it up now!* My brain is shouting.

"OK, I have never had time for any relationships, really."

Oh... how lame does that make me sound, she's going to think I'm really sad now.

"The truth is, no-one has ever caught my attention like you have."

I am not sure where this is coming from, but these words are just pouring out of my mouth... so I just run with it.

"The way you make me feel has taken me completely by surprise, and I didn't understand it at first. I am beginning to get my head around it now... you make me feel..."

Stop now! You are talking too much... you are sounding really crazy again.

"I make you feel, what?"

I feel myself going very red... I don't know what to say...

"You make me feel alive... excited... like I can't wait to see you again!"

Before I have the chance to gauge what she is thinking about what I have just said, she pulls me through a gap in the fence and we are surrounded by trees. She pulls me closer to her, and whispers in my ear that that is exactly the way I make her feel too. Oh yes, that is exactly what I wanted her to say. I try to speak, but I find that I can't because she is gently biting my neck. She lets out a little moan.

"You have that perfume on again, and it has been driving me crazy!"

I hear a noise, and look around.

"Don't worry" she says, "there's no-one around, and it's very secluded here."

What am I doing...? Do I want this...? Fucking right, I do! I pull her hair gently back so that we are staring into each other's eyes.

"Kiss me!" I hear myself saying.

"Are you sure?" she says, but my tongue is in her mouth before she gets the last word out. We stand there, kissing softly. Her hands are on my waist... I think... oh, this is it... this is what I want... I hear her moan again... she's kissing me a bit harder now. Her tongue is exploring every inch of my mouth. My legs go weak, I am going to fall over! She feels this, and turns me around so that the tree is behind me. She pushes me up against the tree, while still kissing me passionately. One of her hands is slowly going up inside my top... oh yes, find my nipple… please find my nipple! Oh yes… that is my nipple… oh, that is definitely my nipple!

"I don't know what to do!"

"Just do what you want to, just touch me!"

Oh God, I must have said that out loud. She is biting my neck again… I pull back a little. I am not sure about that.

"I won't mark you, trust me" she whispers, "Just enjoy it!"

I relax a little. She is gently biting my neck and her fingers are playing with my nipples. My legs are going to give way. This is so nice… I run my hand through her hair, and she arches her back, offering me her neck. So I bite it gently… oh, she is moaning! I lose all control when she does that. Now she is running her hands down my sides, to the hem of my t-shirt, and before I know it, my t-shirt is off… and then my bra… oh God, I am in the middle of nowhere, half naked, and I absolutely love it! She runs her hands back up my sides, and along my arms, all the way down to my wrists and then she raises my arms gently above my head… she's kissing down my arms and along my shoulders… oh, back to my neck again… oh yes, she knows what I like… I am putty in her hands… I try to kiss her lips.

"No" she whispers, "I am busy!"

She nibbles down my chest and starts licking around my nipple. I push my chest out, so that she can reach more easily.

"Oh, you like that, do you?" she says, as she sucks my whole nipple into her mouth… I don't know how I am still standing… my hands travel down her body, and I lift her top up over her head. She stands up and kisses me.

"What are you doing to me?" I gasp.

"This is just the beginning, Sam! We are going to have so much fun, I can tell!"

My hands find their way to her breasts… I run my fingers around her nipples, they are very hard. My mouth follows the route that my fingers took, and my tongue circles her erect nipple.

"Oh Sam, that is so nice, but I have to go soon! I have another lesson booked."

"I don't think so!" I hear myself saying. My tongue is enjoying this far too much.

"Suck it!" she says, "Suck it hard!"

Oh God, this is so horny, I think, as I suck her nipple, and then nibble it gently.

"Is this OK?"

"Oh fuck, yeah, it's really OK!"

She cups my head in her hands and guides my mouth back to hers.

"I'm so sorry", she says between kisses, "But I really have to go."

"No," I moan.

"Sam, this is just the beginning of 'us' but for today we have to go. My next pupil will be waiting for me."

We both get dressed.

We stand face to face... hearts racing and smiling, and I say,

"One last kiss?"

"You are bad!" She says. "And I love it. I don't know how I'm going to concentrate for the rest of the day!"

She kisses me again, and we hold each other close for a couple of minutes before walking back to the car.

"Are you sure you haven't done this before?" she asks me, as we walk.

"Positive, but I want to do lots more with you!"

"Oh we will, don't you worry!"

We get back into the car, and the radio comes on as she starts the car engine.

"Do you want an extra lesson next week?"

I smile at her and ask her if she thinks that I need extra lessons.

"Driving lessons, I mean! You only have two weeks left before your test. If we were to have a Tuesday lesson, that will give you Tuesday and Friday next week, and Tuesday of the week after that. So just three lessons, and if you are a very good girl then you might get a really nice reward!"

"So, I have to wait four days before I see you again?" Will I be able to do that? As I get out of the car, 'How would you feel' by Ed Sheeran is playing – *ironically it's the line about sitting in a parked car.* We look at each other, and smile.

"I think that's going to be our song!" She chuckles.

Our song... I love Ed Sheeran... I think to myself, as I play with my necklace.

Chapter 5

I don't want to get up yet. I'm just going to lie here and enjoy the thoughts running through my head… I want her here beside me in my bed… Dad, this is Nicole… she drives me crazy and I really want her… oh, how do I tell anyone…? Who do I tell? No-one yet! I think… oh, I don't know what I think… for now, I'm just going to enjoy whatever it is that we have.

I am meeting Louise, Cassie and Christopher today. It is less than three weeks till our camping weekend now, I am strangely looking forward to it. I think it has been far too long since we all had a fun time… I wonder if I could sneak Nicole in…

I'm taking Little Harry and John to the cinema today to see the Lego Batman movie. I can't say I'm looking forward to the film, but I love spending time with the boys and I'm sure that they will love it. I have to meet Jess there at 12.30, so that gives me… an hour! God… an hour! Have I really laid in bed that long? Shower, here I come!

"Auntie Sam, you're here!"

"Hi boys! Harry, I can only just see you behind that huge popcorn box! Jess, I would have got their treats!"

"It's nice that you're spending time with the boys. I can buy them popcorn. Boys, be good for Auntie Sam, please!"

"They always are… go… go… go do some shopping on your own. I will text you when we are out."

"Bye Mum, come on Auntie Sam, let's go!"

Jess and I exchange smiles… Yay, Batman… here I come!

Sitting in Nando's with Jess, after the film, the boys are telling her how amazing the film was. I just look at her and shrug my shoulders. We both understand… No words needed!

"You OK, Sam? You don't look too clever."

"No, actually I don't feel very well. I feel like I'm getting a cold, or something. Dad's here now, anyway. If you don't mind I'm going to go home, dose myself up and go to bed. Bye boys! Great seeing you both, and be good for Mum!"

"We will, Auntie Sam, and thank you for taking us to the cinema!"

"That's OK, see you all soon, love you loads!"

We all say our goodbyes and I go out to the car park where I can see Dad sitting patiently in his car. I almost collapse into his car and he says,

"Hiya, I can't wait until you pass your driving test, and then you can start giving me lifts and picking me up!"

He turns to look at me,

"You OK?" he asks.

"I'm alright, just a bit of a cold, I think. Take me home, please, I think I need to go to bed and get over this bug."

I spend what feels like months in bed feeling sorry for myself, however, it's actually only two days. It's Monday afternoon and Dad has just got in from school. I'm snuggled up on the sofa wrapped in my quilt, watching a film… "You had me at hello…" I will always think of Nicole when I hear that line.

"Fancy some soup?" Dad shouts through from the kitchen.

"Yes, please!"

He makes us some piping hot tomato soup, and cuts us some nice thick slices of fresh bread to dip into the soup.

"Do you think you will be OK for your driving lesson, tomorrow?"

Of course I will, how could he even ask such a question?

"I will be fine, I am feeling so much better now, and my test is in eleven days, I need all the practice I can get."

"OK," he says, "but don't you go over-doing it!"

Oh, the irony…! I couldn't over-do it if I tried at the moment.

"I was going to go out tonight, but I think I'll stay in and look after you"

"Dad, there really is no need, honest. I feel much better, and I think an early night tonight and I will be as good as new in the morning."

I finally managed to persuade him to go out and have a good time with his friends, I watched another film… well, I say watched… I slept…

I was due to meet Louise for a run tomorrow morning, although to be honest, I don't think she'll mind too much that I'm not fit enough to go. She wants to go running. I have told her that I will have no problem starting at the beginning with her, following a starter's program, but she is embarrassed. I am sure in time she will get there. We all feel that way when we first start. I phone her to tell her that I can't make it, just to find out that she couldn't make it anyway. It seems that she has also had this cold bug, and is just getting over it too.

Only three lessons until my driving test! What if I pass and never see Nicole again… no, that won't happen … she feels the same as I do… she is single… I'm so pleased about that… just three lessons, I'm so excited! What if I pass? What if she wants to go somewhere where people might see me? See us, together!

Tuesday morning… I have to wait all day for my lesson… but at least I'm feeling much better… Probably shouldn't be kissing anyone… I wouldn't want to pass whatever I have had to Nicole… I think I'll go shopping and cook Dad a nice dinner… Toad in the Hole… we both love that.

When I get home, there are three messages on my answer phone. The 3-message symbol was flashing away at me from across the room. Do I want to listen to them? … What if it's Nicole saying that tonight's lesson is cancelled? Oh, I don't want to listen… it might be Dad or Jess, though…

Message 1: "Sam its Louise, I really need to speak to you. Can you call me?"

Message 2: "It's Cassie! Where are you Sam? Call me!"

Message 3: "Sam, its Louise… it's really urgent. Can you call me ASAP?"

What's happening, I wonder… I really must get a new mobile phone… I dropped mine in the bath a couple of weeks ago… it never recovered and I still haven't got around to replacing it… I picked the phone up to call Louise or Cassie… who should I call first? That decision was taken out of my hands, as the phone started to ring as I picked it up…

"Hello," I say.

"Sam, where have you been? Christopher has been in an accident! He's just going into theatre. It's his legs, Sam… they're both really badly broken… they are concerned that he might not walk again!"

"What," I say, as I collapse down onto the sofa behind me. "Slow down… what happened? When…? Is he OK?"

"Right, sorry… he is stable. We are not exactly sure what's happening. We are waiting to speak to a doctor. They are operating on his legs, and we are not sure about his back."

"What!" I say again, shocked.

Twice now I have said "What" – come on, Sam, think of something more intelligent to say!

"What happened?"

Louise tells me that Chris was crossing a road and they think that a car might have jumped a red light, hit him and threw him up into the air.

"They're really concerned, and he has been unconscious ever since."

"Oh God! Who is there? Shall I come? What hospital are you in?"

"To be honest, his parents and brother are here, and Cassie and me. I can't stay because of this bloody cold, and you won't be allowed in... but Cassie has promised to keep us informed. She said... oh hold on... she wants to talk to you..."

"Sam!" Cassie is sobbing... "It's awful!"

"Oh Cassie, I'm so sorry and I'm really sorry that I can't be there with you! My cold has nearly gone, so if I can, then I'll be with you tomorrow. I don't know what else to say. Please keep me updated with everything that is going on. I will sit by the phone."

"You have your driving lesson, don't you?"

"Don't worry about that!" I hear myself saying... my heart is sinking... but... Christopher... I have to make sure that he's OK... don't I?

"I am going no-where until you call me back!"

I sit by the phone for the next few hours, waiting for it to ring.

When it finally rings, I put my hand on it and freeze... what if it's bad news...? What if he has died or is paralyzed? I take a deep breath and pick it up.

"Hello!"

"Sam, it's Cassie," and she bursts into tears.

My heart is in my mouth

"What has happened? Is he... OK?"

"Yes," I catch, in between her sobs.

"He is going to be OK... his back is not broken, like they feared, but both his legs are, so he'll be in traction in hospital for a long time, but they are hopeful that he will make a full recovery in time."

"Oh Cassie, I'm so relieved! Have they found the bastard that did this?"

"No, not yet... Christopher is very groggy and not with-it at all, and they're saying that he'll sleep well tonight as he still has lots of drugs in his system."

"OK, and are you OK?"

"I'm really numb at the moment, Sam, to be honest. I need to get back in with him now."

"Give him my love, and I will come in to visit him tomorrow, if that's OK? Can you find out what the visiting hours are?"

"I will, and we can come up together, I will call you in the morning."

"OK, Cassie, love to everyone! Give Christopher a cuddle from me. You take care, and I'm here if you need me."

I put the phone down, and it rings again, straight away.

"Hi Sam! I am outside!"

Outside? Who is outside? Oh my God... it's Nicole! I meant to cancel, but I guess I might as well go now.

"Hi, sorry" I say, as I jump into the driver's seat. Oh, what have I sat on?

"Er, sorry, I think I just sat on something," I say, picking up what feels like a bag. "I hope I haven't squashed it, whatever it is."

"So do I!" She grins. "Look in the bag!"

I open the bag to see the sweetest teddy with "Be Mine!" on its t-shirt. A tear runs down my cheek.

"OK, that's not quite the reaction I was looking for, I am not sure what to say. What is wrong?"

I give her a big hug and say,

"That's the sweetest thing that anyone has ever done for me. I am so sorry... I'm feeling very emotional, my friend is in hospital. He got knocked over this morning… a hit and run, apparently."

"God, is he OK? I'm so sorry to hear that!"

"I just literally got a phone call, saying that he's out of surgery. He's got two broken legs, but thank you so much for the teddy, I love it! I have been really looking forward to seeing you… I've had a stinking cold and this is my first day of feeling better. I wish I could cuddle you right now!"

"Are you up for a lesson, or would you like to just go somewhere and talk?"

"Well, I'm not doing very well at talking right now, but somewhere quiet would be good."

"OK, would you like to come to my place? It's not far and we could just watch a film or something, if you like?"

"Sounds great!"

"What a lovely place you have, and so close to the beach! I often run along this part of the beach!"

"You run?"

"Yes, I love running." I say

"I don't believe it… I run too, but only on the treadmill. We will have to run together once you have passed your test."

"You are on!"

"Tea, coffee, hot chocolate? I have so much to learn about you?"

"Hot chocolate, please, every time." I laugh.

"Sit down, make yourself comfy. I won't be a minute. Oh actually, have a look through the DVDs and see what you fancy."

"Nicole, I don't think I'll be very good company tonight."

"Don't panic, we're just watching a film."

This is quite scary… what is she expecting… any other night, I know what I would want, but tonight I am just drained…I should have said no, but it's too late… here she is… holding two steaming hot chocolates…

"Picked a film?"

"Oh no! I forgot to look!"

"I've just remembered…I got this the other day." she says, holding up Bridget Jones's Baby.

"Oh yes!" I say, I've been meaning to get that myself."

She puts the film on, and sits on the sofa beside me. She holds my hand, smiles and kisses me.

"Want a cuddle?" she says.

Yes, I actually do… that would be lovely… just what the doctor ordered… I really appreciate her being supportive at this time, with all that is going on with Christopher.

"Yes please!" I say and kiss her back. We cuddle up on the sofa and watch the film.

It was really lovely… the cuddling… not the film… the film was funny… when the film ended she asked if I'd like another drink. I said that I'd better be getting back.

"OK," she says, standing up.

"Can I have a kiss first?" I say.

"Yes, you can," she says, pulling me to my feet and kissing me passionately.

"Right, let's get you home. I hope your friend is OK,"

"So do I, we're meant to be going camping in a few weeks' time. I don't suppose he will be doing that now."

"A kiss for the road?" she says.

"Oh, alright then, seeing as how I will have to go a whole 3 days before I see you again," I say. My brain is screaming… *Three days*… as I feel her tongue dancing around in my mouth… can I wait three days? I want more… so much more…

As we get into the car, she puts the radio on… it's really weird that she's driving me now… I feel like saying, "take the third exit on the roundabout… next left"

"It's our song again", she laughs. Ed is singing, 'How Would You Feel?'

Before I know it, we are outside my house.

"Thanks so much for tonight, I really enjoyed it."

"Me too," she says, gently squeezing my knee.

Is she not leaning in for a kiss because she knows it would completely stress me out… my dad could be looking out of the window… someone might see…

"Are you forgetting something?" She asks.

I look at her, worried.

"Your teddy!"

"Thanks, she is really lovely, and thanks again for tonight."

"You will have to work extra hard on Friday!"

"During my driving lesson, or afterwards?" I ask, cheekily.

"Both!" she grins. Her blue eyes are sparkling.

God, I want to kiss her again… but what if he saw me?

"Nicole, I… I …"

"I know… Get out of here! See you Friday and I hope your friend is OK."

Chapter 6

Thankfully, my cold is now completely gone, so I spend most of the day at the hospital with Cassie, visiting Christopher. Louise still has her cold, so she won't be visiting today. We do stay in touch with her though, keeping her up to date. Not that there is much to tell… Christopher is still a bit spaced out from all the drugs. We sit in his room, talking to him a bit when he's awake. He came around at one point and he started apologizing that he could not come camping with us now, and insisting that we still go and take someone else with us in his place. You know exactly what I am thinking… Nicole… could I get away with Nicole being my friend? Would she go…? Does she camp? Would she go…? Poor Christopher, he was really looking forward to it as well. We tell him not to give it any more thought, and to concentrate on getting better.

"I'm going to the shop, do either of you want anything? Christopher, would you like a magazine, for when you are feeling a bit more awake?"

"Not really, Sam. Oh, actually, a Sudoku book would be good, if they have one down there?"

"No worries, do you want anything, Cassie?"

"Yes please, could you get me a Dr Pepper, please?"

I wander down the corridor, feeling very sorry for Christopher, and very guilty about the fact that I feel excited that maybe Nicole will be able to take his place on the camping trip. Could that work…? I want it to work… or do I? Because then Louise and Cassie would see us together. Would they be able to tell that something is going on…? Could I keep my hands off her? Do I want to tell people…? No, not yet… it's all too soon… too new to me…

Right, what am I buying in here? Hot chocolate for me, a Dr Pepper for Cassie, and a Sudoku book for Christopher.

"Sam!"

"Hi Cassie, I thought you were waiting up in the ward?"

"He's asleep again, I thought we could sit down here and have a bit of a catch up"

"Cool," I hear myself say… however, my brain says, *Be careful what you say now…*

"So, how are things with you? I mean… before all this happened, were you and Christopher getting on OK?"

"Oh Sam, I can't believe how well it's going. I wonder why we didn't get together sooner. But this accident… it's a complete nightmare, but we'll get through it. All we need to do now is to get you and Louise hooked up!"

"Me and Louise?"

Me and Louise… does she know? Does she know I have… have what? Been having crazy feelings for a woman…

"Yes, not together, obviously! We need to find you both a nice man!"

"Cassie…" I say. Should I tell her? Am I ready to share my secret with her? No… I don't think so… I'm not ready to share with anyone else yet… not yet… I have just said her name, so I need to say something…

"Erm… I know the camping weekend is still three weeks away and we don't need to decide anything yet, but I was just thinking that I have a friend who may be able to come, if you want me to ask her? But I will understand if you don't want her to go."

"Are you kidding? Do you think Christopher would let us not go! Ask your friend, and Louise and I can share. I don't

62

think she'll mind. I'll give her a ring tonight and check. But do ask your friend, because if she can't go, then we will need a Plan C."

Oh… a whole weekend… I wonder what she'll say… I hope she says yes.

"I'll have to make a move soon, Cassie."

"That's OK, he'll probably sleep for a while now, anyway."

"Will you give him a hug from me when he wakes up, oh, and take this Sudoku with you, there's a pen with it, so that's all good. I have something to do in the morning, but I can come back here around 1p.m."

"Thanks, I will be here, and don't forget to ask your friend about camping."

"I won't, don't worry! See you tomorrow!"

Forget to ask… I don't think that will happen… I know that won't happen… I want to go and buy a teddy to give Nicole on Friday… I love the teddy that she bought me, I've named him Ed the Ted, after Ed Sheeran!

There are so many teddies in this shop… which one should I buy? I don't believe it… a lovely teddy wearing a t-shirt… the t-shirt says, "You had me at hello." That's the one! It has to be!

I'm cooking Toad in the Hole for dinner tonight, as I didn't get around to it yesterday. Dad comes in from work,

"You look very happy, how is Christopher?"

"Hi, I am good, cooking dinner for my favourite Dad! Christopher is tired, sore and in lots of pain, however, the doctors are saying that he should make a full recovery, so that is excellent news. But it's going to be a long road for him… poor guy!"

"Have they got any updates regarding the driver of the car that hit him, yet?"

"No, nothing yet, sadly. Dinner will be ready in about 20 mins, Dad."

How do I ask her…? I think I'll spray some perfume on the teddy on Friday, before I give it to her… just over a week until my test! I've not really had time to think about that, which is probably a good thing!

"Have you remembered that you are dropping me off at Jess's in the morning, Dad?"

"Yes, as long as you are ready by seven, that's fine. You know I can't be late for school!"

"Get a detention, would you?"

"I can't believe you still find that joke amusing!"

"That was a lovely dinner, thanks darling!"

"No worries… can you please do the washing up tonight? I want to make a playlist for Christopher… he's going to get so bored in hospital."

I sit for ages, creating a playlist for Christopher… it is really difficult… I find myself wondering what songs Nicole likes… Adele? … She must like Adele… and Whitney, of course. I'm not sure I could be with anyone who did not like them! Be with anyone… am I with her, then? Well, we have a song… that's a start… I think I have finished Christopher's playlist, it probably would have been a good idea to ask him what songs he likes… to be fair, though, he was asleep most of the time that I was there… I'll give him this iPod tomorrow and tell him that I can change the songs if he just writes me a new list. Dad knocks on my door,

"Night, don't be late in the morning!"

"I won't, I'm going to bed myself soon. Night, night."

Half an hour later I am in bed.

"Night, Ed," I say, as I give my new teddy a kiss on the cheek, and smiling at the memories that come flooding back whenever I see him.

"I'm up, Dad! Nearly ready! Would you like a cup of tea?"

"Yes, please!" he replies. We sit at the table and eat our breakfast together. I love the simple things in life that we do together.

"Good luck with Little Harry!" he says, "I'm sure he will be fine!"

"Thanks. See you tonight, don't forget to pick me up, please! 7p.m. at the hospital."

"Hi, Auntie Sam!"

"Hi boys! Hi Jess!"

"Morning, Sam. I have to leave as I have to get John to school. Harry has had his breakfast, but please make sure that he brushes his teeth before you leave for the dentist!"

Little Harry looks up at me and raises his eyebrows. I smile at him. I tell Jess to get a move on, and to get out of here, before they are both late. "Harry and I have got this! See you both after school!"

"Right, little man, what are we going to do?"

"Mario Cart on the Wii!"

"What, that again? Are you never going to bet bored of beating me?"

"No."

Just no...? OK, then... he always makes me smile... I love my nephews... I wish my mum had met them... she would have absolutely adored them!

"Come on, Auntie Sam!"

"OK, OK," I say, letting go of my necklace.

After about the 30th time of Harry beating me at Mario, it's time for him to brush his teeth, and for us to walk to the dentist. Luckily, it is just a 15min walk. Little Harry is not big on walking... he's used to being driven everywhere. He has this appointment at the dentist because he keeps saying that his teeth hurt. The dentist was pleased, though. She said,

"It just feels a bit uncomfortable, as new teeth are coming through. But his teeth are fine!"

Harry is happy. He says he's glad that he can still eat sweets.

"More Mario, Auntie Sam?"

"Sandwich for lunch, and then we play? Deal?"

"OK," he says, then the phone rings,

"Hi Sam, I will be there about 4 o'clock. Be ready and I will take you to the hospital. Did everything go OK at the dentist?"

"All OK, will tell you all about it when you get here! We will be ready!"

I did not stay very long at the hospital today as Christopher was very sore, and his older brother was there too. If I am not mistaken, Cassie was trying to set me up with him!

Christopher woke up and thanked me for his playlist. He asked if my driving test was tomorrow.

"God, no!" But it's only a week tomorrow… That is scary… really scary!

"I have to go, Christopher, Dad will be here soon. Take care of yourself, and see you soon!"

"Hi Sam, fancy a Chinese?"

No, I am sure she is English!

"What are you grinning about?"

"I was just thinking… in just 8 days I could be driving you, and yes, Chinese sounds lovely!"

Chapter 7

Today feels like it's just dragging because I want it to be 6 o'clock. I want her to be waiting outside. I must remember to spray her teddy with my perfume… Will she think that is silly… will it make her horny all through the lesson… I hope so… I like it when she's horny… when she lets out those little moans… Oh, there's the phone…

"Hello, it's Cassie!"

"Oh good, I'm glad he's a bit better today. No, I haven't seen my friend to ask her yet… I'll try and get hold of her later." I really will too… and kiss her…and…

"OK, I'm hoping to pop up there tomorrow. Can you let me know when would be a good time? I don't want to get in his family's way. OK, give him my love."

It is so good that he is going to be OK, he's a really nice guy… bless him!

This day really couldn't go any slower. I've done all the washing, including the bedding, the ironing and even made a curry for later. I'll leave a note on the fridge for Dad, telling him that I won't be in until about 11p.m., and to eat without me, if he wants to.

It's almost time… I've sprayed the teddy with my perfume…I hope she likes it… I feel a bit silly doing it, but also a bit excited… I can't wait to see her… this feels so right… and here she is…

"Hi, gorgeous!" I say, as I get into the car.

"Well hello yourself!"

"I've got you a little gift" I say, handing her the bag, and suddenly feeling a bit embarrassed that I am giving her exactly the same present that she gave me. Why didn't I think of something more original to get for her?

"Thanks, I'm going to put it in the glove compartment, until after your lesson. You really have to concentrate... just two more lessons before your test, but I must just say two things... One... I love the present already because it has your perfume on it, and two... Can I gently peel your clothes off after your lesson?"

"So, you tell me you want to take my clothes off, and also that I need to concentrate. You really need to think about what you are saying and rethink your teaching methods!"

"Well, I am only human, and I have a gift for you later on, as well."

"You are such a tease! Are you like this with all your female learner drivers?"

"No, not all, just the ones that throw themselves at me. Or, should I say, just the one... now concentrate, babe!"

"You've just called me "babe"!"

"Yes, I did, don't you like that?"

"I've never been called that before, but yes, I like it a lot, when you say it."

"Good! Now drive!"

Babe... she called me babe... that's hot... I like it a lot.

"So, tell me, Nicole, is it a coincidence that my hour is nearly up, and we are very near your house?"

"Oh, are we?" she replies, all innocence, "Shall we go in and then we can get your present?"

"Oh, OK!" I say, and smile.

"Do I get to see your bedroom on this visit?" I say, holding my breath.

"Why, someone is losing their shyness, aren't they? Is that what you want?"

"Sorry am I being too… er… "

"God, no! I've been wanting to get you into my bedroom since the day that I met you. I just didn't want to rush you, or put you off."

"Oh you have, have you?" Great news… what am I saying? I don't know what I'm saying…

"You couldn't put me off, you're a good teacher and I love learning!"

Sam, shut up now… stop talking…

"We can go as slow as you need to, there is no rush, babe."

Ah, there it is again… I love it when she says that…

"Right, we are at your house, so now open your present. It's only a little thing, so don't get too excited!"

"Oh, Sam! I love it! 'You had me at hello!' We need to watch that film together, one day. And the teddy smells of you. I will take it to bed with me every night, and think about you as I fall asleep. Let's get inside, and then you can have your present."

What is it? I must remember to ask her about camping… but if she says no, I will be mortified. If she says yes, will I be able to keep my hands off her, in front of everyone? When do I tell people? How do I tell people?

"Sam, come on!"

"Sorry," I say, letting go of my necklace and getting out of the car. I hand her the keys.

"Are you sure you are OK with this?"

"Let me think… YES!"

"I want to learn lots tonight."

Her face lights up.

She has bought me a mobile phone!

"It's too much!" I say.

"No its not, your old one died, didn't it? How else am I going to get dirty texts from you?" she laughs.

"Why are you laughing at me?"

"It's your face! You don't really have to send me dirty texts, if you don't want to!"

"But I do," I reply, perhaps too hastily.

I just don't know if I can… I have never done that before… where would I start…?

She cuddles me and says:

"Only ever do and say what you feel comfortable with. If I'm going too fast, or you don't like something, then you have to tell me. You… are… so horny, and get me so excited, I forget that this is your first relationship!"

Relationship? So this is a relationship, then… she obviously thinks so… I want to think…it is… I'm in a relationship. A big smile curls along my lips and I kiss her.

"It feels like I have been waiting forever to do that. Three days is too long."

"Far too long", she agrees. "Oh, listen to this… hold on, where's my phone? I have taken the liberty of putting my number on your phone, and have personalized that number so that when I ring, this ringtone will play. You can, of course, sort out what ring tone you want for other people, when they call you!"

Her own ringtone… I wonder what it is. How do I explain the different ring tone to… to Jess, she will know that it is different. Dad won't notice, but Jess will. I hear 'How would you feel' by Ed playing… our song… that is so lovely… but Jess will know.

"Nicole, that is so sweet, I don't know what to say!"

"Just kiss me again, then!"

"No problem, you don't need to ask twice for that, I love kissing you!"

"I'm very pleased about that because I love it too, and you have been driving me crazy with your perfume, it just turns me on so much. Right then… drinks, I have beer, cider, wine…"

"Are we allowed to drink in the bedroom?"

"You can do whatever you want in my bedroom, babe!"

"In that case I will have a cider, please!"

"While I get them, do you want to put a CD on?"

"Yes, which one?"

"You choose…"

Pressure… mind you, she will like what I pick as they are her CDs. No Ed? Mental note for a gift! Maybe she doesn't like him… well, I know one of his that she does like. Ah, she does like Whitney though… so Whitney it is. I am putting it on as she comes back into the room.

"No Ed, I see!"

"Actually, I bought it today, but it's in the car."

"Good choice, and, by the way, I love Whitney!"

I feel nervous… what should I say…

"I need to be home about 11," I say.

"Are you nervous, by any chance?" she says, smiling at me.

"Yes… no… yes… oh God, I do feel nervous, but very excited as well, I really want to do this, I really want you, I want to kiss you, touch you… it's all I can think about."

"Me too… Let's sit here and have our drinks, and talk a bit, there really is no rush, other than you have to be home by eleven!"

We both laugh, and sit on the sofa. She holds my hand, I gently kiss her.

"I want you, Nicole, show me your bedroom, please!"

She stands up, without saying a word, takes my hand and leads me to her bedroom. The curtains are drawn and there are lots of candles lit… when did she do this? Ah, when I was picking the CD… what a lovely thought. I don't feel scared now, I feel safe… she makes me feel safe.

"Are you sure?" she whispers in my ear. Between kisses.

More sure than I have ever been about anything.

"Yes, I am sure, if I ever feel uncomfortable, then I'll say, honestly, I will."

"Promise?"

"Yes, gorgeous, I promise."

I walk over to the bed, and she follows me. I turn and kiss her and before I have a chance to think, I realise that I'm slowly taking her top off and she is mirroring me, kissing me gently, nibbling my neck while she unclips my bra and dropping it to the floor. She cups my breast in her hand, and I let out a gasp.

"I want this! I want this so much."

"So do I," she whispers.

Her body looks amazing, feels amazing and I can't stop running my hands all over her, and my hands and lips explore her. All my fantasies, and so much more, since that first kiss in her car, seem to be coming true and are amplified a hundred times, no, actually a thousand times better than I could ever have imagined.

We fall back onto the bed, and carry on kissing and touching each other. Her hand is running gently down my body and I feel her undoing the button on my jeans. I hold my breath. I don't realise this until she tells me to breathe.

"I can't," I say, "you're amazing, you make me feel amazing!"

Her hand is now gliding into my knickers. Oh fuck, this feels so nice. Her fingers pass gently over my clit, barely touching it. Her fingers keep going, very gently. Are they going to go inside me? Yes, please… I hope so… please put them inside me. She then brings her hand back up to my breast. I am breathing now, and breathing very hard. I am kicking my jeans off at the same time as my fingers are undoing the button on hers. She groans. I hesitate,

"Oh don't stop, please don't stop!" she says.

I don't need telling twice. She is pushing her jeans off. We get under the duvet, both wearing just knickers. My hand caresses her silky skin, and eventually I can no longer resist and I slide it into her knickers, and my fingers find her clit. They are playing with it, gently flicking it. She rolls on top of me, her legs are pushing mine open. Her fingers are rubbing me on top of my knickers, rubbing my clit. Oh God, I am going to explode! Her legs push mine wider apart, her hand has pushed my knickers to one side so that her fingers are touching me… touching my clit… now they are inside me… fuck… this is good! She is good! Oh, what is this feeling? I love it, I want more of it… I want more of her… her fingers are back on my clit, circling and squeezing it gently and then rubbing it.

"Oh Nicole," I moan, "You are fucking amazing!"

"You are so horny! And I want to hear you come!"

Keep doing that, and I think I will… it is blowing my mind! It feels like time has stopped and I have no idea how long we spent exploring each other's bodies… this is heaven! Total heaven! I want to touch you… I am going to touch… her fingers are inside me again… my hand is touching her knickers… my fingers are inside her, she is touching my clit… she is rubbing my clit… my breathing is getting faster and faster.

"Oh Nicole," I moan, "I'm coming! I'm coming! "

I think I yelled quite loudly. It must have been several minutes before I could breathe again, following my very first amazing, mind-blowing, earth-shattering orgasm. I start rubbing her clit again, I am not sure when I stopped, but I did at some point. But I am squeezing it again now, just the way she did to mine. My fingers then push inside her… Oh, she is very wet now! I slide my fingers in and out, and then back along to her clit. It is not long before she is panting heavily. She is having an orgasm! Wow, she is having a fucking orgasm. I can't believe this… is this really happening… have I made her feel like this…? Did I really make her have an orgasm…? Her body collapses onto mine. We both roll onto our sides and hold each other.

"That was fucking amazing!" I say.

"I agree," she pants. "Are you sure you have never done this before, because it feels so right between us."

After what felt like a few minutes, but was actually a few hours, Nicole whispers,

"Are you OK, Sam?"

"Fuck, yeah!" is all that I can manage to say.

Much later, she told me that it was just after that short conversation that I fell asleep in her arms, and she held me tightly.

Chapter 8

"What time did you get home last night?"

"Morning, Dad. It wasn't too late. You didn't wait up, did you?"

"No, sorry, I didn't wait up – I was really tired."

"That's fine, I didn't expect you to. What are you up to today, have you got any plans?"

"No, I am having a relaxing day today, you?"

"I am going up to the hospital to see Christopher, then I might go shopping. A bit of retail therapy. I haven't bought any new clothes for as long as I can remember!"

"What is that noise? Sounds like a message coming though on a mobile."

"Oh yeah, you have just reminded me, I didn't tell you that I got a new mobile yesterday, Dad."

"At last!"

"Leave the number on the fridge, and I will put it into my phone. But who has the number already… who is that texting you?"

"It's probably the phone company, telling me how to top up, or something like that. Can you remember how to add new numbers on your phone, or do you want me to add it for you? I'm going to go and get ready now."

How do I manage to lie to him so easily and quickly? He hands me his phone and I add my new number to it in a couple of seconds.

I'm not going to get ready just yet... I need to check my phone...

- *Morning babe, last night was amazing! I didn't want to wake you, I wanted to sleep holding you all night. I hope you are OK this morning?*

- *Morning, thank you for last night. It was so gentle and natural and very, very hot.*

- *I'm working all day, but do you fancy dinner tonight?*

- *That sounds perfect! How about we order an Indian take-away and watch a nice chick flick? I have just the DVD. Also, I meant to say last night... you know that Christopher can't come camping the weekend after next, so do you want to take his place?*

- *What, share a tent with Cassie? Is she my type?*

- *No, share a tent with me!!*

- *I need to have a look at my diary to see what I can do, but I am loving the idea. Can we discuss it tonight? And do you want me to pick you up?*

- *Please, and thanks again for the phone. You have really spoiled me! I will text you later x x x*

- *I'm looking forward to it x o x*

I feel… erm… I don't know how I feel… it's all like a dream, really… is this really happening to me? Anyway, I'd better get ready and go to the hospital.

"Hi Louise!" I say, as I bump into her going into the hospital. "How are you now?"

"I'm good now, thanks. It took a while for that cold to go, but I am really pleased I can come in to visit Christopher, at last!"

We go into Christopher's room, but Cassie is not there! We all exchange hellos and I ask him where Cassie is.

"She won't be long," Christopher says. "She's taking her Nan shopping, and then will be in. I thought she would have been here by now, actually."

Just as he finishes his sentence, she walks into the room. She looks very tired, bless her, it's been a stressful time. We all sit and have a good catch up. I ask Christopher whether he liked any of the songs that I put on the iPod and he laughs! Some of the songs that I have downloaded onto it are a bit avant garde, but he is very grateful, none the less. He said he gets really bored at night. He has his iPad now, though, so that is good. He can Skype people and access music and games and the internet while the rest of the world is sleeping. The conversation moves on to our camping/festival weekend. Christopher tells us about the bands that will be playing, not that I've heard of most of them, but I'm sure we will have a good time regardless. They ask who my friend is that may be coming. I tell them all about Nicole, well… not ALL about her… obviously I leave out the bits about me being obsessed with her… me kissing her… her giving me my first orgasm… yes, I think it is best that I leave those parts out, and just tell them what they need to know.

"She is going to text me tonight, and let me know if she can make it."

I think saying 'text', rather than 'when I am there tonight' works better. Now my mind is there… it's remembering how I feel when she looks at me with her lovely blue eyes… kisses me… touches me… Oh, I need to stop thinking about this while I am sitting here with my friends.

"Talking about Nicole, when is your test? Not long now, is it? Christopher asks, snapping me out of my lovely memories of last night.

"No, not long enough," I reply, "In fact, it is just six days away and that makes me feel a bit scared."

"You will be fine!" They all try to reassure me.

"Just treat it like a normal lesson," Cassie says helpfully, although that's not very helpful to me… what my brain is saying… think about kissing the instructor… stop… stop… we start discussing the finer details, and how it's going to work. Luckily Cassie's family has two tents, and we can use them both. Another added bonus is that she knows how to put the tents up! I wouldn't have a clue! At the moment, Cassie is the only one of us who drives, and she is happy to drive us all there.

"If Nicole comes, she will probably drive too, as there will be four of us and all the equipment."

And… I will have her all to myself during the two-hour drive. God, I hope she can make it!

At that point, Christopher's brother and his friend walk into the room. Louise and I make our excuses a few minutes later, and leave. In the lift, I ask her if she wants to come running in the morning. I haven't been for what feels like forever.

"I can't tomorrow," she says, "I'm spending the day with my Nan and Grandad, sorry."

"No worries, maybe one day during the week, then?"

"Yes, let's make that happen! What are you up to now?"

"I'm going to do a bit of shopping, you?"

"I'm going to the cinema with my mum, just for a change. We hardly ever go out."

"Oh, that's really nice," I say, fiddling with my necklace.

I'm looking forward to my shopping trip… I want to get a couple of pairs of jeans, a new top… and I should probably get a nice warm jumper to wear in the evenings at the festival.

Wow, it's busy here. I guess Saturday is not the best day to go shopping. I send a text to Nicole, just saying,

- *Thinking about you x x x*

No reply, but she's working today, so may not be able to reply while her pupil is driving.

I have all the items I wanted to buy, and I also got Dad a new shirt. I like to treat him sometimes, he always appreciates it. Walking out of the shopping centre, I spot a lingerie shop. It can't hurt just to have a look, can it? I think to myself. As I walk into the shop, my phone beeps,

- *Thank you for my lovely text. I have been thinking about you too, all day, in fact. I can't wait to see you x o x*

- *Me too, I am just about to buy something for tonight x x x*

- *I am intrigued. What are you buying? x o x*

- *Well, if I told you that, it wouldn't be a surprise, would it? x x x*

- *Now, I am really intrigued! x o x*

- *I think you will like it!!!!! x x x*

Should I go for the black basque, or the lacy red two-piece set…? Erm… I don't know…

- *Can I have a clue?*

- *No gorgeous, just be patient, you will see tonight x x x*

- OK, I'll pick you up around 7 x o x

- OK, see you then x x x

- You certainly will, babe x o x

Oh, I hope so, I think, as I pay the lady shop assistant, who is probably wondering why I have a huge smile on my face… but then again, maybe she sees expressions like mine all day long in her shop!

"Have a good day!" I say, as I walk away… I'm going to… I can't wait… where shall I tell Dad I am going? He might see her car… Maybe I will say I am going for a drink with her… I don't like lying… but I'm not lying if I say I am with her… he might think it's a bit strange… but I can just say that we have become friends… he wouldn't think it was weird if she rings or texts then, either. Yes, I will say that, I think… it wouldn't matter if I mention her name then, either… and if she comes on the camping weekend… yes, I think I will just say that we are going out for a drink… I could say that Louise is coming too. No, don't over-complicate things, and start lying… I am going out with her, that is the truth… he does not need to know that she is all I think about… that I love kissing her… touching her… love her touching me… bringing me to orgasm… Oh God, Sam… just stick with the 'going for a drink'.

"Hi Dad!"

"How was shopping?" he says.

"Busy… I can't believe how busy it was there today."

"It's Saturday, it's always busy on a Saturday. Did you get everything you wanted?"

"Yes, thank you."

And more… I got some sexy underwear to wear for my girlfriend tonight… Oh… girlfriend…? Where did that come from?

"I got a little something for you too, actually"

"What have I told you about buying me things? Don't waste your money on me."

"It's not wasting money, and it's only a little thing. Here…" I say, handing him the bag.

"That's really nice, thanks." He says, holding up the shirt. "I can wear that tonight. I am going out with friends from work. It is Nathan's birthday."

Here is my chance… how do I say it… erm… I am going out for a drink tonight… that's all I have to say. I purposely walk into the kitchen, so that he can't see my face.

"Oh, that'll be nice, Dad. I am out tonight too. I am going for a drink with Nicole, you know, my driving instructor."

"Your driving instructor?" he says, as he joins me in the kitchen.

"Yes," I say, keeping my back to him.

"That will be nice."

Nice… you have no idea…

"Will you be late then, Sam?"

"Probably, you know what it's like when the girls get drinking and chatting… will you be late?"

"More than likely, we are going out for a meal and then out to the pub."

"You are such a party animal Dad!" I say, trying to deflect the conversation away from my plans for the evening… I guess at some point I will have to tell him… I don't want to tell anyone yet…

"You don't want to eat then," I say.

"No thanks, but you carry on, though!"

"Actually, I'm going to jump in the bath, because we'll probably grab something to eat when we are out too."

"What you mean is… you want to save room for the drink!"

I laugh… no… we are actually going to order an Indian take-away, but I can't really tell you that.

"Can I jump in the shower, before you get in the bath, Sam? I have to leave soon."

"Of course you can!" I say.

- *I have just told my dad that I am going out with you tonight x x x*

- *No, you haven't... really? x o x*

- *I have, he thinks we are just friends, but at least I have introduced the idea of you being in my life to him x x x*

- *Are we not friends? x o x*

- *Stop teasing me! I have to go and get ready now, I am meeting a very hot, sexy woman tonight! x x x*

- *Is that after you have seen me, then? x o x*

- *Not listening... can't wait to see you! x x x*

- *Me too, babe, see you soon x o x*

Chapter 9

Here she is… bang on time! I get into the car with a big coat over my arm.

"Hi," she says, giving my knee a little squeeze as I get into the car.

"Hi," I say, "I really want to kiss you, but I can't right here."

"Don't worry, you can give me an extra one when we get back to mine. What were you buying for tonight, then? That coat?"

"No," I say, laughing, "the coat is because my dad thinks that we are out drinking tonight!"

I throw it onto the back seat, "and as for what I bought for tonight… if you are a good girl, I will show you later."

"Oh, well… just for the record, I plan on being a very good girl tonight!"

"I'm very pleased to hear that," I say. "I think we should order dinner for about 9.30 and then we've got time to work up an appetite!"

"I like your thinking, Sam! And if that is what you want, babe, then that is what we shall do!"

I'm not quite sure where I am getting all this confidence from… but I like it… I like the new me… very much… easy to say when sitting here… but will I feel the same when we get back to her house? … Yes… I think so… I hope so.

"What time do you have to be home?" she asks.

"Don't be horrible or you won't get your surprise. You being very good didn't last very long, did it! Dad is out and I told him I would be late."

"I was thinking that next Friday night, after you pass your driving test… we could celebrate? We could go out?"

I think she saw the horror on my face, because she said, "Or, we could stay in and I could cook us a nice dinner. We could have a drink and you could stay over?"

"Stay over?" I love the sound of that but… what do I tell Dad? I could say that I was staying at Louise's, or Cassie's… or… or… what?

"You don't have to… it was just an idea!"

"I would love to, but…" What? Think, Sam! "I might not pass…"

"You will pass. You have had an excellent teacher, the best, some might say. Is that the only problem?"

"Yes, no, erm…"

"Your dad?"

"Yes, obviously I can stay out, but I don't like lying to him. But I am sure I can think of something, though," I say.

My mind is reeling, trying to think of what I can say to him… what would he believe…? I don't really stay out, ever… he would probably think it was weird… or would he? Nicole is staring at me… we are sitting at red traffic lights.

"You don't have to stay," she says, "It would be really nice, but you don't have to."

Oh… I want to… more than anything… a whole night… with her… in her bed…

"Nicole, I can think of nothing I want more than to spend the night with you, yes… yes please! I will think of something to tell Dad."

I don't know what… but I will think of something.

"That's really exciting, thank you… but what if I don't pass?"

"You will, I'm sure of it… and afterwards we will have an amazing night! And more good news, I have moved a couple of lessons, so the weekend after next, I am yours, all weekend!"

Oh God, how do I explain that…? That is amazing… scary, but amazing…!

"Fantastic," I say, fiddling with my necklace and smiling the broadest smile ever.

We arrive at Nicole's house. She has left some lamps on inside, so it is all cosy and welcoming when we go in. She quickly goes around lighting candles. It looks like a house from the outside, but she owns the top floor and someone else owns the ground floor. It is a very nice apartment, and she has decorated it all really tastefully. She has lived here for five years, she bought it when she was only twenty-two. I am finding out lots about her tonight. So that makes her twenty-seven… the same age as Jess… And there is just a three-year age gap between us… all good… she has no siblings… I can't imagine how that feels… I can't imagine being without Jess. We discuss which career I want to embark on… I think I have finally decided that I want to be a Social Worker… I have the application form for University at home… they run the course at the same Uni that I was at, so at least I will still be local… I hope Dad is OK with me not wanting to follow in his footsteps… I think he will be OK with it… he has always told Jess and me to follow our dreams and told us that he will support us with whatever we want to do … as long as we are happy, then he is happy!

"You seem like you are miles away, Sam, are you OK?"

"Yes, I am fine, better than fine, in fact… I am here with you!"

"Let's have a look through this menu then, I can put the order in. What time shall I say?"

"Erm, nine, or nine-thirty?"

"Let's go for nine-thirty," she says, grinning.

"Do your friends know that you are gay?" I ask.

"Yes, they do. My mum doesn't. But she doesn't live around here, so it's never really been an issue. She lives in Dubai, so obviously I could not be "out" over there anyway. I have often thought about telling her, but she has early on-set dementia, so it just would not be fair to tell her, as I would have to keep on telling her, day after day, and dealing with her shock day after day. Anyway, why all the questions… have you been thinking about telling people?"

"Yes."

But I am not ready yet… I want to tell Dad… and Jess… probably Jess first… and Louise and Cassie… but not yet…

"How do you think they'll react?" she asks.

"I think that they will be alright. Dad raised us to be proud of who we are and to be happy."

I really hope that he will be alright… I'm sure Jess will be OK with it, she has a gay friend, Lauren… it's different when it's in your family, though… I don't know… who knows…? I will cross that bridge when I get to it… but not yet…

"Have you decided what you want from the menu?" she asks.

"Yes" and I tell her what I want, then I cheekily ask, "Shall I go and warm the bed up while you are ordering?"

"That sounds like a perfect plan!" she says.

"OK, let me just get some money out."

"Sam, I am buying this… no arguments… go and warm up our bed!"

I wanted to get into bed first because then I can take all my clothes off except for the basque, and surprise her… I turn the lights off, but leave the candles flickering. It is very romantic… she is so very thoughtful, and within minutes she is in the room, my heart is racing as I watch her slowly undress. She is watching me watch her. It's very hot… she strips completely naked. Her body is perfect, such smooth lines and curves. I notice that she has a little scar just below her perfect breasts. As she climbs into bed beside me, I run my finger along her scar.

"What's that from?" I ask.

I regret asking that the second the words leave my mouth. She might be embarrassed about it, or shy, or...

"Oh, I had my gall bladder taken out... the scar is from the keyhole surgery three years ago."

"Oh sorry, I shouldn't have asked."

"It is fine, Sam, you can ask me anything!"

"Anything?"

"Yes, anything!" she says, and giggles.

"Are you going to make me have my second orgasm tonight?"

"Do you mean the second in two days?"

"No, I mean second!"

"Do you mean that yesterday's was your first ever?"

Now I feel embarrassed... I feel very conscious of the fact that I am under this duvet with her and she still has no idea that I have sexy underwear on... for her...

"Sam, I think there is a real danger here..."

Danger... what does she mean, danger? Have I said something wrong? Done something wrong? I don't understand!

"Danger?" I whisper. "I don't understand."

"Yes, a serious danger that I could fall for you!"

I don't see that as a danger... not for me... not at all... because I think I am already falling for her... what else can it be? She's in my head 24-7... I want to talk to her... touch her... look into those amazing blue eyes... gently pull her blonde hair back... so I can kiss her soft lips... I want to feel her touching me... have I fallen for her? Is it too soon? Oh, I know nothing about this... is she just saying that... does she mean it?

She pulls me in close to her, and as she does, she feels what I am wearing. She turns away.

Doesn't she like it? Have I done the wrong thing? She turns her bedside light on… turns back and gently throws the duvet off…

"Oh my God!" she says. "What are you trying to do to me? There's only so much a girl can take, you know! This is what you were buying when you texted me! I'm glad you kept it as a surprise… I would never have gotten through the day if I had known!"

"You like it, then?"

"Like it? Like it? Are you joking? I fucking love it, babe! I don't know where to start!"

"Kiss me!" I offer, as a suggestion.

And before I know what's happening, she is sitting astride me, and she's just staring at me.

"You are beautiful, Sam! Your personality, your body, and then you add this! I feel under-dressed now!"

"I love what you are wearing… your birthday suit works for me, Nicole! Now, kiss me!" I say, pulling her beautiful body down on top of me.

Her hands are everywhere. Gently, she is caressing every part of my body. I can't help but let out a little groan. I run my hands down her back,

"Scratch me!" she whispers in my ear. Then she nibbles my ear.

"I like that!" I tell her, as I very softly scratch her back.

"Oh, and I love that," she pants.

She sits up, still astride me, and asks what I am doing to her, whilst looking into my eyes… into my soul. I smile as I run my hands up her legs. I stop at the top of her inner thighs.

"Don't stop!" she pleads. "Touch me Sam, like you did last night!"

My hands carry on up her body,

"You tease!" she groans, smiling at me.

I cup her firm breasts; her nipples are very erect. I pull her down on me, so my tongue can dance around one nipple, while my fingers play with the other one. I roll over, pushing her onto her back, so I am now on top of her... I start undoing my Basque.

"Oh no, please don't take it off yet!"

I look at her.

"Please!" she says, "Not yet!"

But she undoes the top ribbon, so that she can see my breasts.

"You are perfect!" she says. "I love your body, especially these beautiful breasts! Can I please suck your nipples?"

Oh, yes please! I think... please do something before I explode... make me come again... she is staring at me... why is she staring at me? Oh, she is waiting for an answer...

"Yes, please! Suck them... touch them like you did yesterday!"

She didn't need telling twice... she was on top of me again... *How did she do that?* My brain is asking. I don't care... my body is saying... go with it... enjoy it... she is running her hand up the inside of my thigh while still sucking my nipple. Yes... touch my clit! Fuck me with your fingers! Make me cum! Did she make me cum? Three times... each time more powerful than the last! I don't want this to ever end, I think, as my fingers slide inside her. It is very warm... she is very hot... I love the way she feels... I tell her that I love how wet she is...

"How wet you have made me, I think you mean!"

Me... how wet I have made her... wow...

"Nicole, do you know how horny you are?"

"How horny we are together, you mean. You are amazing, Sam!" she smiles as she starts to rub my clit again.

Oh God, surely not... surely I can't cum again... oh yes I can! And I do... Once my breathing has steadied again, my hand goes from her breast, down her tummy and finds her clit again... I need to hear her cum again, I love hearing that! Later, we collapse into each other's arms and just lie there, cuddling.

"Nicole, what are you doing to me?"

"Nothing that you are not doing to me!"

The doorbell rings.

"Who is that?" I ask, in a panicked voice.

"The delivery driver, I guess." smiles Nicole.

I look at the clock. Two hours have passed since we got into bed together! I can't believe it!

"Two hours, have we really been in here for two hours?"

"Two hours of heaven!" she replies, hurriedly putting her dressing gown on.

I start getting up,

"No," she says, "let's be naughty and eat in here!"

She comes back into the room with the food, some plates and two forks.

"Oh hold on!" she says, rushing back to the kitchen. She grabs two ciders. We sit on the bed, feeding each other pieces of poppadum, and eating delicious curry.

I can't believe how complete I am feeling... how alive... and how tired! Wow, I feel really tired.

"Penny for them?" she says.

"I think I am falling for you," I reply. "I am sorry, but..."

"Why are you sorry?" she says. "I feel exactly the same way!"

She takes the dishes out to the kitchen and then climbs back into bed with me.

"Here is your drink," she says, handing me my bottle.

I think I only have one or two mouthfuls before putting it down.

"Can we have a cuddle?" I say.

She wraps her arms around me... don't fall asleep, I tell myself... I need to go home... I don't want to... I want to stay here forever...

"Shall I get a cab?" I say.

"No, I'll take you. Let's just lie here for a while, and then I'll take you home."

I look into her big blue eyes, smile, and snuggle up into her.

Chapter 10

What's that noise, oh, it's a text! What time is it… 10 o'clock! God, I never sleep that late… she is up and texting early, I think, with a big smile on my face… Oh no… it's not Nicole… it's Cassie,

- *Morning, is your friend coming camping?*

- *Yes, sorry I forgot to text you. Yes, she can come, and is happy to drive.*

- *Excellent! I might as well take the tents and chairs and other things with me, as it will be just the two of us in my car now.*

- *OK, I'm really looking forward to it. In two weeks' time we will be there.*

- *I know, and the bacon will be cooking!*

- *You cook bacon?*

- *Oh yes, bacon and fried egg rolls are a must for breakfast when you are camping!*

- We will have to get together to make a shopping list during the week, and then all put some money in to a kitty.

- Good plan!

- Have a good day, talk soon x

- You too Cassie, x

I hope I have done the right thing asking Nicole… I will have to be really careful not to show my feelings for her in front of the others… that won't be easy… mind you, given the choice of that, or her not coming, I know which I would choose… and we will be all alone in our tent both nights!

- Morning, gorgeous! Are you still feeling as horny as I am? x x x

- Morning, babe, more so, I think! Last night was something else! I haven't stopped smiling yet and I can't wait till next Friday. You can fall asleep in my arms. Will you wear your Basque again, please? x o x

- Oh, so you liked that, did you? x x x

- Couldn't you tell? x o x

- Well, I kind of got the feeling you liked it! x x x

- What are you up to today? x o x

- Dad and I are going to Jess's for Sunday lunch, if I can ever get out of bed x x x

- You're still in bed!!!!! Don't tell me things like that x o x

"Sam, are you awake? Was it a heavy night last night? I have a bit of a sore head myself!"

"Morning, Dad, no, it wasn't heavy at all, just late."

Not much drinking… but lots of other things! Lots and lots of other things…

"Fancy some eggy bread?"

"Yes, please, I'm getting up now"

- I wish you were still in my bed, I can still smell your perfume, and my sheets smell of you x o x

- I wish I was still in your bed, too. Dad is making me eggy bread, I have to get up x x x

- What is eggy bread? x o x

- You have never had eggy bread? Get eggs and bread, and I will cook you some on Saturday morning x x x

- That's if I let you get out of bed! x o x

- Don't say things like that, when I have to get up! x x x

- Have a good day, baby, talk later x o x

- You too, missing you already x x x

- Me too x o x

"Did you have a good night, Dad?"

"Yes, it was a really good night, thanks! I drank too much, though!"

"Dad, I've got something to tell you…"

How do I tell him…? How will he react…? I'm just going to have to tell him… there is no easy way.

"I've decided to go down the Social Work route."

"OK, well I'm glad you've finally decided."

"You don't mind?"

"Of course I don't! As long as you are happy, that is all I want for both my girls."

"I have the forms, so I will fill them in tonight."

"Another year for you at University, studying."

"Two years, actually. So you are stuck with me, I'm afraid!"

"Sam, you know this is your home for as long as you want it to be. I'm lucky that I have no mortgage left now, so money isn't an issue. And, most importantly, I love having you here, you know that!"

"I know, thank you for everything, I do love you!" I say, giving him a big hug. "Now where's my eggy bread!" We both laugh.

We had a lovely time at Jess's, apart from her asking me to babysit next Friday night. I had to tell her that my driving test is next Friday and Louise and I plan to go out to either celebrate or commiserate, and have lots to drink. In fact, I told her that I am staying at Louise's, I hated lying to her.

"News to me!" Dad said.

"Oh, I thought I'd told you… sorry Dad!"

"It's fine," he said. "It's about time you started letting your hair down, and yes, Jess, of course I will babysit for you next Friday"

"You are the best dad in the world!" we both tell him.

I also told her about my plans to apply for the Social Work course. She was very happy for me, I couldn't stop thinking about what Dad said… 'It's time to let my hair down'… If only he knew! I also gave Jess my new phone number,

"About time!" she said.

She and Dad grinned at each other. If I hear another 'about time'…!

On the way home, I asked Dad if we could decorate my room. He seemed delighted with the idea.

"Why didn't you say earlier, we could have gone to B&Q and picked out what you want? Shall we do that tomorrow night?"

"Yeah, that would be nice, Dad. Listen, I'm having an early night tonight, I'll think I'll just snuggle down in my room and watch a DVD, or something."

"Yes, I think we could both do with an early night tonight."

- *How has your day been today, sexy? I am so tired, I am in bed already! x x x*

- *In bed… it's only 8 o'clock! And stop telling me you are in bed! x o x*

- *My girlfriend tired me out last night x x x*

- *Oh, I'm your girlfriend now, am I? x o x*

- *Yes, you are, and I told my dad that I am staying at Louise's on Friday night x x x*

- *Excellent… it will be really nice, not having to watch the clock x o x*

- *Yes, I can't wait….night night gorgeous x x x*

- *Night night babe, sleep well x o x*

I didn't see the last text until the next morning, as I had fallen asleep as soon as my head hit the pillow.

- *Morning, I am going out for a run x x x*

It feels like forever since I have run along this beach.

"Morning!"

It's a nice day… well it's dry, a little cold, but you don't notice that when you are running…

"Morning! No, you are right, I haven't run for a little while."

Same people walking their dogs, apart from Rosie and her owner… I wonder if they have moved house… I miss seeing them…

"Hi, how are you… yes I'm good!"

I hope they are both OK… one driving lesson, and then test day… well, really I have two lessons, as I have a lesson for the hour before my test on Friday… Friday! Test! Then a whole night with Nicole…! That will feel strange, I have never woken up with someone else… in someone else's bed… running is hard work, this morning… I need to get back into running more often… I miss it, and as they say… 'Use it or lose it!' I'm going to go up to the hospital at lunchtime to see Christopher… Cassie can't make it today, she did tell me why, but I can't remember now… I clearly wasn't paying enough attention…

"Morning!"

I hope their relationship works out for them, they both seem so happy… B&Q tonight with Dad… it will be nice to freshen up my bedroom… we haven't decorated for so long… I wonder if she will ever see inside my bedroom?

- *Morning babe, I hope you enjoyed your run? I'm working all day today, so I will text you tonight x o x*

It's taking much longer than I thought it would to fill out this application form. I need to get it finished so that I can drop it off on the way to the hospital, as it is near enough next door.

I have a sandwich for lunch and start to think about what colour I would like to paint my bedroom. I might go for red… or yellow… or blue… perhaps… I think I'll decide later when I get to the shop.

Christopher seems a bit down today, which is understandable. I tell him that I have put my application in to become a Social Worker. He was surprised, he thought that I would apply for teaching. He, Cassie and Louise have all applied to enrol on a PGCE course. I think that they will be brilliant teachers.

- Missing you, babe x o x

- That's sweet, thank you. I was just thinking about you too, x x x

Christopher looks at me enquiringly.

"It's my sister," I lie… and lie so easily…

"Do you want me to get you anything from the shop before I go?" I ask Christopher.

"No, I'm OK thanks, and thanks for coming up again," he says, "I do appreciate it, it's really boring in here when no-one is visiting."

"Do you want me to stay a bit longer?"

"No, it's fine thanks, my mum should be here soon."

His mum is getting out of the lift, as I get in… we say quick hellos… I warn her that he's a bit down today.

"Thanks," she says, "It's lovely that you all keep visiting him. I know it is helping him a lot."

- On my way home, Sam, so be ready and we can go straight out to B&Q. Dad x

- OK x

It cracks Jess and me up that Dad still signs every text… he just does not get it that the text appears with the name of the person who sent it already on the screen... bless him... but at least he's texting now, I guess... he's slowly crawling into the twenty first century. We get red and magnolia paint for my room. I am going to have two walls of each colour, and I also convince him that he should paint his room. He picks out a nice blue... well actually two nice blues. I think they will look very good together.

"Shall we get fish & chips on the way home?" he suggests.

"Yes, please!"

We sit and watch *EastEnders* with dinner. It was very depressing, we don't watch it very often, so we don't really know the story lines. I do the ironing... Dad does the ironing sometimes... he is very domesticated really... but as I'm not at Uni just now, I like to do as much as I can... he works really hard, and often brings marking home with him to do in the evenings. Teaching is definitely not a 9-3 career, like a lot of people seem to think!

- I hope you had a good night, and I am looking forward to my lesson tomorrow x x x

When I wake up, I see that Nicole has not texted back. I make Dad's packed lunch, and head off for a run... I wonder why she hasn't texted back?

"Morning!" I might start the prep work for the decorating today... I can take down all my pictures and start filling holes. Dad bought some Polyfilla in the shop last night.

- Morning babe, sorry, I thought I had lost my phone, but I just found it in my car. I am looking forward to seeing you today x o x

- Oh good, I'm glad you found it, that would have been ironic if you had lost it after buying ME a phone, so that I can text you x x x

- I didn't get you a phone just so that you can text me. x o x

- I know, I'm sorry, I am just teasing you. See you at 6. Don't work too hard. x x x

- I'll try not to… I'll save all my energy for you x o x

I finish prepping my room… We forgot to buy masking tape for when we paint. I am going to pop to the shop and buy some, and then I am going to cook something nice for dinner… Shepherd's Pie, I think, Dad will love that.

"Dad, I have my driving lesson soon. I have made Shepherd's Pie, do you want it now, or when I get in?"

"I will wait for you, thanks Sam. You are not going to be late, are you?"

"Errrmmmmm."

Chapter 11

"Hello, sexy!" I say, as I get into her car.

"Careful, someone might hear you," she teases.

"How is my favourite student today?"

"All the better for seeing you, of course. I'm a bit stressed though. I don't know if I've told you, or not, but I've got my driving test on Friday."

"Oh really," she laughs, "As I am your driving instructor, you should really have shared this information with me. Now start the car please, madam, and show me what you can do!"

"Very demanding, aren't you!"

"On a serious note, Sam, is there anything that you want to practice… anything that you feel less confident with?"

I turn and look at her,

"With your driving, Sam… focus!"

"Could you focus if I told you that I was wearing my Basque?"

"What! Are you?"

"No, but I was just asking. I was wondering how well you could focus. Now, teacher, where would you like me to drive?"

"Go to the end of the road, and then turn left, you bad girl."

The lesson goes very well, and I actually feel very confident about my test, although I'd never say that to anyone.

"Are you coming in for a while tonight, babe?"

"I'm sorry, I can't tonight," I look down, sadly, "Dad is waiting for me so that we can eat together, and we are then decorating. So, you're going to have to wait until Friday."

"Three whole days!" she moans.

"I know, but you will enjoy it, enjoy me, all the more after your wait."

"Are you kidding… I always enjoy you!"

"I can't even kiss you!"

"Focus!" I tell her, laughing, as I get out of the car.

She catches hold of my hand, and I look deep into her eyes.

"How is your friend… the one in hospital?" she asks.

"Bored and getting very fed up of being in there, but other than that, he's fine… the doctors say that his legs are improving… the bones are beginning to heal."

Looking around nervously, making sure that there was no-one around, I lean into the car and give her a quick kiss on the lips.

"Thanks, babe! See you at 2 on Friday and try not to worry."

I smile and shut the door… she slides over into the driver's seat, and waves goodbye… try not to worry… how can I not worry… I guess I do have Friday night to look forward to… that could help take my mind off my test… Oh God… my test! Just three days to go! Three days…

"Hi Sam! Did your instructor say that you are doing OK?"

"Hiya Dad, what do you mean…?"

She says I am doing amazingly well… and… Oh… you mean driving, don't you!

"She said that I should have no problems with my driving test. The only issue will be dealing with my nerves on the day, though."

"You will be…"

"Please don't say 'fine', Dad. Everyone keeps saying that I will be fine. If I hear that once more…!"

"OK, OK, I won't say 'fine', but you will be!" he says, putting our dinner out on the table and patting my shoulder.

"The shepherd's pie looks really good," he says, "I've cooked some cabbage to go with it to compliment all your hard work"

"Nice! Let's dig in! I thought I would start painting tonight, would you like to help?"

"Why not, and then when we have done your room, then you can help me with mine," he says… here comes Noel Edmunds… "Deal!"

We spend the evening decorating my room. We get the two magnolia walls painted after sanding down all the blobs of filler.

Next morning, I get up early and go for a run, after texting Nicole. I enjoyed being out this morning… still no sign of Rosie and her mum, I think they must have moved out of the area.

I get back to work with the decorating. I start in Dad's room… we thought it would make sense to do the prep work there, so we can then rub it all down once we have finished painting in my room. My mobile rings… Ed is singing to me… it's Nicole!

"Hello you!" I say, picking the phone up.

"Hi babe, just wanted to hear your voice. How are you?"

"I'm good thanks… just doing some decorating."

"Ooh, is there no end to your talents?"

"Well, what can I say…? I've put my Social Worker application form into Uni."

"Oh that's good… oh, sorry, here comes my next pupil, got to go, have a good day!"

"You too, talk soon!"

That was nice… wasn't expecting that… I can't understand why she makes me feel this way… but I love it… Ed's latest top ten single comes on the radio. I'm singing along before I know it…shall I make lunch? … No, I'm going to phone Jess, first.

"Hi Jess, how's things?"

"Hi Sam, we're all good thanks… how's you?"

"I'm really good," I say. "I've been really busy. I feel like I've neglected you and the boys a bit, I don't see you half as much as I would like to. I was wondering if you'd fancy coming to the cinema on Saturday afternoon? We could take the boys to see 'SING'."

"That would be really nice, but we are out at lunchtime on Saturday. Could we make it early evening, instead?"

"Yes, that's fine… I'm at Louise's on Friday night, so that will give me the whole day to get over that," I laugh.

What I actually mean is… I won't have to rush away from Nicole's… on Saturday.

"Cool, have fun on Friday night, and I will see you on Saturday! Oh Sam… how is Christopher?"

"He is doing OK thanks. And, guess what? Dad and I are decorating our bedrooms!"

"Wow, how did you talk him into that?"

Laughing, I say, "He was actually OK with it. I am going to go and make my lunch now; shall I ask Dad if he wants to come with us on Saturday? We could do dinner after the film as well."

"Yes, good idea, let me know what he says, and then I can book the tickets."

"OK, take care and give the boys a kiss from me!"

"Always do… see you Saturday!"

I have lunch and then give Cassie a call. Christopher is getting better, she says, he doesn't stop moaning, bless him! He must be so bored... I'm glad he and Cassie seem to be getting on so well.

I look out of the window and hope that now that it is nearly June that the weather might start getting better... I hope we have dry weather for our weekend away... I know we will have fun anyway... it would just be much nicer watching the bands play if it is dry... but maybe I need to invest in a pair of wellies... maybe Jess has a pair I can borrow...? I will probably never use them again... so would grudge buying a pair.

I'm going to make Dad his favourite for dinner tonight... spaghetti bolognaise, so I need to pop along to the shop for a few bits of shopping. As I walk down the road, I see Nicole drive past. She has a pupil in the car with her... my heart rate gets faster and faster... wow... how can she make me feel this way just by driving past me? I still struggle to understand how she makes me feel... my mind races through some of the things that she has done to me... some of the things I have done to her... lots of the things we have done together... before I know it I am at the shop... I have fantasized my way here!

"Hi Sam, something smells nice! Have you cooked my favourite?"

"Hi, have you had a good day? And it might be your favourite!"

"Yes it was good, and it just got better... how has your day been?"

"Good, I have done the prep work in your room," I also told him about the plans with Jess and the boys and he said that he would love to go, and would treat us all to dinner after the film.

"Thanks Dad, you are the best!"

"Do you mind if we don't decorate tonight... I am really tired."

"Of course not, I'm pretty tired myself, actually. I think I might have a night off, too. I can finish off the other two walls in my room tomorrow. I think I'll go for an early run, then go and visit Christopher, then I will have the whole afternoon free to paint"

Later that evening, I texted Nicole and told her that I saw her with another pupil, so I didn't call or text her... I wanted to... I really wanted to... I wanted to jump in front of her car... pull her out and kiss her... but I settled for my memories... settled for knowing that we will make many more memories together... many more...

- Hello baby, I am out tonight with a few of the other driving instructors. We often go out for a pay day meal. This month we are having a curry! It's nice to catch up with them because, unlike other professions, we don't see each other at all during the day. Missing you and looking forward to Friday more than you know x o x

It can't be more than I know, I know how much I am looking forward to it... it can't be more than that... she is out with friends... I hadn't given that a thought... how do I feel about that...? It's OK, I guess... I see my friends... I wonder how she feels about that... it's just hard when you have no idea who the friends are... at least she will meet my friends next week at the festival... wow, that has come around really quickly.

- OK, have a good night x x x

- X o x

Thursday has gone by in a flash and I am getting nervous about my test... but looking forward to after it very much... people keep calling me... wishing me luck... which is really nice... but it's all making me very nervous. I do manage to finish painting the other two walls in my bedroom, which is nice, although it has taken me all evening to put my room back together, and to hang the pictures back up. The end result is great through and I feel very proud of my efforts.

- Hi babe, how are you feeling? x o x

- *Nervous x x x*

- *I will be there at 2pm tomorrow x o x*

- *I'm not sure if that will lower my heart rate, to be honest! x x x*

- *Get a good night's sleep. Are you going to go running in the morning? x o x*

- *Yes I think I will, its helps me to de-stress x x x*

- *OK, baby, can't wait to see you tomorrow, sweet dreams x o x*

- *Sweet dreams, I think I will have them now, no problem! x x x*

Chapter 12

Today is the day… my day… our day… my mind is reeling… I run in a daze… It's just as well my legs know the route. I don't remember much about it really… hopefully I nodded at all the usual people I meet… oh I'm sure I would have… understandably, my mind is a little otherwise engaged. It was flicking between… oh shit, my driving test… to… I can't wait to spend the night with her… her… the woman who has stolen my heart… taken over my mind… my body… Oh, she can take over my body any time she likes… she knows exactly what to do with it… oh shit, my driving test!

I stand in the shower for what feels like hours… it was probably only about 10 mins. Nicole is picking me up at 2pm for my pre-test lesson. I still have three hours to wait till then… what can I do for three hours… I know… pack my bag for tonight… right… that's done… that wasted 10 mins… next… erm… I go into the kitchen and make myself a drink… Oh bless, my dad is so sweet… he has written a good luck note on the fridge noticeboard. He is a lovely guy… a perfect dad and so thoughtful… the phone is ringing… the home phone is ringing… it can't be Nicole, can it…? It's Jess…

"Hi Sam, I just want to wish you good luck, today! I will be thinking about you. I have bought the tickets for tomorrow. The film starts at 6.30p.m. Shall I meet you and Dad there at about 6.15?"

"Thanks for the luck," I say. "And 6.15pm sounds great."

"OK, stay calm and smash it!" She says, so… stay calm… really… and 'smash it'… smash it? Really? Could she not think of any other word to use? I do love my sister and I'm looking forward to seeing her and the boys… I used to see them a lot, but Uni took over for a while… especially around exam time… that's a really stressful time. But now that I have finished the course, I should have more time again… mind you… I think… well, I'm hoping… that from now on Nicole could be taking up a lot of my time… I'm sure she will… I will make sure she will… still two hours till she picks me up… two hours… is this clock going backwards, or what? I know… I'm going to lie on the sofa and put the music channel on and chill out… Little Mix… really! I start flicking through the channels… Lionel Ritchie… better, but not quite Ed… I somehow manage to totally chill out…

- *I'm on my way, babe x o x*

What… is she really early… no… Oh God… am I ready? Would I ever be ready for this day? No… no… right, pull yourself together, I say to myself… I hear Nicole pull up… Oh God… it's time… I pick my bag up… pick my keys up and put my phone in my pocket. I walk out to the car and she is standing by the boot… she's smiling… her smile melts me… she sees I have a bag, and opens the boot for me, as I put the bag in, her hand gently brushes mine.

"I was hoping you'd have a bag, and that you hadn't forgotten about tonight!"

Forgotten… forgotten… is she kidding… I don't miss the brush of her hand over mine either, and I feel that familiar tingle. I am standing next to her looking straight into her eyes.

"I have to get in the car," I say, "or I will have to kiss you!"

"That's fine," she says, smiling, "kiss me!"

"Not here," I say, looking around nervously, "Nicole, don't make me even more nervous, please!"

"OK, sorry, listen, you jump into the passenger seat…"

"Why?"

"Just get in, Sam, trust me!"

She drives us to the quiet car park. Then parks and takes her seatbelt off. The car park is empty.

"Right then," she says, "Can I have a hug now, please?"

We have a hug, which then turns into a few kisses.

"Feeling better?" she asks.

"Much, thanks."

"Now get your sweet little ass into this seat and show me how well you can drive!"

"OK," I say, after stealing another kiss.

I make a few silly mistakes, and Nicole says that's normal because of nerves… is she just saying that…?

"Right babe, you are ready for this test! I wouldn't put you in for your test if I didn't think that. It would be really bad for my reputation if my students kept failing."

She smiles at me,

"Oh nice one, Nicole, more pressure!"

"I'm joking, go and get them and whatever happens, I will be here waiting to take you home where we are going to have an amazing night! I know you can do this, Sam, just drive how you normally do."

"See you in an hour," I say, in a quiet voice.

I pull out of the car park, with the driving examiner in the car. I purposely don't look Nicole's way. I follow all the instructions that are given to me by the examiner. I'm not sure how I managed the hour, I couldn't tell anyone where I had driven, or much else, really. As we drive back into the car park I see Nicole pacing up and down. She sees me and goes over and sits down in her car. I park the car carefully and the examiner turns to me. I sit there for what seems like forever, and he says:

"Miss Meade, I am pleased to tell you that you have passed!"

He carried on talking, but I wasn't really listening… I've passed! I signed something, I think.

I get calmly out of the car and start walking over to Nicole, with my head down, pretending to look as though I had failed. She gets out of the car, I look up and smile. She starts running towards me, she swings me around and hugs me.

"Well done, babe, now let's get out of here!"

She starts asking me lots of questions about the test.

"I don't know, Nicole, and at the moment I don't care much! I've passed! Thank you, Nicole!" I say.

"For what?"

"For being such a good teacher!"

"Let me just text Dad, Jess, Cassie and Louise to let them know."

"You carry on babe, you clever girl!"

I spend 10 minutes letting them all know, and receiving many 'well done' texts.

"Right gorgeous, I'm all yours now," I tell Nicole. "Now I can start enjoying my night with you!"

"Now you are talking… my place or yours?" she giggles naughtily.

"You are so bad! Can we stop off at an Off-License on the way, please?"

"No need," she says, "I went yesterday."

"Thought of everything, haven't you!"

"I hope so, Sam. This evening is special. It's our first proper night together."

We get to her apartment, park the car and she says, "Can I kiss you again now, please?"

"Oh yes," I say, pulling her towards me. We kiss passionately.

"I needed that!" I tell her.

A few minutes later we go inside.

"Sit down here," she says, pointing to the sofa. She's lighting all the candles. I love the candles. She goes to the kitchen and comes back with two glasses and some nibbles. She goes back to the kitchen again,

"Can I help?" I offer.

"No, I'm done now," she says, walking back into the room, with a bottle of champagne.

"Do you like champagne?" she asks.

"I don't know... I have never tried it!"

"Well, let's change that right now!" she says, handing me a glass with a strawberry in it.

POP! Goes the cork. What a lovely sound!

"You should keep that cork," she says, pouring the champagne into our glasses.

"Well done, Sam... congratulations on passing your test!"

I sip the champagne... Oh I like it... I like it a lot!

"I won't be a minute," she says.

"Where are you going now?" I ask.

"Just putting the oven on... I have prepared a beef bourguignon, it will take about three hours in the oven, so do you think we can think of anything to do while it cooks?"

"Oh yes," I say, "Come and have a drink with me! I'd like a cuddle, please."

She smiles, "I'm on my way, I have been looking forward to tonight so much!"

We have a nice cuddle on the sofa while sipping our drinks.

"Do you fancy having a bath?" she asks.

"Are you saying I smell, sweetheart?"

"No, I am asking if you would like to join me in the bath. You can bring your drink."

Oh, a bath with her… she never said 'with you'… now that is interesting…

"Yes, please! I thought you… never mind! Go and run our bath, please!"

These bubbles are going to my head… I could get used to this… how my life has changed in just a few weeks…I love it…!

"Sam!"

"I'm just putting my bag in the bedroom… is that OK?"

"Of course it is, make yourself comfortable here, babe. You never need to ask things like that, OK? If you want a drink, get one. Treat it just like home."

"OK" I say, walking into the bathroom with our drinks, which I have topped up.

She finishes lighting the last candle, and then just stares at me. I offer her drink to her… she's still staring… I am starting to feel a bit awkward…

"Wow, fucking wow!" she says. "You are one sexy, hot woman, and you have no idea, have you?"

"I'm just me," I say, "You like my new underwear, do you?"

"Like it…? Are you serious…? Stay there, I'm going to get my phone, I need a picture of this!"

"You can have a picture, if I can have one of you!"

My God, that is the drink talking… I would never normally have agreed to that… never in a million years… however, I do manage to get a beautiful picture of her… she knows what I am thinking… I am sure she does…

"Are you brave when you drink?" she asks.

"Apparently!" I giggle. "Top my glass up and take your clothes off, I want another picture… no, actually, hang on… can I take your clothes off?"

"Undress me then, you sexy woman and let's get into the bath."

I take her clothes off very slowly, gently running my hands over every inch of her smooth skin. As I take her bra off I cup her breasts and kiss her nipples, I run my hand down her stomach. She is trembling.

"Are you cold?" I ask.

"No, that's pure excitement!" she says, dropping to her knees, "That's what you do to me. That is what your touch does to me!"

She slides my knickers off, and pushes my legs open. She nibbles up the inside of my thigh, then pushes my legs open wider… her tongue is darting inside me… yes, it is inside me! In and out, in and out… Oh My God… so slow and sensual now. She is now sucking my clit… oh God… suck it hard… Oh I'm sure I shouted that.

Her fingers are inside me now and she is still licking and sucking my clit. My legs are like jelly… I am going to fall over.

"Oh Nicole!" I call out, as I have an orgasm. When I can breathe again I cup her face and pull her up to me, "That was absolutely amazing!" I say. "Can I do that to you?"

"Later, let's get in the bath, baby. We've got all night, all night long together, remember?"

"Oh God, I remember, don't worry!" I pant in reply.

We get into the bath and chink our champagne glasses. I could get used to this… I could definitely get used to this…

"Nicole, you are very horny, and turn me on so much!"

"Sam, you do exactly the same to me, do you know that your toes are playing with my clit, by the way?"

"Oh sorry, are they?" I say, feigning innocence, and then smile, "You have to remember that I am new to all this!"

"Hmmmm… I'm not so sure about that… you are so horny!"

"I think your toe has just slipped inside me... oh Sam!"

I lean towards her and stroke her breasts, play with her nipples, they become very hard. I put my hand between her legs and play with her clit. She is panting very heavily in my ear. I think she is going to cum. She is shaking.

"Don't stop, Sam, please don't stop!" she screams.

I suck her nipple, and circle her clit with my finger... ah... there it is... she is calling my name... as she cums. That is so horny!

I sit back in the bath and we smile at each other...

"You are amazing, Sam!"

We pick our glasses up and finish our drinks. Later on, we get out of the bath, and gently dry each other. Nicole gives me a dressing gown.

"Are you OK just wearing that while we eat?"

"Yes, are you going to do the same?"

"Do you want me to?"

"God, yes... that is sexy! Next Friday, when you drive us to the festival, I think I will wear jeans and no knickers. Would that work for you?"

"Sam, you are going to be very good for me... are you really going to have no knickers on?"

"You will have to wait and see, gorgeous!"

Just at that moment, her oven starts beeping.

"Good timing! Are you ready to eat, babe?"

"Oh yes!" I say, with a huge grin. I watch as she puts her dressing gown on. What a shame she is covering that beautiful body up. I will have to rip it back off again after we have eaten. I could just sit and look at her naked body for hours... It's so... perfect!

Dinner was mouth-wateringly delicious.

"Is there no end to your talents?" I say, between mouthfuls.

After we have eaten, she asks,

"Where is Jerry Maguire… would you like to watch that?"

"Yes!" I say, "Shall we bring the duvet out here, and take our dressing gowns off?"

"You want to lie naked on the sofa and watch the film?"

But before I have a chance to answer, she has gone to get the duvet. I take my dressing gown off, and am lying naked on the sofa. When she comes back in, she stops and just stares at me. She drops her dressing gown, and I stare at her. Stare at her beauty… at her silky soft skin… she walks slowly over to me and joins me on the sofa, pulling the duvet over us both, over both our naked bodies. We lay there in each other's arms, exploring each other's bodies… just touching and stroking. It was amazing, just getting to know every part of her gorgeous body. Her head is getting heavier on my shoulder… she's falling asleep… I cuddle her tightly… I listen as her breathing gets heavier and slower… yes, she's asleep… I'm not going to move her, I like the fact that she is sleeping, naked in my arms.

We lie there for about an hour, until she wakes up and looks up at me…

"Tell me I didn't just fall asleep, please tell me I didn't!"

"It was perfect, Nicole, holding you close and feeling your lovely body close to mine. Feeling your heart beat on my chest. It felt just magical and I hope I get to watch you sleep often."

"I invite you here for a night that you will never forget, and then I go and fall asleep! I can't believe I have done that!"

"Hey, I will never forget this night. It has been romantic, very horny and I got to hold you while you were sleeping… you were so sexy and hot and yet so gentle, I like that"

"Do you?"

"Shall we go to bed and be a little bit more 'sexy and hot and gentle' then?"

"Yes please!" she replies, "And, while I think about it… I have been meaning to ask you something… don't laugh at me, but is the Alphabet Tongue thing you talked about really 'a thing'?"

"Well, I overheard some teenagers talking in the canteen at Uni, and they were saying that you should spell the alphabet with your tongue on your partner's clit."

"I think we should try it… What do you think?"

"I think I want to try lots of things with you, Nicole!"

She stands up, holds my hand and leads me back into her bedroom. As we walk in I watch her beautiful back. I look down her body and I think to myself… what an amazing sight!

We lie on the bed, touching each other. She is on top of me, her mouth goes from kissing me on the lips to nibbling my ear… Oh! … That drives me crazy! … I try to touch her, but she gently puts my hands above my head, just like she did that time in the woods… she holds my hands there… I try to pull them down so that I can touch her.

"No, leave your hands there, or do I have to tie them to the headboard?" she says, with a twinkle in her eye.

Oh… tie them up… what do I think about that…? I would trust her to do that… I'll have to think about that one… I'm not discarding the idea though…

"Oh, she says… you like that idea, don't you?"

"It's hot!" I hear myself saying. The words leave my mouth before I realise what I've just said. She gets the dressing gown belt and very gently and loosely ties my hands to the headboard.

"OK?" she asks.

"Very OK!" I hear myself reply.

"They are very loose and you can take your hands out any time you want, OK?"

I don't want to… I like it… I like it a lot… I'm giving her control over me. She smiles and starts kissing her way down my body. She kisses every inch of me. Her hands are pushing my legs apart, she is touching me, making me wet, Oh, wow, I think she is writing the alphabet! I must remember to thank those teenagers, if I ever see them again... it feels amazing! I think she probably gets to about L or M before I cum in her mouth...she is moaning almost as much as I am, I notice. And, surprisingly, I am loving the feeling of being helpless, of my hands being tied... it's amazing! She kisses her way back up my body... *My turn, my turn*, my brain is screaming. I want to show her what the alphabet game feels like. I have a feeling she will like it. She unties my hands,

"Did you like that?" she asks.

Did she not hear me? Did she not feel the way that she made my whole body tremble under her control? Oh hold on... did she mean the alphabet, or the tying up? It doesn't matter, I loved both!

"I loved it, and now it's your turn," I say, as I gently roll her over.

I do to her exactly what she did to me, except she wanted her hands tied tighter, so that she could not get them loose. "Horny!" I say out loud... I meant to say it in my head.

"It works for me too!" she pants, her eyes are closed with anticipation of the ecstasy that I am about to create for her.

I kiss my way down her body, with an added little bite here and there. Just little gentle bites. I work my way down to her clit and I give it a little nibble.

"Oh yes... Yes...!" I hear her mumble.

I start, slowly and sensually... a, b, c, d...k, l...

"Sam, you are fucking great at this!" she says, very loudly.

m...n...o...

O was the one that tipped her over the edge and she had a powerful, beautiful orgasm. I nearly had an orgasm too, just watching and listening to her! I kiss and caress my way back up her body and I spend some time playing with her nipples. I eventually untie her. She wraps me up in her arms and holds me tight.

118

"Thank you!" she says. We fall asleep in each other's arms, at peace and smiling.

I wake before her, it is morning already. I slip her dressing gown on and go to the kitchen and start making eggy bread, just as I had promised that I would do. I hear her move around in the bedroom, and she then joins me in the kitchen.

"Do you need any help", she asks.

"No, it is all ready for you!" I say, giving her a kiss.

She loves the eggy bread and asks if I will make it again for her, next time.

"Next time? I like the sound of that!" I tell her. She cuddles me and says,

"You don't think I'm letting you go, do you?"

I smile… we both feel so comfortable together… this relationship is just perfect! I had never imagined that a relationship could feel like this. I have never allowed myself to be in a relationship before and I feel like such a novice, but I have a wonderful teacher.

After breakfast, I ask if I can have a shower.

"Only if I can come with you!" she says.

"I was hoping you would say that." She lathers a puff ball up and washes every inch of me. I do the same to her and then I wash her long blonde hair. Before I know what is happening, she is on her knees, and sucking my clit again. I fall against the wall as she brings me to orgasm again, for the… oh I don't know, I have lost count of how many times… she stands up afterwards and nibbles my neck. I begin to play with her clit and my fingers slide inside her. I have to catch her and hold her up as she cums. Her legs just give way. Her whole body is trembling. Later, we dry each other gently, not missing an inch of each other's bodies. We smile at each other, no words are needed. It was the perfect end to a perfect night.

She drops me off at the end of my road, so that Dad does not see her. We stare into each other's eyes and smile.

"I will text you!" I say, as I get out of the car.

"You better had!" she says. "Oh, Sam, don't forget your bag"

I walk into the house, grinning like a Cheshire cat, happier than I have ever been.

Chapter 13

There is a message on the fridge.

Sam... I've gone out, I will pick you up at 5.30pm for the cinema... Dad x

I go to bed and try to remember all that happened last night. I just want an hour's sleep, my body needs to recover a bit... I never knew I could feel like this, like anyone could make me feel like this... I then set my alarm... but just before I go to sleep, I text Nicole,

- *Wow... just wow x x x*

- *Right back at ya, babe! I have to try to work, somehow. I'll text you later. Have fun at the cinema tonight x o x*

That can't be my alarm already, surely? But it is... I get up and jump into the shower... remembering what happened last time I was in the shower, and smiling to myself... I grab a quick bite to eat... I see Dad's car pulling up... he comes in and puts a clean shirt on.

"Hi Sam, did you have a good night?"

"Hi Dad, yes, very good, thanks... You?"

"Yes, it was really good thanks! Oh yes, Jess said to me to tell you to pack a bag and stay with her and the boys tonight, as Matthew is staying at his parent's because his mum is not well again. She said that you and she could have some girly time, because she has really missed that."

"OK" I say, "That will be nice!"

I throw a few things into an overnight bag and off we go. We meet Jess and the boys at the cinema, as arranged… Jess is giving me that 'big sister' look… the look that only big sisters can give you…

"Did you have a good night, last night, Sam?" she asks.

"Yes," I say, trying not to look at her, "You?"

"Yes, really good. Where were you, again?"

"At Louise's," I say, still not looking at her.

"Oh nice… was Louise OK?"

"Yes, good, thanks."

Why is she asking me all these questions… she isn't normally like this…?

"Did you pack a bag for tonight, are you up for some sister bonding time?" she asks.

"Yes, sounds really good!"

Dad asks us what we want and then takes the boys to get their popcorn. They love having a big box while watching a film. Jess catches my arm.

"I'm glad you can stay over," she says, "Because then you can tell me where you really were last night, and who you were really with!"

I look at her in shock. She leans in close to me and whispers,

"I bumped into Louise last night, and I asked her when she was meeting you. She had no idea what I was talking about. I said I must have got mixed up, as I thought that the two of you were going out."

My mind went into blind panic for a moment… what can I say? But thankfully Dad and the boys returned at this point, rescuing me, for now… but later… what do I say to her later?

"I just need to pop to the toilet," I say, "I won't be a minute." I get in there and close the door, and try to breathe… oh God… what do I say?

- *Shit! Help! I am sitting in the toilet in the cinema. My sister knows I wasn't with Louise last night. She wants to know where I was and who I was with. What should I say? x x x*

- *Oh Sam! Just tell her the truth, I will come and talk to her with you, if you like? x o x*

Oh just like that! Just tell her…? What… how… what do I say…? Oh I can't believe that this is happening!

- *I'm staying at hers tonight. She wants to talk!!*

- *Sam, baby… just tell her, it will be better in the long run, she loves you, it will be fine! x o x*

There it is again… you will be 'fine'… I wish everyone would stop telling me that everything will be fucking fine! What if it's not… what if she hates me… hates what I have become?

- *Sam, I will do it with you, if you want me to, baby x o x*

It's not about what I want anymore. I have to tell her something.

- *I have to go, they are waiting. I will text you later x x x*

- *My next pupil is just getting into the car now, but remember that I will do anything that you want me to x o x*

We go in, find our seats and watch the film… Well… they all watch the film. I sit there wondering how I tell my sister that I have fallen for a woman… that she's all that I can think about… that she makes me feel amazing… that she makes me feel alive… that I can't stop thinking about her… Oh God, how do I tell my sister all that? I can't get out of this one… I can't lie to Jess… she will know… oh God… how do I tell her…?

The film is ending... oh no... it can't be ending... don't let it end yet... please! I'm not ready!

We are all sitting eating and the boys are both excitedly talking about the film... I can't join in... I can't remember a thing about it... I can't believe this is happening to me... I'm not ready to share my secret, but I don't have much choice now... shit... why did I lie to Jess? ... And why did she have to bump into Louise?

"Are you alright?" Dad is asking.

"Yes, sorry Dad, just tired. This is a lovely treat, thank you."

Dad drops me, Jess and the boys off at Jess's house... Oh God... please don't leave me... I can't do this. Jess baths the boys and gets them ready for bed...

"Auntie Sam, can you read to us?"

"Yes, of course I will!" I say, a bit too hastily, and Jess gives me that look again.

- Are you OK, baby? Have you spoken to your sister yet? x o x

- Not yet, soon, I will text you x x x

I read to the boys, it is typical, they are so tired after their exciting day that they fall asleep after just 10 minutes.

I sit there wondering what I am going to say to Jess... the truth...? I don't know... what should I say? How do I say it?

I pluck up all my courage and walk down the stairs. Jess is sitting on the sofa with a glass of wine.

"Why don't you grab a cold can of cider from the fridge, and then come and tell me why you are lying to me?" she says, with a little smile playing on her lips.

Oh fuck... I very slowly get the cider out of the fridge, wondering what the hell I am going to tell her.

"Well," she says, as I finally walk back into the room, my stomach churning. "What is going on? It's not like you to lie. You know you can tell me anything?"

I burst into tears, I don't know where the tears suddenly came from. She stands up and hugs me.

"Sam, what on earth is going on… are you in trouble?"

I shake my head, and then my brain starts thinking… well, I guess that would depend on what you class as trouble… no I'm not in trouble… I'm in love… Oh my God, I'm in love… that's what I have been feeling… that's how she makes me feel…

"Are you pregnant?" Jess asks, quietly.

I shake my head again, and let out a small ironic chuckle.

"Sam, you are starting to worry me now…" and at that point my phone beeps.

"Not drugs, please tell me it's not drugs? If it is drugs, I'll…"

"No…" at last I found my voice.

- Can I come round and be with you x o x

- Not right now, I will text you in a bit x x x

"Sam, is that the problem, have you met someone? Is that him?"

I burst into tears again.

"I have met someone!" I hear myself saying.

"OK, at last, we are getting somewhere… so are you ashamed of him? Is he married?" Jess is determined to get to the bottom of this.

I look at her… once I say this next sentence… I can't take it back… ever.

"No I'm not ashamed… I'm, I'm…"

"Sam, you are scaring me now, who is he?"

125

"He is a she!" I say, almost in a whisper.

That's it! It is out there now… I can't take it back… I actually don't want to take it back now.

I look up and see that she is smiling. She cuddles me.

"Do you think I care whether you are in a relationship with a man or a woman? I love you, Sam, and as long as she treats you right, that is all that matters! Does she make you happy?"

"Oh Jess, she makes me so happy… but I didn't know… I don't understand it at all… I've never liked a woman… or a man, in my entire life come to that! But she is just perfect!"

"I feel sad that you felt that you couldn't tell me, and that you've been going through this alone. Does Louise know?"

"No one knows, and Jess, please don't tell Dad yet!"

Oh God, she is going to tell Dad.

"I won't tell anyone, it is up to you who you tell, and when you tell them. Tell me about her? How did you meet? What is her name? How long has it been going on? Was it love at first sight?"

"Jess, slow down please!"

I realise that I'm shaking and I drink the rest of my can in one.

"Can I get another one, please?"

"Of course you can, you know you don't need to ask!"

I go and get another cider and walk back into the sitting room.

"Come and sit here," she says, patting the seat beside her.

I sit down, choosing a chair that is at an angle so that I am not looking directly into her eyes and I start talking…

"She is amazing, I say, in a whisper, "Her name is Nicole, she has the most amazing blue eyes, and long blonde hair."

"How long has it been going on?"

"Not very long, but it feels like forever."

- Babe, I am very worried, can I come and be with you? x o x

"Is that her?" Jess asks…

I think about lying… but what's the point, she knows now… I can stop lying to her now… it feels like… like…a weight has been lifted… it feels good…

"Yes, it's her! I texted her from the cinema toilet earlier tonight and told her that you had seen Louise. She is worried about me and wants to come and meet you and talk to you"

"Invite her over, then and let me meet the woman who has stolen my little sister's heart!"

"No!" I say.

She can't come over… can she? What if Jess doesn't like her… it would feel really weird her being here… with … with my sister…

"Are you ashamed of her?"

"No!"

"Invite her over then!"

It might be good, especially as Matthew is not here and the boys are asleep… Oh, I don't know! Should I…?

"OK", I hear myself saying. Oh God, am I really ready to do this?

- Jess says come over x

- Have you told her about us x o x

- Well, not all the details, obviously x

- Is it what you want? x o x

- I think so x

I text Nicole the address.

- Is she OK about us? x o x

- I think so x

- I will be there in about 20 mins x o x

"What's happening?" Jess asks.

"She will be here in 20 mins," I say, not quite believing what's about to happen.

Jess starts bombarding me with questions. How old is she? Where did you meet?

I need another drink, so Jess gets us both one, and I carry on telling her all about Nicole.

"She's the same age as you, and she was my driving instructor… that's how we met!"

After lots more questions from Jess and lots of laughs, hugs and smiles between us, there is a knock on the door… oh God, I think my heart is going to burst right out of my chest!

"Are you going to let her in, Sam or just leave her on the doorstep?"

I think about this one… shall I let her in… shall I leave her on the doorstep… oh God, what am I doing?

I get up to go and let her in. Jess catches my hand.

"Don't worry!" she says, "it's OK!"

"Jess, this is Nicole, Nicole, this is my sister, Jess."

Nicole seems very calm… can she be…? I mean… really… how can she be?

She has a pack of ciders, and a bottle of wine.

"Hi Jess," she said, handing her the drink, "I wasn't sure what you would prefer?"

"Wine is lovely, thank you. You didn't have to do that. Although the cider is also good, I think Sam has drunk most of mine this evening, already!"

She smiles at me. Oh God, she is being cool... very cool... it is a lot for her to take in.

"Wine or cider, Nicole?" Jess asks.

"Wine please!"

Another cider for you, Sam?"

"Yes, please!"

She goes into the kitchen, leaving us alone. Nicole gives me quick hug.

We all sit and chat and it's not awkward at all. Jess asks Nicole a lot more questions, but she is really cool, other than saying.

"You are right, Sam, Nicole does have amazing eyes!"

I blush, and they both laugh.

"I think you will fit in fine, Nicole." Jess is saying, smiling broadly. "But hurt my little sister, and I will find you!" she says, feigning aggression.

"Jess, please...!" I say.

"It's fine!" Nicole says, "I don't plan on hurting her, anyway."

After about an hour, which felt like five, Jess said that she needed to go to bed because the boys would be up soon... Sunday morning, or not, they are early risers.

She told Nicole that is was lovely to meet her, and that she was welcome anytime, and that she was welcome to stay and finish her drink.

When Jess had gone to bed, Nicole said,

"So you think I have amazing eyes, then, do you?"

I blush again, and she puts her arms around me. We hold each other tightly, and kiss gently on the sofa. I could not do more, as I was a nervous wreck following my revelation to Jess, and we were on her sofa in her house. It was also my time of the month, as well as Nicole's... what a co-incidence! *At least we will be OK for the festival next week*, I thought.

Nicole said that she thought that Jess was lovely.

"You looked like a rabbit caught in headlights when I first came in," Nicole said to me.

"That's exactly how I felt," I said.

It was nice just sitting there, cuddling. I felt so relieved, and a little bit tipsy after all the cider I had drunk. Nicole had only had one glass of wine, as she was driving.

"Thank you, gorgeous!" I said.

"It's OK!" she said, looking into my eyes... "We're a team now... your dad is next?"

"Oh God, I don't want to tell him yet..."

"That's fine, whatever you want! We will do this at your speed, Sam."

And I relax back into her arms.

Chapter 14

I woke up with quite a hangover. I can smell eggy bread!

Oh God… Jess knows! She seemed really cool about it last night. I hope she feels the same way this morning… I'm glad she knows… but hope she doesn't try to convince me to tell Dad… I'm not ready for that… I'm not ready to tell the world yet… Jess is enough for now… maybe I should tell Louise and Cassie as we will all be spending time together next weekend… if they knew then I wouldn't have to watch how I behave towards Nicole… I will give this more consideration later on today when I am feeling more human.

"Knock! Knock! Auntie Sam!!"

Oh no… here come the boys! I smile, knowing that I am about to be jumped on!

"Sam… eggy bread is ready…!"

"Coming!"

Jess is dressed and the housework is done. She has set the boys up on the X-Box which is a Sunday morning treat for them. Jess and I sit in the kitchen.

"I'm really pleased to see you so happy, Sam, Nicole seems really nice and obviously adores the ground that you walk on. Are you ready to tell Dad now?"

"No, I'm not ready for that yet. I'm glad you know but I don't want to tell anyone else yet."

"OK, that's your call, but, for the record, I think he will be fine with it. Can I tell Matthew, though, because then we can all go for a drink?"

Oh God... she wants to double-date!

"Really... I haven't been out... out... with Nicole yet."

"How about Wednesday night?" she says.

Easy tiger... I think... will Nicole want to? Do I want to? Might be quite nice...

"Sam!"

"Sorry, I'll ask her and let you know."

"Will Matthew be OK with it, do you think? OK with Nicole, I mean?"

"Erm, OK... let me think... will it interfere with him being fed, or watching the football?"

"No," I say.

"Then he will be fine with it!" And we both chuckle!

"Does Nicole like football?"

"I don't know, I will ask her for you."

"I'm going to jump into the shower and get dressed," I say.

- *Morning gorgeous, thanks for being here last night. Jess really likes you. She wants to know if we want to go for a drink with her, and her husband Matthew on Wednesday night. x x x*

- *Morning babe, I am really glad I came around too, and I think Jess is lovely, apart from the time when you were not in the room, and she said that she would re-arrange my teeth if I mess you around!! She was smiling when she said it, but she still meant it... I'm glad you have such a caring sister lol x o x*

- *Oh... she also asked if you like football. x x x*

- *Arsenal, and I can make Wed evening, if you want to go? x o x*

- *Oh no!!! Matthew is Chelsea mad. I am not sure about Wed. Do you think it would be a bit weird? x x x*

- *Yes, it will at first, but I'll be there to hold your hand x o x*

"Jess, are you ready?"

Oh no, I haven't even had a shower yet… I'd better get a move on!

- *I've got to go, I've got to get ready, talk soon x x x*

- *So are we going on Wed? x o x*

- *Yes I think so x x x*

"At last… I didn't think we would ever see you again!"

"Sorry Jess, I was texting and finding out all the answers to your questions. And she's an Arsenal fan!"

"Oh no!" said Jess. "That's going to be fun, isn't it? And is Wednesday night OK?"

"Oh yes, she is free and would love to come! She thought you were lovely apart from the re-arranging teeth thing… what are you like?"

"I'm just looking after my baby sister!" she says, and we both laugh.

"So, where do you want to go on Wednesday?" I ask. "And you're not going to question her all night, are you?"

"Of course not, trust me Sam!"

It's Wednesday before I know it. I feel really nervous. I hope Jess doesn't ask Nicole too many questions. I hope Matthew is OK about us… or me… come to think about it… that would be really embarrassing… I try talking Jess into going to the cinema... but she says that she wants to meet Nicole properly... she would like to talk to her. Yes... that's kind of why I suggested the cinema... so we finally agreed on bowling, instead. I have not been bowling for so long... I warn Jess to be nice and to not ask too many questions.

"Sam, will you relax... what do you think I'm going to say?"

"Erm, teeth... re-arranged... ring any bells?" I say, holding my necklace.

"We'll be fine, don't stress about it. The babysitter is coming at seven, so shall we meet you there around seven thirty?"

"OK, and be nice!" I say, as I put the phone down.

- Hi gorgeous, are you OK with bowling? x x x

- Of course, that should be fun! x o x

- Can you pick me up about 7pm? x x x

- See you soon, looking forward to seeing you again x o x

We have a really good night at the Bowling Alley. Matthew was really cool, and Jess didn't ask too many questions. At the end of the night, Jess hugs Nicole and kisses her cheek, which was very nice.

She whispers to me that Nicole is a keeper. She said that she's glad that I'm so happy. I feel so relieved... maybe I can, in fact, live my life as a gay woman after all, and not feel that I have to hide my relationship away behind closed doors. This is a good feeling....I hadn't realised how much I was stressing about that.

During the drive home, Nicole and I discuss the music festival camping weekend, and what we need to take. I'm meeting with Louise and Cassie tomorrow to do the shopping, and then the next day we go! It's getting really exciting now! It's going to be hard not giving anything away... it's too late now to tell them though... even if I wanted to. Nicole stops a few doors away from my house so that we can have a goodbye kiss and cuddle without Dad seeing from his window.

"Thanks for dropping me off!" I say, squeezing her hand. "I wouldn't like Dad finding out about us that way."

I don't want him to find out at all... not yet... let ME get used to it first... I wonder if Dad has managed to put his pictures and mirror back up in his bedroom. We finished decorating yesterday, and both our rooms look so much better now, they really needed decorating. I suggested that we tackle the living room next, but Dad wants to wait a while.

- *I really enjoyed tonight, I can't wait for the weekend to be here, two sleeps and then we get to spend two nights away together x x x*

- *Oh, I see... got plans for those nights, have you? I really enjoyed tonight too and Matthew and Jess are a lovely couple. It's really nice that we can all go out like that x o x*

- *It is nice because Jess and I are really close, and as for the two nights, I have a few things in mind...the alphabet tongue, for instance! x x x*

- *Oh good! Have you got any more tips from any teenage boys? x o x*

- *No... LOL, I was hoping you might have a few tricks of your own up your sleeve? x x x*

- *I'm sure I can think of something. You seemed to like being tied up, how about handcuffs next? x o x*

- *I quite like the sound of that, but not sure about that in a tent with my friends close by? x x x*

- *That would just make it more exciting!! x o x*

- *You are making me very horny and you are not even here? How do you do that? x x x*

- *I know, I am sitting here with my hand in my knickers! x o x*

- *Really, are you really? x x x*

- *Yes, aren't you?*

- *Erm… I… no… I … never have x x x*

- *Seriously?*

- *Never! x x x*

- *Maybe on Friday night we could watch each other touch ourselves?*

- *I like the sound of watching you… oooo, that has just sent an electric shock right though my body x x x*

- *I am looking forward to Friday night even more now!*

- *Have you still got your hand down your knickers? x x x*

- Yes, and it is very wet… you make me VERY wet! x o x

- Tell me what you are doing…

- I've just made my fingers wet and now I am going to rub my clit.

- Oh God… I wish I could hear you x x x

All of a sudden, Ed is singing 'How would you feel?' My ringtone… very apt timing, I chuckle.

"You are very bad!" I say.

"Or very good?" she pants.

"Oh fuck, I'm even wetter now, hearing your voice… I'm going to cum Sam, I'm going to cum…"

Wow, this is so horny, I push the phone hard on to my ear, just in case Dad can hear from his room. Like he could! I slowly run my hand down my body, open my legs and feel how wet I am… how wet she has made me.

"Nicole…" I whisper… "I'm very, very wet too!"

Just as I say that, I hear her have an orgasm… wow… that was mind blowing! I feel like I'm going to explode… I touch my clit…

"Touch your clit!" She's gasping.

"I am, but it's not as good as when you touch it!"

"I will touch it lots for you over the weekend then!"

"Nicole, will you touch yourself and let me watch?"

"Fuck, yeah!"

"Can you cum again… Just for me… so I can hear you again?

"You liked that, did you?"

"Just a little bit! It made me feel amazing, like my whole body was on fire! I just wish I was there, next to you."

She giggles and then I hear her breathing getting very heavy again… I know she's touching herself, I want to be there watching her… oh God… she is cumming again… this is just amazing…

"Nicole, you are so hot!"

I am guessing that she can't talk just yet, so soon after her orgasm… so I lay there just listening to her very heavy breathing.

"Are you OK?"

"Mmm!" is the only reply I get.

Her breathing is getting much quieter, and slower… very slow… I think she's falling asleep… I just lay there listening to her breathing… I close my eyes… And I can almost imagine that she is asleep beside me. At 3a.m., my phone beep wakes me.

- *I am so sorry I fell asleep x o x*

- *God, don't apologise… it was amazing… you are amazing x x x*

- *Night night… sweet dreams x o x*

Four hours later…

- *One more sleep, baby x o x*

- *I know… I can't wait, it is really exciting! I need to get ready now, cos I am meeting Louise in an hour to get the shopping x x x*

- *Can you get some baby oil x o x*

- *Why? x x x*

- I will show you on Friday, if you are a good girl. Have a nice day x o x

- How do I explain that to Louise? And you too, sexy x x x

Dad has already left for work. When I'm shopping I'm going to buy the ingredients for spaghetti bolognaise. I want to cook him a nice dinner as I'm away for the weekend.

- Hi Sam, really enjoyed last night. Nicole seems really nice. Are you all set for your dirty weekend? X

That makes me smile… I'm so pleased that Jess is being so good about all this. It feels as though a heavy weight has been lifted from my shoulders.

- Almost… have you got a pair of wellies I can borrow? X

- I'm not even going to ask… and yes, I have x

- In case it rains! I am going shopping later, can I drop in at around 4p.m. and pick them up, please? x

- Yes, see you then x

Dad appreciated the spaghetti bolognaise. It really is true that the way to a man's heart is through his stomach!

"Have you got everything you need for the weekend?" he asks.

"Yes, all sorted, thanks… I'm even borrowing some wellies from Jess"

"Good thinking… I did look at the weather forecast… it says dry all weekend, but you never know!" he tells me.

"Brilliant news!" I say, so excited that I can't keep from smiling broadly.

- Hiya, we have got the shopping and we are all good to go! x x x

- Excellent... my 5pm tomorrow has just cancelled, so I can pick you up after my 2p.m. If I put my bag in the car in the morning, I will be with you at 3.15 ish x o x

- Great, I will tell the girls... they are hoping to be there for 2p.m., so hopefully they will have the tents up by the time we get there LOL x x x

- Bless them! Will they be OK with that? I was thinking that we should have met up, so that they know who I am x o x

- Don't worry, they will love you! x x x

- I'm going to bed... night babe... can't wait until tomorrow x o x

- Me too, it's very exciting... night sexy x x x

Chapter 15

I say bye to Dad as I will be gone before he gets home from work tonight.

"Have a good weekend," he says, as he walks out of the door… "I have left you something in the kitchen"

When I look, it is £50 in an envelope… he is so sweet… he spoils us… I text him to say thanks… and then go to visit Christopher in the hospital. He's very happy as the doctors have told him that they think that he can go home in a week or so, if he carries on with the physio etc. This is very good news because he is going stir crazy in there… he is gutted that he is not going away with us for the weekend, but glad that we are still going.

- *Not long now! x o x*

- *I am so excited… see you soon x x x*

I am also a bit worried… more excited than worried… we will just have to be careful… I think I have packed everything… I will wear my new skinny jeans… and no knickers… I wonder if she has remembered about that… I have packed my iPod so that we can listen to music in the tent… that was Jess's idea… good old Jess!

- *Are you all excited? X*

- *Hi Jess, yes I am actually x*

- Have a great time and send me some pictures please X

- I will do x

Two whole days, and two long nights… I can't wait… I make some sandwiches and pack some nibbles for the journey… I don't even know which bands are playing… I don't even care what bands are playing… two days and two nights with Nicole… that is what I care about… I hope Louise and Cassie like her… I'm sure they will… what's not to like? The post lady has just delivered our mail… I have a letter from the University… I have an interview next Friday for a place on the Social Work course! Everything seems to happen on a Friday… well, everything good… maybe it is an omen… hopefully, I will be offered a place… I haven't even considered the possibility of NOT getting a place… what if I don't… where would I go from there? No… think positively, Sam!

At last, I have made it through the day, and Nicole is pulling up outside. She's waiting at the boot of the car, which she opens as I walk out with my weekend case and a few bits of shopping, (Cassie has the rest of the shopping in her car) and Jess's wellies.

"Wellies! Really? Do I need wellies?" she says. She helps me to load my gear into the car and then stands back, looks at me and says, "Fuck!"

"What's wrong?" I say, looking around to see if anyone is near or can hear her… No, all clear…

"Wrong… nothing is wrong… you just look really hot!"

I laugh and tell her to get into the car.

"Sam, you look really hot, and I mean really hot…those jeans really work for me! Are you wearing any knickers…?"

Oh she didn't forget!

"A lady does not divulge secrets like that! You should know that! You will just have to wait to find out!"

"You have got that perfume on as well… what are you trying to do to me, babe?"

"Just getting you into the mood for later!"

"Mission complete then, Sam… I am in the mood!"

As we drive along, I find myself singing… *I sing my favourite line…*

"That's our song! And you can sing!"

I feel comfortable singing in her company

"You can really sing!"

I have always loved singing, but I have only ever sung in front of Dad and Jess and once in a school show when I was about 11… that was the night Dad gave me my necklace. I give it a little twiddle remembering that night.

Embarrassed, I ask, "Can you sing?"

"Well that is a matter of opinion! In my opinion… yes… however the rest of the world says NO! Maybe one day you will be unfortunate enough to find out!"

"I look forward to that!" I laugh.

"Sam, tell me it's a 6 o'clock bedtime tonight, and… I need to know… Have you got any knickers on?"

Feeling really naughty, I say, "Pull into the next service station, and maybe you can find out!"

"Sam!"

"Yes, Nicole?" I tease.

"Services 8 miles, the sign says. Not far!" I smile at her.

"Too far," she moans, but we are soon there.

"Right! We are here! You better hope that the toilets are empty…"

"What? You want to…? Sam! You're so bad!"

As we walk into the toilets, a lady is walking out. No-one else is in there. Nicole almost drags me into a cubicle… her hand is down my jeans before I even know what is going on.

"Fuck, I don't believe it, Sam... you really are so bad!"

"Excuse me... I'm not the one with my hand down someone else's jeans!"

"That's soon solved!" she says, pulling my jeans down, and completely off the end of my right foot.

Her hand is back between my legs.

"You can't do that!"

"I've done it!" she's grinning.

"If anyone comes in, they could see our feet, and probably hear us..."

"Why would anyone look under the cubicle, and we would hear if anyone came in"

"They would see our feet..." I whisper, feeling stressed, but very aroused.

She puts the toilet seat down, sits on it and pulls me onto her lap so that we are face to face.

"Now they can't see your feet!"

At that moment, someone comes in... she puts her fingers to her lips, whispering "Shh," as her other hand travels back down between my legs, her fingers sliding through my wetness and inside me. The person leaves after what seems like an eternity.

"I cannot believe I'm half naked, your fingers are inside me and you are fucking me... anyone could come in here!"

"Exciting, isn't it!" she says.

"Very!" I say, as I pull her top off over her head. She's fucking me hard with her fingers, as I bite and suck gently on her very hard nipples. She closes her eyes and starts breathing very deeply...

"Someone else is coming in..." I whisper, as I put my hand on hers to stop her touching me. Oh fuck off, please, whoever you are... I want to scream.

They are soon finished and leave the toilets, and she continues.

"Nicole… I am… I'm… I'm going to cum! Oh… yes… yes…!" I say.

She puts her hand over my mouth, still bringing me to my climax. I realise after a minute or two that someone else has come into the toilets… I didn't hear them come in… I don't actually care, anymore.

When we are alone again, she starts putting her top on.

"Oh no you don't!" I say, just managing to stand up. I push her against the back wall, pull her cargos down, completely off one leg, just like she just did to me,

"You are a quick learner!" she says.

We have to pause for a minute as another family comes in and eventually leaves. I pleasure her with my tongue. It feels fantastic to be so intimate with her and to bring her to orgasm so quickly. Afterwards, we stand together, holding each other close, lost in our own thoughts. After a few minutes, we get our clothes back on and walk back into the Services giggling like naughty school girls.

"I'll have to wear no knickers more often, if that is the effect it's going to have on you!" I say twiddling my necklace.

She quickly agrees. We grab a drink and hit the road again.

"I'm still horny and still wet, I think," she says.

"So am I!" I confess.

"Put your hand down inside your jeans, and check!" she says.

"No… you need to concentrate on the road… I'd like to arrive in one piece, please, and you are a driving instructor! How could you suggest such a thing?" I say, laughing.

"I am also a woman, and currently a very turned on woman," she says.

We arrive at the campsite and the girls have put the tents up. I make introductions, and we put our gear into our tent. We all go and have a look around. There is a big field, with a main stage and three smaller stages, which are all in big marquees. The music doesn't start officially until tomorrow, but there is lots of activity, impromptu musicians playing in small groups and plenty of drinking going on. There are mobile food caravans and bars galore. We decide to eat pulled pork wraps. Louise and Cassie get a pizza to share. We all sit down to eat and drink, lots! It is a really nice evening and the girls seem to really like Nicole. No-one would have guessed that they had only just met. All the normal questions are asked… "Are you seeing anyone, Nicole?" Nicole said that she had her eye on someone that she really liked. She held my hand under the table as she said that.

"You should have brought him along with you, Nicole!"

"No… not him… her!" Nicole says.

I try not to show the terror that I am suddenly feeling…

"Does that bother you, girls?" Nicole finishes her sentence.

"Of course not… live and let live, I say!" I hear Louise saying.

Don't beat around the bush, Nicole… just come straight out with it! Don't be shy!

As I come out of my shock, Louise is asking me whether Nicole is any good…

"What!" was all I that could manage.

"Keep up, Sam! Louise is asking if I'm a good driving instructor."

"Oh yes," I say, nervously. "She's very good, I passed first time, after all!"

"Maybe I could take Sam's old lesson slot?

"You'll have to take my number and call me next week when I have my diary to hand."

Oooh… that's going to be weird… very weird…

146

"Sam, can you give me a hand at the bar, please?" Nicole asks.

At the bar, she tells me to chill out.

"I didn't know that you were going to tell them that you are gay," I said. "It threw me!"

"Well, I am, but don't worry, I have no intention of outing you, so stop worrying, they are going to work out something is wrong if you keep acting like that... relax, get drunk... I have plans for you tonight!"

We all end up getting drunk... very drunk, in fact. So drunk that when we get into our tents and into our sleeping bags we fall asleep immediately.

I wake very early in the morning to see Nicole asleep beside me. We have zipped our sleeping bags together, so we are cuddled together in one big sleeping bag. We are both naked. It is very quiet outside. I cuddle closer in to her, and she wakes up gently.

"Sorry," I say. "I didn't mean to wake you."

"It's fine," she says. "Did we fall asleep?"

"Yes, its morning... very early, but it is morning!"

We have a kiss and a cuddle, and things start heating up.

After some time has passed, I hear movement and voices from the other tent, and then Cassie is outside our tent, saying,

"Morning, ladies! Who would like an egg and bacon roll?"

We look at each other...

"We have all weekend," she whispers to me.

"Both of us, please!" we call out to Cassie. "We are just getting dressed."

"I'll have to keep my little surprise for tonight," Nicole whispers to me.

"You can't say things like that!"

"Oh yes I can, and actually I just did!" smiles Nicole.

We all enjoy a deliciously unhealthy breakfast while Cassie shows us a program of who is playing and on which stages. I have never heard of any of them, but I am quite happy to go with the majority and just wander around and enjoy the atmosphere. We come up with a plan for the day over a cup of coffee, then wash the dishes and wait in the queue for a shower. Eventually, we are ready to hit the festival! The guys say that they really like Nicole.

Good, I think, because I am hoping that she will be around for a long time! I suddenly feel very guilty that I haven't told them we are together or even that I am gay... gay... I am gay!

We didn't stay with the other two all day, we had some time on our own. It was a lovely day, but now I feel that I really want some alone time with Nicole. We all say that we are NOT going to get as drunk as we did last night. Nicole and I do drink less, however the other two do end up getting very drunk again. This is very good for us, as they flake out and stumble into their own tent at around ten thirty. They appear to go straight to sleep. It's been a really good day! The bands were brilliant... well most of them were, and we really enjoyed it. We have a last wander around the stages, and on our way back to our tent I whisper,

"Right... what is this secret surprise, then?"

"Once we are back in our tent, I will show you! Did you bring the baby oil?"

"Yes, I did," I say.

We rush back to our tent.

"Oh yes, before I forget to tell you... I have an interview for Uni on Friday!"

"Oh good!" Nicole says, "You might get some more sex tips!"

"Stop it..." I say, getting all embarrassed.

We get back into the tent, I get the baby oil out, and she gets something out of her bag but does not let me see what it is. It is very dark in the tent, which is good, as we really don't want any shadows through the tent walls giving away what we are doing. She takes the baby oil and rubs some on her chest. We get into our sleeping bag and she is rubbing her body up and down mine. My hands are all over her body. It feels even more amazing with the baby oil on… I can't believe how erotic this feels. Her breathing is very heavy…

"What did you get out of your bag?" I pant.

"Funny you should ask, I will show you in a minute, but first I need to do something else…"

I am intrigued. She lies beside me and takes my right hand. She rubs my hand all over my body. Her hand is on top of mine. Our hands slide over my chest… my nipples are very hard…

"Nice!" she whispers, then she slides my hand down in between my thighs, down the inside of one thigh, and then back up, then down the inside of the other thigh and back up. *What is she doing*, my brain screams, and then my hand, which is still underneath hers, starts rubbing my clit. I go to pull my hand away…

"No "she says, and my hand is really rubbing my clit and it is sliding around in the baby oil, I am getting very aroused. I take control and rub my clit. She slowly takes her hand off mine, I keep rubbing. She leaves her hand at the top of my thigh. I guess so that she can still feel that my hand is touching my clit, getting faster and harder. I am bringing myself to orgasm… do I want to do that… myself? Yes I do… I couldn't stop now, even if I wanted to… but I am also very aware that I am in a tent… I can't make a sound…

"Nicole, I am going to cum!" I whisper in her ear.

"Enjoy it baby, enjoy it, like I am!"

My body goes as stiff as a board as I come to orgasm. My mind blows and then I am trembling… oh my God… I just did that…!

"And that's how you masturbate!" she said… I know she is smiling, I just know she is!

"So now when we talk late at night on the phone, we can do that together!"

Now I am smiling… "Your turn!"

"No," she says.

"What do you mean, no?"

"I will do it, but not tonight, I will do it one day back at home, when the lights are on… I want to see you watching me!"

That's hot… I think… I will look forward to that day… she is getting out her surprise… I don't know what it is… I can't see anything… I don't know right up until the moment when she clicks it onto one of my wrists.

"Handcuffs!" I say.

"Not just handcuffs, but fluffy handcuffs!" she quietly chuckles.

She puts my hands above my head and puts my wrist with the cuff on it around a little pole above the sleeping bag, and clicks the other cuff on my other wrist.

"Where did that pole come from? What if someone comes in?"

"I might have put the pole there earlier, and who is going to come in… it's nearly midnight!" she whispers.

"Oh you did, did you? Confident that I would want to do this then, were you?"

"Don't you? I think you like the thrill as much as I do… you were fine in the woods… I think you like the thought that you might get caught, admit it, it turns you on."

Oh God, it does, she is absolutely right…

"You have no control now, and I can do whatever I want! I think that also turns you on."

She is right again… I love it…

"I trust you," I whisper. "It's exciting me!"

"Not just you, babe, one day I am going to do this to you outside!"

"One step at a time," I say. "Now what are you going to do with me?"

"I've brought another friend with me," she says.

"What!" I say, trying to look around, panicking, but it is pitch black, and I can't see anything.

"Don't worry, it's not a real friend... it's just a toy!"

She stands up, I can hear her doing something, but I can't see a lot.

She is still very close to me... she is by my feet... she is kissing my ankle. Slowly kissing up my leg... her tongue is lingering in certain spots... she's kissing and softly biting right up to my nipples... I can hear myself moaning... she's kneeling up, pushing my legs open.

"Are you warm enough?"

"Yes," I say, far too quickly.

Her fingers are playing with my clit, which still has baby oil on it, or is that just how wet she is making me? I don't know? I don't care... still playing with my clit with the fingers of one hand, she is raising my hips with the other hand, which is on my lower back... what is she doing? 'Go with it, Sam,' I tell myself...

"I want to touch you!" I pant.

"Later" she says. Her fingers are driving me mad. She is being very tender, hold on, something is going inside me... hold on... that's not her fingers... Oh God... what is it? Do I like it?

"Yes..." I say, out loud, without meaning to. She is fucking me with... with... with what?

"What are you doing to me?" I ask.

She pushes further inside me, she is sitting up on her knees. I can tell because her knees are just underneath me and her hands are on my pelvis area, but still something is slowly pushing inside me… in… out… in… out… getting deeper inside me with every thrust…

"Are you OK?" she checks.

"Oh yes!"

She starts going faster… I can feel her hips thrusting. She is wearing a strap-on, and is using it to fuck me. I relax and feel it going even deeper in to me. I have never experienced anything like this before. She goes slowly and then gets faster… all the time checking that I am OK. She is thrusting into me, then she gently pulls right out and gently slides back in. She does that a few times, I can hear her moaning. I am trying to be so quiet. Then she thrusts really quickly, banging against me… then again, she goes really slowly, then she lays on top of me, somehow pushing my legs to where she wants them to be… which is wrapped around her waist. She starts thrusting again, while passionately kissing me… it feels amazing… then she gets back onto her knees and goes really slowly again… in… and then right out… Oh this is so horny… now she is rubbing my clit at the same time…

"I need to touch you!" I moan. "Undo me, please!"

"Not yet" she says, as she starts thrusting more and more quickly, while still rubbing my clit.

"I'm going to cum!" I tell her.

She pulls out and puts her mouth on me… fucking me hard with her tongue… Oh God… I cum… and I cum hard.

"Fuck me!" I say, once I have regained the power of speech and control of my panting body.

"I just did!" was her reply, and I can hear her smile!

"Oh God… Was I very loud?" I panic.

"No baby, you really weren't," she pants.

"Undo me now and let me touch you please!" I beg her. I put her in the handcuffs and play with her, touching stroking, licking, biting. Then I start on my alphabet. She keeps saying…

"Take the cuffs off and let me join in"

"No," I said. "Like you said to me, it's my turn!"

After she had cum three or four times, I let her free.

Oh my God… that was absolutely amazing!

Hours later, we lay cuddling. I was thinking how content I am, but that does not start to cover it.

"Can I use your toy on you, one day?"

"You certainly can… did you like that?"

"I love everything that you do to me," I said, just before I fell asleep in her arms.

"Ladies! Are you awake?"

"Oh God," I whisper, "Nicole, Louise is here!" I say looking around our tent, scattered with toys that Louise really should not see.

"We will be… give us ten minutes and we will be with you!"

"OK… we will get the bacon on!" she says.

"Nicole, we have to get up and tidy up!" I whisper into her ear.

"OK, OK, just give me a quick cuddle first!"

"It will have to be quick, gorgeous… they are cooking breakfast, and will be back over here if we don't go to their tent soon" I say.

I snuggle closer in to her and say,

"Last night was amazing, thank you!"

"You are amazing!" she replied. "And I'm glad that you enjoyed it!"

"Oh yes, I enjoyed it very much!" I say, remembering back and probably flushing a bit red.

"Right, Nicole, we really need to get up, and pack away some of this stuff!"

"One minute more, please! I just want you to myself for one more minute! And who can blame me!"

We have breakfast with Louise and Cassie and we offer to wash up, as they had done all the cooking AGAIN. We all decide to pack up the tents once we are contentedly full of bacon and eggs. We can then load the cars up with all our bags, so that we can relax and enjoy the rest of the day knowing that all the work is done. Also, it's warm, sunny and dry, so a perfect time to take the tents down. We are all following Cassie's instructions, as none of us have a clue about tents! I have a real struggle trying to pull two poles apart. As I am battling with these poles, a voice pops up…

"Need help with that, darling?" a very nice young man asks.

"No she doesn't!" Nicole answers, before I have a chance to open my mouth.

"OK, maybe I'll see you later…?" he says, winking at me.

Nicole stares after him. We finally get the tents all packed away neatly into Cassie's car, and head off with just our small rucksacks into the throng of the festival.

The first moment I have alone with Nicole, she says,

"That man fancies you!"

"No he doesn't! He was just being nice!"

"He wasn't… he fancied you!"

"Does that bother you, Nicole?"

"No, or I would have been unhappy all weekend. You really haven't noticed how many people have looked your way, have you?"

"What?" I say, laughing.

Nicole laughed and said,

"Just makes me see how lucky I am, because it's me that you're choosing to be with, and that makes me very lucky and very happy!"

154

"Good!" I say… what is she talking about… no-one has looked at me… have they? That man was only offering to help… wasn't he? Anyway, she is right… I choose her… I want to be with her… I want her.

"Sam, Nicole! We are over here, come and join us for a drink!"

"I guess you are on soft drinks like me" Nicole says to Cassie. "Since we both have to drive later!"

"Oh excuse me… it's Christopher!" she says, looking at her ringing mobile. We all smile, and tell her to send him all our love.

Louise goes off to the toilet, and Nicole whispers in my ear,

"I wish our tent was still up! Can we just slip away and go back to mine?"

"No, that would be horrible!"

- *Where are my pictures? X*

- *Hold on… I'll do a selfie of me and Nicole x*

"Nicole," I say, "Jess wants a picture of us… I forgot… I said I would send one."

So we take a selfie and send it to her.

- *Ah, that's a lovely picture, thanks. I hope you are having fun!*

"I do like your sister, Sam!"

"Good, I'm pleased about that, as she's the only one that I have!"

The other two come back and join us. Cassie tells us that Christopher is doing really well and will be home soon, which will be good for everyone involved.

"Oh, I had a letter… I've got an interview on Friday at University for the Social Work course!"

"That's great news!" Louise voices, and the others agree. They all wish me luck.

"And congratulations again on passing your driving test! Was it really nerve-wracking?" Louise asks.

"No, I had a good teacher," I say, nodding towards Nicole.

"Did you get your tent down OK, gorgeous?" It was the same guy that had offered to help earlier.

"Yes, all done, thanks, we can relax now!"

"That sounds good, can I buy you a drink now?"

"I'm alright, thanks," I say, "I am with my friends."

"Told you so," Nicole whispered. "Why don't you just follow me into the gap between those trees?" she says very quietly.

"Stop it," I whisper, "behave yourself!"

We have a really good day, listening to some bands, and just having fun. Louise had us all in fits of laughter with her jokes. I can never remember jokes. The girls told Nicole some of the silly things that we got up to in Uni, including putting permanent marker on the cup that Christopher was drinking out of, which I must admit, was quite funny at the time! And how he drew on the back of Cassie's ear during a lecture.

"I am so glad you all took your degrees so seriously!" Nicole said, "And I feel really comforted that the three of you are planning to go on and teach the youth in this country, and become pillars of society!"

"Do you definitely not want to be a teacher, Sam?" Cassie says, "I think that you would make a great teacher!"

Nicole smiles at me,

"Yes, I could imagine you teaching people," she says... I am sure I blush... has anyone noticed... I don't think so... I can't make eye contact with her... just one more band to listen to... it has been a really good weekend... we all agree.

"We will have to do it again," Cassie says. "And hopefully Christopher will be able to join us next time... he would love it!"

We all agree that we should meet up for a post-festival drink next week.

"Next Saturday?" suggests Louise.

"Sounds like a plan!" Cassie says.

"That means you too, Nicole, you're one of the gang now!"

"Thanks," she says, "that sounds great!"

"I will call you about driving lessons as well", says Louise. "If that is OK?"

"Of course it is" As she hands Louise her mobile number.

We all say goodbye, and we ask Cassie to give Christopher our best wishes. We get into our cars and head home.

"It's only early!" Nicole says. "Fancy stopping somewhere for dinner?"

"Why not, got anywhere in mind?"

"Mine," she says.

"You are shocking…! Let's do it!"

- *Hi Dad, having a really good time… not finished yet, and then we are going to go out for dinner, so don't wait up for me x*

- *OK, Sam, thanks for letting me know. I'm glad you are having a good time. I'm going to have an early night, so will see you tomorrow, Dad x*

- *I might as well stay at Louise's then, so that you can lock up before going to bed x*

- *OK see you tomorrow, Dad x*

"Guess what?" I say to Nicole.

"Erm… what? You have to be home by 10?"

- *Hi… you having a really good time still? X*

- Hi Jess, we are heading home now. Dad thinks that I am going to say at Louise's, but I am actually staying at Nicole's x

- OK, take care, say Hi to Nicole for me. Call me tomorrow! X

- OK x

"So?" Nicole is saying.

"So what?" I ask.

"Do you have to be in at 10?"

"Yes I do, actually... well, 10ish, anyway... tomorrow morning! Do you know anywhere I could stay tonight?"

"Umm... I suppose you could stay at mine! Now that I am one of the gang!" she giggles.

"Yes, that didn't go over my head!" I try to look sternly at her but I fail miserably. We both laugh.

"We are nearly home, shall we pick up a pizza or something on the way?" Nicole asks.

"Why not," I say. "Can we have a bath too? It was good fun camping, but I really want a bath now!"

"Whatever you want, my lady!"

"That makes me sound really old." I scowl and get the look just right this time.

"What are you? 24?"

"Yes."

"When are you 25?"

"August, I am a sweet little Virgo!"

"Me too, what date?"

"27th," I say.

"No way... that's my birthday too!" Nicole says, "And it's only three months away! Can you believe that we have the same birthday?"

"Hold that thought," I say. "We are at the pizza place!"

Nicole is asking me what I want, and passing me the menu.

"I have a problem…" I whisper to her.

"What?" she says back, looking concerned.

"It's a very big problem!"

"What's up?"

"You are not on the menu!"

"Oh don't worry, I will be once we get back home!"

We order our pizza and take it back to Nicole's. I can't believe that we have another night, just the two of us… we can relax tonight… and I will be able to see what she is doing to me… while we were driving home in the car we discussed what she did to me last night. It was very hot… strange not knowing, or being able to see what Nicole was doing to me… she said that's why she kept asking me if I was OK…

"I'm not moaning!" I told her…

"You were last night, quite a few times, in fact!" we both giggled at that comment. She reminded me that I don't ever have to do anything that I don't want to. I told her that I was completely happy with it, and would tell her straight away if I wasn't.

We ate our pizza, well half of it… and then had a lovely bath. We were touching and caressing each other's bodies.

"Can I see what it was that was inside me last night?" I ask her, as she is drying my body.

"Of course you can, wait there!" she says, wrapping the towel around me.

She walks back in with her little friend strapped on to her.

"Is that what… it's not…?"

"Yes, this was inside you!"

"Oh, I'm glad I didn't see it first"

"Do you want me to show you?"

"Ummm..."

Before I could answer, she was standing behind me, gently, oh very gently caressing my body. Her hands were everywhere, and then she put them on my neck, pushing my chin up and biting my neck, and playing with my nipples.

"Oh Nicole, you're so hot!"

I feel her mouth curling up into a smile on my neck. One of her hands is slowly going down my body, tenderly touching me, while the other one stays on my breasts. Her fingers expertly playing with my nipples, then slide down and cup my breast. Her other hand slides between my thighs. The hand that was cupping my breast is now on my back, pushing on my back so that I bend over in front of her. Her fingers do their work, they are playing with my clit, and then they are inside me. *How, how is she doing all that?* My brain is screaming. She has one hand round the front of me and her fingers are inside me, coming from behind. Is she going to put that thing inside me...? I want to feel her thrusting inside me again... oh God... I'm going to explode... my poor little brain just can't keep up... her fingers are still inside me... I can feel the tip of it now... she's gently pushing it inside me... she pulls her fingers away... her hands roam up my back to my shoulders... I go to stand up but she pushes me back down to bending position... her hands slide down my sides... sending shivers through my body... she has hold of my hips, gently pulling me onto her... I can feel it going deeper inside me... she starts thrusting, very gently and very slowly, and it is going deeper in to me with every thrust. She's now holding me still and moving her hips in a slow rhythm... I hold on to the towel rail in front of me to keep myself steady... it's making my whole body tremble... I fall down to my knees, she carefully gets on her knees and re-inserts with slow thrusts, pulling my hips up and in towards her... pushing it into me gently... I turn to the side and see that she's watching, as it slowly goes inside me and out. I watch her in the mirror watching it...

"Go faster...!" I pant.

"I don't want to hurt you."

"Fuck me faster!" I beg, "I want to feel it… really feel it!"

She goes faster, still watching it going in and out, smiling. One of her hands slides between my legs, her fingers are playing with my clit… I'm shouting her name… she slows down again, pulling it slowly out, and sliding it slowly back in.

"Harder!" I say.

She gets harder and faster, and her fingers find my clit again. This brings me to orgasm. I collapse down onto the floor and turn over and look at her. She's still on her knees, smiling. She's undoing the strap. She throws the strap-on aside, and sits astride me.

"Fuck!" is all I can say. She is playing with my nipples, but they are too sensitive right now… I put my hand on them to stop her… just for a moment, just until they become less sensitive.

"You are going to kill me!" I gasp.

"What a way to go!" she says, smiling from ear to ear.

She moves up my body a bit, rubbing herself along on my chest. I run my hands up her beautiful body and play with her very erect nipples, and she moans. I put my hands on her hips and encourage her to keep moving up my body. She looks at me, and I nod. It is her turn to hold the hand rail now, as my tongue explores inside her. I can feel her body shake as my tongue teases her clit. I put my tongue right inside her and then back to her clit again. She lets herself lower on to me a bit more, rubbing herself onto my mouth, so that my tongue can get everywhere a bit more easily. I lick every inch of her, her hips start moving wildly so that she's rubbing herself on my mouth. I hold her hips still so that I can gently bite her clit. She moans.

"Suck it!" she says.

I take her clit into my mouth and suck it very hard and, within a few seconds, she cums. Every inch of her body is trembling. She moves her hips back down onto mine, so she is straddling me again. We lie like that for a while, I hold her tightly to me, she is still shaking. She moves so that she is lying beside me, her hands roaming up and down my body.

"You are very wet," she says, as she puts her hands between my thighs, "You play... you touch yourself!"

I do, but I look away as I touch myself,

"No, look at me Sam... look into my eyes as you cum!"

I smile at her, it feels strange... but a nice strange. She plays with one of my nipples, as my fingers play with my clit. That gets me very excited. I rub my clit as she looks deep into my eyes. I look away again, but she gently holds my chin and turns my head, so I am looking at her.

"I'm going to cum!" I pant, looking straight into her eyes. She looks from my eyes, to my hand rubbing my clit, and then back to my eyes... just in time to see me orgasm.

"Wow!" she says. "Wow, I can't tell you what you do to me... you are amazing! Are you OK?"

I just lay there... OK? ... OK does not even begin to describe how I feel... I smile at her...

"Are you OK?"

"I'm in heaven, in heaven!"

"I am too, Sam!"

We lie there for a little while... then we put our dressing gowns on and go into the kitchen. We finish the pizza, eating as if we have never eaten before, and then have a drink.

"Bed time, I think!" she says.

We just lie in bed, holding each other, discussing tonight and the events of weekend that we have just shared together.

"Are you alright with everything?" she asks.

I reassure her for the twentieth time that I would tell her immediately if I was not.

"We have done so much! Is it normal to do what we have done?" I ask.

"What do you mean, normal?"

"Well, does everyone do what we have just done?"

She giggles.

"You are laughing at me!" I say, feeling suddenly embarrassed.

"No, I'm sorry, everyone is different, and there are no rules. We do what we feel comfortable doing. I am not laughing at you, you ask whatever you want to ask."

"OK, have you had many partners?"

"Sam!"

"You said to ask you anything!"

"OK, you are right, I did. I have had a couple of relationships that never really went anywhere, and one that lasted about a year, but…"

"But what…" I ask.

"I was about to say that it feels different with you… very different"

"In what way?"

"It just feels nice, I can't explain how you make me feel, it's like we just fit together. Nothing is forced, or hard work… it's just natural," she says and holds me very close, our naked bodies entwined. We fall asleep in each other's arms, comfortable, relaxed and smiling.

Chapter 16

I wake up next to Nicole... again... I really like it... no... I love it... I snuggle in to her warm body.

"Morning gorgeous!" I say, as she opens one sleepy eye, and smiles at me.

"Morning to you too!" she says, kissing my cheek, "What, no breakfast ready his morning... I'll have to trade you in!" We both laugh.

"I just wanted to lie here and have a cuddle, if it's OK with you. My girlfriend tired me out this weekend!"

"Did she?" Nicole asks. "That's not good, is it!"

"Au contraire," I smile. "It's been an amazing weekend, but I'm guessing that you need to get to work"

"Oh shit!" Nicole jumps out of bed. "I have a pupil in 25 minutes she gasps as she looks at the clock!"

"You jump in the shower and I'll make you a cup of tea!" I say.

"I won't have time to drink one, sorry babe. However, my pupil lives very close to your house, so I can drop you off, or you can chill here for a bit, it's up to you!" she shouts as she runs into the bathroom.

She is back in the bedroom clean, but dripping wet within 5 minutes.

"I'm going to go home, if that's OK… I want to have a run. Dad will be at work, so you can drop me at the house, if you are sure that is OK with you?"

As we pull into my road, I see something very pink on our driveway. It's a bright pink KA. It has a huge pink bow tied right around it. On the windscreen is a cardboard sign saying,

"Well done, Sam X"

As I get out of the car, Jess jumps out from behind the bush and takes a photo. I burst into tears.

"Dad's surprise for you!" Jess is saying, but it's not sinking in. Nicole and Jess say, "Hi!"

"I really have to go, sorry Sam! That's great, I will call you later."

As I hug her goodbye, Jess says, "This is a really good inconspicuous car for you two, isn't it!"

We all laugh.

"So this is why you have been texting me to see what time I will be home… very devious!"

"Well, I had to take a picture, as Dad wanted to see your face when you saw the car!"

"Have we got the best Dad in the world… or what?" I start to cry.

"Is everything OK with Nicole?" Jess asks me whilst laughing and giving me a hug.

"Yes, really good… she has to rush off because she's running late this morning."

"Oops… your fault?" She giggles.

"No, actually… it isn't, this time!" I smile.

"Well, are you going to take me out for a spin in it, or what?"

"Do you think we should? What about the insurance for me to drive it?"

"Dad has sorted all that out for you."

"OK, let me dump my bags, and we can go if you are sure that you are ready to come out in the car with me."

"Oh yes, and if we have any issues, we can just ring Nicole!" she teases.

"That reminds me… Nicole asked me to ask you whether you fancied bowling again on Wednesday evening."

"That sounds like a great idea… just let me ask Dad if he can come over and sit with the boys. Shall we make it a regular Wednesday night event?"

"Yes, sure, if you can bear losing every week!"

- *Thanks Dad, the car is amazing! You are the best Dad in the whole wide world. I am just going to take Jess out for a drive x*

It feels really strange driving without Nicole sitting beside me.

"This car is something else, Jess, isn't it. We are so lucky having our Dad!"

"We sure are… we couldn't have bought our house if he hadn't given us the money for the deposit."

We drive around for a while discussing how lucky we are… we also discuss my exciting weekend and, of course, Nicole.

"I think I love her, Jess!" I confide. "She makes me so happy, I go all gooey just thinking about her, like I can't breathe with the excitement… was that how it felt when you when you met Matthew?"

"Yes, and I can't imagine life without him and the boys now. The 'new' excitement of it all gets less but turns into a different feeling. It's still love, just a different love, he really is my best friend, and I love him with all my heart!"

"That's really sweet, Jess!"

"I'm so glad that you have found someone that makes you feel this way. Are you going to tell Dad, now?"

166

"Not yet, Jess, I am not ready for that yet. I wish you could understand."

"It's up to you, of course, but I think that Dad will understand, you know?"

"Shall we get some lunch?" I say, changing the subject, and I park the car in the car park of a carvery.

Well I don't just park… I actually reverse into the space!

"I'm impressed!" says Jess. "You're a good little driver!"

"Thanks!" I say, with a huge smile on my face.

- *How is the car, babe x o x*

- *Really good, but strange driving without you sitting beside me x x x*

- *What are you doing now? x o x*

- *Just going to have lunch with Jess x x x*

- *OK, I will call you later… have fun, and say Hi to Jess for me x o x*

- *Jess says Hi back, and are you ready to lose at bowling on Wednesday? x x x*

- *Fighting talk… huh! Does she not know that we are the dream team lol x o x*

- *He he he! … I will tell her… talk soon x x x*

We have a lovely lunch and discuss the boys and their achievements on the football pitch. They obviously take after their Dad. Matthew's mum is still not very well, Jess tells me.

We talk about Christopher and the fact that he will hopefully be coming home soon.

"I have an interview on Friday for the Social Work course!" I tell her.

"It will be strange at Uni without your mates there, won't it?"

"Yes, although all three of them will be at the same Uni doing their PGCE course, however, we won't get to see each other as much because we will all be out in the real world on placements."

"Look at the time, Sam... are you going to drive me home?"

"Yes, of course!"

Oh God, I will have to drive home by myself, after dropping Jess off... that's scary... very scary... It will be the first time that I am alone in a car... somehow, Jess must realise what I am thinking.

"Will you be OK driving home by yourself?" she asks.

"Yes, I will have to do it at some point and at least the roads are quiet at the moment."

I drive her home, and we arrange a time to meet on Wednesday.

- Can you talk or have you got a pupil? x x x

I hear Ed singing to me... her special ringtone...

"Hi baby, I have 5 mins before my next pupil. Are you OK?"

"Yes, I'm OK. I have just dropped Jess off and I am about to drive home... by myself!"

"You will be fine!"

Oh, no... not 'fine' again... why do people say you will be fine... how do they know that? They don't know that... but everyone always says it... you'll be fine...!

"Sam!"

"Sorry, I'm just a little nervous. I have never been in a car alone" I say, clutching sub-consciously at my necklace.

"Just drive how you normally drive, Sam. Put your mobile on silent and put it in the glove compartment, so that it won't disturb you."

"OK... I'll be fine, thanks!"

Oh God... I'm saying it now... I will be fine!

"It's only a five-minute drive, I will text you when I get home."

"OK, baby. I'm missing being with you, and looking forward to seeing you on Wednesday."

"I'll call you tonight."

"OK text me when you get home though, please!"

"I will do... talk soon!"

Dad gets home at the normal time, and I run and jump on him.

"Thanks Dad... I can't believe that you got me a car!"

"Do you like it?"

"I love it... do you want to come out for a drive with me?"

"I sure do, let me just get changed quickly."

We go for a nice drive, and Dad compliments me by saying...

"Nicole taught you well!"

If only you knew... I think to myself... she has taught me more than you will ever know... more than you need to know... should I tell him... that I'm with her, I mean... not what she has taught me!

"Thanks again, Dad! I can't believe that you have bought me a car... it's absolutely amazing! I am so lucky!"

"You deserve it, Sam... just promise me that you'll always be sensible when you're driving!"

"I promise!"

We both sit quietly for a while, and I fiddle with my necklace…

"Dad, I have an interview on Friday for the Social Work course that I want to do."

"You will be …"

He sees my face and does not need to finish his sentence. We both laugh.

"I've been roped into baby-sitting every Wednesday night so that you can all go and enjoy yourselves bowling."

"Oh!" I say, feeling bad.

He laughs… "It's fine… I love seeing the boys, you know that!"

As I fall into bed later that evening, I text Nicole.

- *What an amazing few days I have had x x x*

- *I am in bed already… just thinking the same thing… I am shattered x o x*

- *Me too… I need sleep. I was thinking that I could pick you up on Wednesday, just for a change?*

- *That sounds good, babe, if you are sure x o x*

- *Yes. Do you think that we could go to the garage too? … I don't know how to put the petrol in x x x*

- *Of course. I might even show you where the oil and water go too! x o x*

- *What… you mean I have to do that too? x x x*

- *Yes, and check the tyres… I will show you it all, don't worry x o x*

- *What would I do without you? x x x*

- *You are not without me… I need to go to sleep now, talk tomorrow x o x*

- *Night night gorgeous, sweet dreams x x x*

Chapter 17

I did plan to run this morning, but I didn't wake up until 10a.m. I have never slept that late! I decide to have a lazy day. I do the housework, and do some ironing and then rummage through the freezer. I make gammon risotto for dinner, and catch up with people on the phone, including Cassie, Louise, Christopher and an old friend, Charlotte, who I was best friends with when we were at Secondary School. It was really nice to chat with her.

"Sorry I've not been in touch for a while, I've been going through a tough time", she tells me. "I'm gay, you see!"

Wow... that was easy... just like that she tells me... I'm gay! Tell her... tell her... I can't... I ask her if she fancies going for a drink one night, maybe I can tell her then? She knows what I'm going through... what I am feeling...

"Are you seeing someone?" I ask.

"No, I was, but it didn't work out."

"I drink in a gay bar," she's saying. "Would you be happy to meet me there? Lots of straight people go there too, it's a really nice, inclusive, comfortable place for a drink, if you fancy it?"

"I don't mind," I hear myself saying... why... I don't know why... maybe I'm curious... curious of what... a gay bar... of what a gay bar is like... so I have just told a single gay woman that I will go to a gay bar with her... how would Nicole feel about this... how would I feel if Nicole told me she was doing that… I don't know… I arrange with Charlotte to meet her… in a gay bar…

"Hi Sam!"

"Hello, Dad, dinner will be ready soon!"

"Dinner! And you have been tidying up, I see!"

"Did you have a good day?"

"I'm glad to be home… it's been a long day."

I lie in the bath later on that night, thinking about how much my life has changed, and about how easily Charlotte was able to say… 'I'm gay'… just like that… I am gay!

"Sam, your phone has been ringing!"

"OK, Dad, I am getting out now"

How do I tell Nicole about Charlotte? I have three missed calls from Nicole… I call her.

"Hi gorgeous… are you OK?"

"Yes, I'm fine… I just wanted to hear your voice," she says.

"Oh sorry, I was in the bath."

"How was your day, baby?"

"It was good" I say, and then I tell her about my conversation with Charlotte… she goes very quiet…

"Are you OK with this?" I ask.

"Should I be OK with this? Should I be worried?"

"Do you need to ask me that?"

"I hope not… I trust you, Sam."

"Good, because you have nothing to worry about… I'm with you… you are all I want and maybe next time I meet up with her, you could come with me. I just need to go on my own this first time… I want to tell her about you, on my own!"

"You want to tell her?" Nicole sounds surprised.

"Yes I do… I didn't know this until just now, but I do want to tell her, is this OK with you?"

"Of course it is... I want to shout it from the rooftops... but as I told you, I will go at your speed, babe!"

I want to tell her that I love her... I do... I love her... but I can't tell her, not yet!

"Sam, do you think that you could go to a gay bar with me, and keep your hands off me?"

"Can I tell you the answer to that when we are there?"

"Are you coming back to mine after bowling tomorrow?"

"Yes, I want to... I won't be able to stay though"

"OK, baby, I can't wait to see you!"

"Me too... night night!"

"Night night, Nicole, sweet dreams!"

She hangs up and I whisper... "I love you!" down the phone.

The day, surprisingly, passes quickly. I pick Nicole up and she looks hot. She only has jeans and a blouse on, but she looks really hot. I tell her so as she gets into my car... my car! We win at bowling again, but I'm not sure whether Nicole enjoys the winning more than she enjoys taking the mickey out of Matthew, as Arsenal beat Chelsea on Saturday! It is really nice that she and Matthew get on so well, and Jess comments on that when we are getting the next round of drinks from the bar.

"Nicole really is a lovely person!" she says. I just smile proudly, and glance back at the beautiful woman, laughing with Matthew on the bench, and think how lucky I am to have found her.

We all have a good evening, and Jess and Matthew tell us that they will definitely win next week!

"Just like Chelsea!" Nicole teases Matthew.

We say our goodbyes and walk to the car. Nicole has a big smile on her face.

"What are you smiling about?" I ask.

"I'm just happy," she says as we get into the car. "And… I have no knickers on…!"

"Really, why are you just telling me that now?"

"I needed you to concentrate on the bowling… we have to win!" she giggles.

"You are SO bad, and I love it!" I giggle with her.

"Great minds…" I say.

"What… you have no knickers on either?"

"That's right… but I also needed you to concentrate on the bowling!"

"OK," she says, staring at me.

"What?" I ask.

"I'm wondering how long it's going to take me to get your jeans off when we get inside my front door."

"Will you text my dad saying no need to wait up because I'm going to be late as we are going to have a girly chat and a cup of hot chocolate… oh and put a kiss on the end, please"

"Of course… anything you say," says Nicole, sending the text. After a few minutes, she says,

"You have a reply… do you want me to read it?"

"Yes, please"

"It says… 'OK, drive safely, Dad'."

We go into her apartment, and the second she shuts the door we are ripping at each other's clothes, trying to get naked. It was different this time… urgent… we could not get enough of each other… kissing… touching… licking… sucking… it was very erotic and very hot and we both orgasmed many times.

"I'll have to wear no knickers more often" she chuckles, "Do you want your hot chocolate now?" she asks.

"No," I say, leading her by the hand to the bedroom. I push her onto the bed, and kneel at the end of the bed, and kiss my way up her leg and right up to the inside of her thigh. My tongue teased her clit…

175

"Suck me!" she begged.

I did as she asked, then I sat up and put her fingers on her clit. I sat and watched her bring herself to orgasm.

"Fuck, you are hot!" she said, when she could talk again. I collapse down on top of her... we cuddled and I said,

"I'm really sorry, but I need to go soon."

"I know... a quick cuddle first, please?"

We just lie there for a while, and then the time came when I really had to leave.

"Text me and let me know that you get home safely."

"I will!"

She kisses me goodbye and said,

"You are amazing, Sam!"

I kiss her back... tell her you love her... NO... not yet... it's too soon... it might scare her.

- I'm home, you sexy woman x x x

- Good I can go to sleep now, thanks for tonight baby. Night night x o x

- Night night, sweet dreams x x x

I awake on Thursday morning with a smile on my face... I wonder why...? I love her... that's why! Dad has left for work already... I go for a run... it has been far too long since I have been for a run... Oh, it's lovely this morning... summer is on its way... it's June already, I don't know where this year is going...

"Morning!"

I really must make more of an effort with my running... it feels really hard today, I must get fitter.

"Morning!"

"Yes, it's lovely weather!"

My interview is tomorrow… I am going to ask Nicole if she wants to go on holiday… a week of sunshine and beach… Oh, I wonder if she likes the sunshine? There is still so much that I don't know about her…

"Morning!"

So much I need to find out… oh, this really is hard work this morning… I'm going to see Christopher this afternoon… he can go home in a few days' time… he is going to need lots of physio, though… so he will be spending lots of time back at the hospital. They have still not found the driver who did this to him. I guess they never will now, what a bastard, how can you do something like that and just drive off? It's beyond me!

I stand in the shower, remembering the things that we did in the shower… I need to get ready and get to the hospital. Christopher seemed much happier, knowing that he can go home soon… he wanted to hear all about the festival. I told him everything… well… all the bits I could, anyway. Cassie came in at that point, and we all agreed that we would go to the same festival again next year. Cassie starts telling Christopher all about Nicole, and how nice she is. I say good bye and leave them to it.

Just as I'm leaving the hospital, Jess calls, and asks if I want to come for dinner tonight. She tells me that Dad is coming too.

"That would be lovely, I'm just leaving the hospital. Shall I just come over to your house now?"

"Of course you can! How is he?"

"He is much better in himself now… still a long way to go, but he's getting there"

We all enjoy fajitas at Jess's house. The boys thrash me at Mario Cart, as they always do, I think I might start practicing so I can surprise them and maybe even win one day… no Sam, back to reality… that will never happen! They have their bath and I read them a bedtime story. I love reading to them. When I come back downstairs, Dad and Jess are discussing my car. I give Dad a hug and thank him again.

"It's a lovely car and I really appreciate it."

"Sam, you don't have to keep thanking me"

I tell Jess about Charlotte…

"You remember her, don't you?" I ask her.

"Yes, of course I do."

"She is gay, did you know that? I'm going to meet up with her next week."

"Oh is she? It will be nice for you to chat with her… and say hi to her from me!"

"So Jess, Sam tells me that she and Nicole are thrashing you and Matt at the bowling!"

"Oh she did… did she? What else did she tell you?"

I look at Jess… what is she going to say…? My heart is in my mouth… I frown at Jess… what is she doing? *Please don't say anything*, I am screaming in my head… Jess carries on…

"Did she tell you that we are going to thrash them next week?"

Dad laughs, "No funnily enough, she did not tell me that!"

I sigh… "We will see on Wednesday…!" I say.

Dad says that we should go as he's working in the morning, Jess has to get up with the boys and I have my interview.

"Good luck with your interview!" Jess says… wait for it… here is comes… wait for it…

"You will be fine!" There it is… right on cue!!

"Just be yourself… text me and let me know how you get on, please!"

"I will do, thanks for dinner!"

"Yes thanks for dinner, and your lovely company!" Dad chips in, and we drive home.

- I hope you had a good day… Jess says Hi x x x

- I guess you are asleep already... I wish I was there with you, next to you, cuddling you! Night night, sweet dreams x x x

I potter around slowly in the morning... there's no rush, my interview is not until 11a.m. I had a nice text from Nicole, when I woke up... she had had an early start this morning, and wished me luck for my interview. She asked me to text her and let her know how I got on.

I only just realised that I have hardly given any thought to my interview... I probably should have... a bit late now... I wonder if there will be many people there... I guess I will find out very soon...I get into my car, and just sit there for a few minutes, admiring her... I am going to call her Sasha, I decide! Hello Sasha... you look after me and I will look after you... I smile... I arrive for my interview dressed to impress, and ten minutes early. I am offered a place on the course and I am given a book list... I am delighted. I thought that I would have to wait for weeks to learn the outcome of this interview... there are quite a few books on the list... but I think I will ask for some of them as birthday presents, to ease the financial pressure.

Dad and I have a curry for dinner and watch a film. I remind him that I am going out with the camping girls tomorrow.

"Are you staying out, then?"

"That's not a bad idea, Dad, then I can drink and leave the car here. Would you mind dropping me off at the pub at seven-ish?"

"Of course I don't mind. I am out all day, and I am planning on being home at around six."

"Are you sure, because I could ask Nicole to pick me up?"

"Well, do you think she will mind, Sam, cos I could just stay out then... silly to come back home, just to go back out again."

"Hold on, I will text her," I say.

"She says that is fine, Dad, what time are you going out, then?"

"About 10."

"OK then, see you in the morning!"

"Night, Sam!"

- *Hi gorgeous… fancy coming to mine for lunch tomorrow? x x x*

- *With your dad? x o x*

- *No, he won't be here x x x*

- *What time do you want me? x o x*

- *All the time, but how about lunch about 1? x x x*

- *I can be there for 1.30 x o x*

- *See you then, sexy x x x*

One thirty on the dot… Nicole pulls up… I have made a quiche and salad… well… I bought the quiche… I hope she likes it… she knocks on the door.

"Come in!" I say, as I open the front door. "I have just done salad for lunch, is that OK with you?"

"That's very nice, Sam. I have been thinking… every time you stay or we are together, we have sex…"

"I know…!" I say, with a grin spreading across my face.

"I want us not to, today."

"What… don't you like it?" I say, suddenly worried that I had done or said something wrong, and upset her.

"I love it!" she says, as she holds my hands and looks deep into my eyes. "I don't want us to be just about sex, though, let's see if we can just kiss and cuddle today… tonight."

"Do you think you can do that, Nicole?"

"Let's try… we can just kiss and cuddle."

"It won't be easy… can we be naked, though?"

"Not in the pub!"

"Spoil sport!" I say, pulling her in to me for a kiss. "Let's eat, and then I will show you my bedroom."

She raises her eyebrows at me.

"Hey, I can do it if you can!" I tease.

After lunch I show her my bedroom.

"We could just have a little cuddle in bed, though?" I suggest.

She's frowning at me again.

"Are you just after one thing?" she asks, with a really serious face.

I turn away from her, and she grabs my hand and pulls me in for a cuddle.

"I'm joking, babe! I want to make love with you, I just want to show you how hot it is if you don't," she says, undoing my blouse. "We can look, but just not touch, other than cuddling."

I stand there while she undresses me, and I slowly undress her. I lead her over to my bed, we both get in. We lie there, just cuddling and stroking. She is right, this is very horny. We lie there for a few hours, just kissing and caressing each other… it is beautiful!

"You are beautiful!"

She looks in my eyes, and melts me just by looking at me… it is madness!

"This is really nice," I say cuddling into her "It's nice to be alone and have some quality time."

She agrees, nodding she says,

"It's nice to see your room, the real you."

"What do you mean, the real me? I don't hide who I am."

"No, I never meant it like that, what I mean is this is the real you, not Sam at work, not Sam in the pub."

"So who is the real you, tell me something I don't know about you."

"Well" she says laughing, "Where shall I start?"

I hold her tighter "Tell me about a dream you have, or what could make your life complete?"

"Heavy stuff, I'm not sure I have ever been asked that! Em...OK, there is something, however, I have never told anyone."

I kiss her neck just to encourage her and reassure her that I'm interested... I didn't realise until now... but I really want to know what she is thinking... who she really is.

"It's a bit crazy really, I want all the normal things in life, I want to get married, have kids..."

I think my reaction prompted a response.

"Don't worry... not yet," she said laughing, don't you want kids?"

Wow...I don't know... do I? I love kids... but do I want my own?

"To be honest I haven't really thought that far ahead."

She looks into my eyes and carries on "I do think about that... a lot."

I'm not ready to think about that... I have just got my head around being gay...

"Anyway," she continues, "before all of that there is something else... my crazy idea! I want to jump out of an airplane! With a parachute, of course!"

Now that I could get my head around... kids are a scary thought... I would rather jump out of an airplane... if I had to pick one of the two, right now... I would choose to jump...

"Wow… I wasn't expecting that! I can understand that though because I have always wondered about doing the same thing myself. Maybe we can jump together one day?"

"Sam?" says a voice from downstairs.

"Oh shit… it's my dad!"

We jump out of bed and get dressed in about one minute flat.

"Hi Dad! What are you doing?"

Nicole makes the bed quickly and sits on it, just as he knocks on my door. I grab a bag and pretend to be packing it.

"Come in!" I say.

"I forgot to take a clean shirt," he says, walking in.

He looks at Nicole…

"Oh you two haven't met, have you? Dad, this is Nicole, and Nicole, this is my dad!"

"Hi," they both say politely.

She stands up and walks over to him to shake his hand. My dad shakes it and then pulls her in for a hug.

"Thanks," he says.

"For what?"

"Well, for teaching my little girl to drive, of course!"

"No problem, Mr Meades!"

"Call me Harry, please!"

Can he see how embarrassed we both are…? I can't look at Nicole…

"I'll let you finish packing your bag, Sam. Are you staying at Louise's tonight, Sam?"

"Ermmm… well, actually, Nicole says that I could stay at hers… she lives near the pub that we are going to."

Dad turns to Nicole,

"Look after my little girl!"

"Dad…!"

"Of course I will, Harry!" Nicole is saying.

"Well, have a good time tonight, ladies, and be sensible! I'll just get changed and I'll be off!"

"Have a good night, Dad, see you tomorrow!"

"Out all day… you said!" whispers Nicole as she falls backwards onto the bed.

"That's what he said, I'm sorry!"

She laughs.

Well, the good thing is that at last I have met your dad, and now he knows that you are staying at mine, good move, Sam!"

"I don't like lying to him, but at least I can now say that I am staying at yours."

"I have never nearly been caught in bed with someone's daughter!" she teases.

"Really, and you think I have!"

She pulls me onto the bed and cuddles me.

"It is all good, babe, you don't have to hide me now, you don't need to tell him we are together, but…"

"I get it, Nicole, it just shocked me… him coming home like that."

She kisses my forehead and strokes my hair.

"I love your hair," she says, stroking my hair right down my back. At the bottom, she gently tugs it, tipping my head upwards. Her lips find mine, and she gently kisses me.

"We need to finish our conversation another time, I would like to know your dreams and plans, but for now, let's get your bag packed, baby, and let's get going!"

"Bye Sam, Bye Nicole!" Dad shouts as he walks to the front door.

"Let's go and meet the rest of the gang!" she says.

"You are not funny!" I say, pushing her onto the bed, climbing on top of her and kissing her. I am sitting astride her, and I look down at her.

"I think I love you!"

She pulls me gently onto my back… she lays beside me and looks into my eyes… into my soul…

"What did you say?"

"I said, I love you… you are all I can think about every minute of every day… you make me so happy! I love you, Nicole, is that OK?"

She keeps hold of my cheeks and kisses me very softly, looks into my eyes, and tells me that she knows exactly how I feel, because she feels exactly the same…

"You … you…?" I can't get the words out.

"Yes, Sam, I love you!"

We lie there smiling at each other, with tears in our eyes. I have never felt as contented as I did at that exact moment. She kisses my tears away, so tenderly.

"We have to go and meet the girls!" I say, eventually, hating to end those few moments of peace and happiness.

"I know, let's go…"

"I can always say that I don't feel very well, and we can get away early?"

And we do exactly that. We spend an hour or so with them, and we talk about the weekend which we all agreed was brilliant. We shared photos that we took. Louise had taken a lovely picture of Nicole and me and she sent it to me. I told them I had got the place at Uni, and they were really pleased for me.

Nicole said she was not feeling great, so we apologised, and agreed to meet up again. We say our goodbyes, and leave.

"Nicole, that was really bad… good… but bad!"

"Yes, but at least we came… we had a nice time. But right now I want to spend time with you, and just you!"

We get into the car and she says, "I forgot what you told me earlier?"

I smile and say, "Take me to yours, and I'll remind you? Shall we get an Indian on the way home?"

"Yes, but next time can we cook together… I'd like to cook a nice meal with you," says Nicole.

"Sounds like a date! I am not very hungry, right now," I say, "Are you?"

"No," she says, we can order a take-away later, if you want? That makes sense."

We both agree.

"It is a lovely warm evening," I say, "shall we go for a walk along the beach?"

"As long as you don't want me to run, Sam", and we both giggle.

We park at her apartment, she gets two hoodies out of the boot of her car and hands me one.

"Thanks," I say. We walk along the beach. No-one is around, it is very quiet, but then I guess it is 9p.m.

My hand brushes hers, she pulls her hand away. I find it again, and this time keep hold of it.

"I didn't think that you would want to… I thought it was an accident, that's why I pulled away."

"I do want to, I'm sorry" I said.

"Why are you sorry?"

"Because I want to tell the world, I want to walk down the middle of the High Street, holding your hand, but I don't think I am quite ready for that yet."

She stops and faces me. It is getting dark so she her face is partially hidden by the shadows.

"Sam… Your speed, remember… I'm not pushing you, I won't… it's all at your speed".

"Thanks," I say, and lean in and kiss her. We carry on walking. I find her hand again and hold it. She turns and smiles at me.

"Nicole?" I say.

"Yes, Sam."

"I have just realised something, I've never walked along holding another person's hand."

"What does it feel like?"

"I don't mean this horribly, but it's quiet here and dark, so it's nice. One day we can do it in the High Street, I want to be able to do it in the High Street in front of everyone."

"Sam!"

"Sorry, yes I know… all at MY speed!"

"Yes."

"I love you!"

"Have you noticed something, Sam?"

"That I am walking along, holding your hand?"

"Which, by the way, I like very much… it is very nice, but that's not what I was going to say… What I was going to say was that I have not stopped smiling since you told me that you loved me!"

Then she stopped, held both my hands and said, "Can I kiss you, please?"

I looked around, no-one was in sight.

"Yes, please!"

She kissed me so gently.

"Oh Nicole! You turn me on so much!"

"Ditto!" she says.

"Shall we go and order some dinner, now and share a bath while we wait for it to arrive?"

"Let's go!" I say.

We have a really lovely evening, we share a bath, eat our dinner and then lie in bed together kissing and cuddling.

"I think I am in heaven!" I say.

"I am there with you, baby!"

We fall asleep in each other's arms.

Chapter 18

I awake before her. I lie there for ten minutes just watching her sleep. I love this intimate time with her. Then I creep out of the room and start cooking eggy bread for us.

"Sam! Sam!" I hear Nicole shouting from the bedroom.

I go running in…

"Oh, I thought you had gone, babe! I woke up and you weren't here."

"Oh sexy! Don't worry, I am just making your breakfast!"

I walk over, bend down and kiss her.

"You just lie there and I will bring breakfast to you."

"I could get used to this, baby!"

"Good!"

- *Morning! We all had a very late night. I'm going to stay here with the girls today, I will see you this evening. X*

- *Thanks for letting me know. Have a good day! Dad X*

"Nicole," I say, walking back into the bedroom, "Two things… the sex ban was just for yesterday, wasn't it? And secondly… are you doing anything today?"

"Yes and no… why?"

"In that order?"

"Yes, Sam."

"Oh good, eat up then, you are going to need your energy today!"

"Oh, I like the sound of that!" she says, "But first come and sit and talk to me."

"What about?"

"Well we never finished our conversation before your dad came home."

"Don't remind me!" I look up at her, still remembering the shock of nearly being caught.

"So, now it's your turn, tell me something I don't know about you!"

I smile and twiddle my necklace "One of mine is similar to yours, well, it's connected to airplanes."

"I'm intrigued!"

"I have, for as long as I can remember, wanted to try wing walking!"

"Wow, now that is a really unusual ambition! It's a bit dare-devilish… wouldn't you be scared? I would be really scared watching you do that."

"Ah that's sweet! I think I would be really nervous going up, but once standing there, I think I would love it… it would be such an amazing feeling, and unlike anything else I have ever done!"

She smiled and said, "You said 'one' of yours, what else is on your list?"

"You will laugh at me." I screw my face up just thinking about my bucket list.

She laughs at me "Come on, now you have to tell me!"

"I want to run a marathon, swim the channel…"

"Swim the channel! I never even knew you swam!"

"I don't very often that's why that one is a bit crazy, but even crazier is the fact that I would love to own a forklift truck!"

Looking at me slightly confused, she laughs "Why"

"I don't know…" I say burying my face in the pillow. "I just love the idea of moving pallets of stuff from here to there and then back to here again! I would be in heaven!

"I don't even know what to say to that, but I did ask you, so thanks for sharing that with me… weirdo!"

We both burst out laughing and she cuddles me.

We then spend the whole day making love, so gentle and sensual, it's amazing. We lie holding each other tenderly, touching, cuddling, kissing, and exploring each other's bodies. I don't want the day to ever end, but unfortunately the time comes when I have to leave.

"Five more minutes?" Nicole says.

"You've said that three times, already!" I say, "I'm sorry, but I really do have to go"

"I know, baby," she says, kissing my forehead. She watches me get dressed, puts her dressing gown on and walks me to the door. We stand there kissing for another five minutes. Finally we tear ourselves apart and I drive home.

"Hi Dad!" I say when I get home, "How are you?"

"I'm good. How was your weekend?"

"Very good!" I smile. "It's always good catching up with the girls"

One in particular… I think… she loves me… I love her. It is crazy… but I do… I love her…

The next week goes by in a flash. Nicole and I beat Jess and Matthew at bowling AGAIN! It's getting too easy now! I was able to see Nicole a few times. She tells me to behave at the gay bar on Saturday with Charlotte…

"I've decided that I'm definitely going to tell Charlotte all about you on Saturday… is that OK with you?"

"Of course it is, babe, I told you if that's what you want then it's fine with me."

"It is, and you can come with us next time, if you want to!"

"Yes, that would be good, I haven't been there for ages. We could take Jess and Matthew there too?" she says, "There are lots of straight people who drink in there too."

"Really?" I ask, looking down... I have never been to a gay bar... I have not even thought about it... what will it be like... I guess I will find out very soon... part of me wishes that Nicole could be there with me... but... I need to tell Charlotte about her first... well... I need to tell her about me first... Oh, how am I going to do that?

I meet Charlotte, as arranged, at half past seven in the car park of the pub.

"Hi!" she says. "How are you? And are you sure you don't mind going in here?"

"I'm fine. How are you? And I don't mind going in here at all... I have got lots of things to tell you!"

"Oh that sounds very intriguing..." she says.

We go into the bar and order drinks... soft drinks, as we are both driving. I look around the bar, it's massive, and there is a little dance area section, where lots of people are already dancing. It is quite easy to see who is gay and who is straight, I think to myself. It is a really nice atmosphere... everyone just talks to everyone.

A lady says hello to me at the bar. She has short, brown hair, lovely green eyes and a nice smile.

"Do you know her?" Charlotte asks.

"I don't think so... she looks a bit familiar, though."

Where have I see her? I can't think... I soon forget about her though, when Charlotte asks what it is that I have to tell her... Oh... where shall I start... how do I start?

"I have a girlfriend!" I announce… where did that come from? I had a whole conversation in my head… but there it is… it's out there now… I have a girlfriend… way to go, Sam!

"Wow, Sam… I wasn't expecting that! You are gay? When? How long have you been with her… wow… details please?"

I smile at her… God, I need a drink! Why am I driving? I tell her the whole story.

"So, does everyone know?"

"No," I tell her all about how Jess caught me out, and how I had to tell her, although no-one else knows.

"Except me!" she says, and we both laugh.

"So, tell me all about you?"

She tells me all about Angela who she has just broken up with.

"Sounds like you are better off without her…" I say, after listening to half an hour about the way she had treated Charlotte… I am so lucky I have got Nicole… I think to myself…

- *Missing you, gorgeous x x x*

- *Do you need rescuing baby, or are you enjoying sitting watching all the gay women? x o x*

I haven't even noticed who is around us, and I have a quick look… Oh that is quite horny… two hot women kissing… quite passionately too… and no-one is paying any attention to them…

- *I'm just sitting talking to Charlotte x x x*

- *I bet you are!! x o x*

"Do you want another drink?" Charlotte asks.

"Why not!" I say.

- Charlotte is getting the drinks in… I have told her all about you x x x

- Not all, I hope x o x

- Well, not quite… I will text you when I get home x x x

"One orange juice and lemonade! For you! And are you sure you don't know the brunette?"

"Thanks! No, I don't know her… why?"

"Because she has not taken her eyes off you all night… you must have noticed!"

"She's probably looking at you," I say, looking up and catching the brunette's eye… she looks away quickly… I do kind of recognise her… but where from? Maybe Uni?

"She's definitely looking at you!" Charlotte says, snapping me out of my daydream. "So when am I going to meet the lucky woman who has set your world on fire, then?"

"How about next Saturday? I will check with Nicole and text you during the week, but I don't think it will be a problem."

We spend the rest of the evening talking about family and school. She seemed to know what everyone is doing now. We have a really nice evening, and I enjoyed my first experience of a gay bar. I can't believe that it is past midnight when I get home. I wonder if I should text Nicole this late at night. I decide that it is too late… but I did tell her that I would… I don't want her to think that I have forgotten… but I don't want to wake her up… what if she is awake and worrying though…

- I hope this doesn't wake you up, I just want to let you know that I am home safe, snuggled up in my bed, wishing that you were here x x x

- Thanks babe… missing you x o x

Dad and I go for Sunday lunch at Jess's.

"How is your mum, Matthew?" Dad asks.

"Not very good, unfortunately, Harry."

"Give her our love!" I say.

Jess makes wicked roast potatoes… I love her roast… she calls me into the kitchen to help her dish up… she doesn't want my help… she wants a gossip… I am so glad she likes Nicole and gets on well with her.

"So…?" She says, the second I step into the kitchen.

"Nicole is fine… we are fine!" Oh God, when did I start saying 'fine'? Is that really the best I can do? We are amazing… fantastic… the sex is out of this world… no I can't say any of that, I just smile.

"What are you smiling about?" she asks.

"Oh nothing, just thinking how happy I am! How happy she makes me!"

"Good… still on for bowling on Wednesday?"

"You want to lose again?" I tease.

"We are going to win this week, I can feel it!"

"Fighting talk, eh!" I laugh.

We all enjoy a lovely dinner and Dad makes a surprise announcement that he is thinking about taking a sabbatical for a year, so that he can travel. We are all shocked… where has this come from, we ask him. He tells us about his friend Tom, at work. His wife sadly passed away a few months ago. He decided to take a year off to travel around Australia, leaving on the 1st September, and he asked Dad if he wanted to accompany him…

"Why not? You will look after each other, won't you? This kind of opportunity does not come along often," said Matthew.

"Yes, but I'm only thinking about it, I haven't made up my mind yet. What do you all think?"

"Go for it!" all three of us say, in unison.

"We will be OK, Dad, it is time you did something for you… you deserve it!" Jess says.

"I don't have to move out though, do I?" I say, only half joking.

"You can move in here!" Matthew offers, smiling.

"Hold on, I have not finally decided yet!" Dad says a bit taken aback that we have all but packed his cases for him. "But if I do go, of course you won't have to move out! It's your home, Sam!"

"Thanks Dad! I think you should go then!"

Everyone laughs, "But, on a serious note…" I say, "It is about time you had some fun. I think it would be amazing and we can Skype regularly, and even come out and see you."

"Yes, we could all come out to Australia for a few weeks to see you." says Jess, her eyes sparkling with excitement.

"Would you really be OK with it?" Dad asks.

We all assure him that we would miss him terribly, but that it would be fine. There it is again… fine…

"I need to check with work that they will actually release me for a year, of course."

Jess and I wash up, and discuss Dad's idea. We decide that he should definitely go.

"He hasn't looked so excited for as long as I can remember." I say, reaching for my necklace.

Jess agrees and says, "We need to support him with this."

We return to the others and we all spend a happy evening together.

Chapter 19

Today is Christopher's big day! He is going home, I think as I am running along the beach.

"Morning!"

Oh, it's been a long time since I did this... I must make an effort to run more... I wonder if Dad will go. I hope so... I will really miss him, but it would be such fun for him... I'm going to go and see Christopher tomorrow.

"Morning!"

Everyone will be going tonight... it's hard running today... probably because I have not done it for so long... and I don't know why, because I really enjoy running... it gives me a real buzz when I am finished.

Dad has already left for work. I stand in the shower. The hot water just hitting me and running down my body... it makes me remember the amazing showers that I have had with Nicole... nice memories... hot memories... I can't wait to see her tomorrow night... my thoughts run away with me...

When I get out of the shower, I do some housework and before I know it, it is 3 o'clock! Louise calls me and we have a chat. I almost tell her about Nicole... who am I? I think I am nearly ready to tell the world... nearly... not quite though... Louise has arranged to have lessons with Nicole on Wednesdays at 4p.m.

Dad is just pulling up on the driveway... I have cooked his favourite, spaghetti bolognaise! He gets in the shower before dinner.

"Dishing up in 10 minutes!" I shout.

As we sit down to eat, he looks at me.

"You are going, aren't you?"

"I need to be sure that you and Jess are definitely OK with it, before I make my final decision. Work have said that it is fine..."

Fine... really!

"Dad, Jess and I have talked about it and we think that it's a no-brainer. You need to do this, or you'll regret it. We love you, and obviously we will miss you, but we'll talk to you all the time on Skype. We are really happy for you!"

"Are you, Sam? Really? Will you be OK?"

"Yes, really!"

I get up and give him a hug. He cries. I can't remember the last time I saw him cry.

"Will you come to Jess's with me, tonight, please, so I can tell her?"

"Of course, I will! I'll text her in a minute to let her know that we are popping around"

"Thanks, I will really miss your spaghetti bolognaise!"

"Oh nice! Not me... just my spag bol!!"

"No, Sam..."

"I'm joking! Eat up before it gets cold!"

We walk into Jess's house, the boys are asleep. She looks at Dad and says...

"You are going, then?"

"Only if you are sure that you are OK with it?"

"Dad! I am over the moon for you. I will miss you... you have done more for us than any other Dad has ever done for his daughters! You raised us on your own. We love you and want what is best for you. It is only a year and we can still talk regularly, so it will be fine! You go and enjoy every second of it. I will keep an eye on Sam!"

"Er… hello! I am standing here, and I can hear you! I am twenty-four, not four, you know!"

"You will always be my little sister, Sam!"

We stay at Jess's for an hour. Matthew was at his mum's… she is not good at all, Jess tells us…

"Let us know if we can do anything!" Dad and I say as we are leaving.

- Can't wait to see you tomorrow x x x

- Me too… lots to tell you, babe x o x

- Me too… night night x x x

In the morning, I drive over to Christopher's. It is still a big adventure being able to drive my own car… I love it! Cassie is there already. Christopher is in a good mood, very glad to be home. He said that Louise had visited him yesterday and was really excited that she was starting her driving lessons… I bet she's not as excited as I used to be… I thought… and excited was the right word… she will be… Oh God! I nearly said 'fine'… in good hands… I'm not sure that is better… I was in good hands… very good hands.

Christopher and Cassie shared some more good news. They and Louise have all been offered places on the PGCE courses that they wanted, so it seems that we will all be back at Uni in September. I tell them all about Dad and his plans to travel around Australia with his friend.

"Holiday in Australia for you next year then?" Christopher asks.

"How do you feel about it?" Cassie asks.

"What a holiday in Australia, or Dad going away for a year?" I ask, laughing.

"Your dad, of course!" Cassie says, scowling at Christopher.

"Obviously I will miss him, but it is such a good opportunity for him."

The week really drags by... Nicole and I win at bowling again, which Jess is not happy about. I did get to see Nicole for two nights which was good. I enjoy being with her so much, it is amazing, and tonight we are meeting Charlotte. It will be strange going to a gay bar with Nicole... it's been such a boring week, apart from the times I spent with Nicole, of course. I think I need to take up a hobby to entertain myself through the summer... what though? It needs to be something I can do on my own... swimming... no... not swimming... knitting? No... just no!

Music... yes! I can do something musical... clarinet... no... flute... no... saxophone... yes! My mum used to play the sax. I wonder if her old sax is up in the loft. I will ask Dad... he may not want me to play it... it might bring back memories that are too hard for him to revisit.

"Hi Dad!"

"Hi Sam! I thought you were out all day today?"

"No, I'm just out tonight with the girls"

"Oh yes, will you be staying out?"

Oh yes, that sounds like a plan... I could do with a night of passion... I want to have a go with the strap-on. I am sure we can think of a few other things to do too!

"Sam!"

"Sorry, and yes, I will stay out, I can have a drink then, and not drive!"

"Very sensible!"

Sensible... yes... that's what it is... it's sensible!

- Can I stay at yours tonight? x x x

- Let me think about that... x o x

- Yes! x o x

- I will drive to yours and leave my car there, then. Let's get a cab and then we can both have a drink! x x x

- Are you planning to take advantage of me? x o x

- Oh yes!!!!! x x x

- I love you x o x

Oh, that is the first time she has texted those three little words... I like it... I like it a lot... should I say it back... do I want to?

- See you about 7pm, then. I love you too gorgeous! x x x

- x o x

"Sam, are you having dinner before you go?"

"No thanks, Dad, I will grab something later, I'm going to have a shower and get ready now."

"Are you doing anything tomorrow?"

"Erm... no I don't think so, why?"

"I was hoping you might come clothes shopping with me?"

"Of course I will, are you thinking about clothes for Australia?"

"Yes, is that OK?"

"That's absolutely great, Dad, I will be home by 2. We could go then?"

"Brilliant! I might even treat you to lunch!"

I'm driving to see Nicole, I don't understand what is happening to me, I still get butterflies when I'm with her, she turns my world upside down and I love it. When I get there I tell her Dad's plans to go to Australia,

"Ooh, how do you feel about that?"

"Mmm… Well, I am sad because I will miss him so much, but I'm also really happy for him. It's the opportunity of a lifetime and he will absolutely love it. And… as an added bonus… you will be able to stay at mine for a change!"

We leave Nicole's house in a taxi at 7.15p.m.

"You are wearing that perfume again" she whispers, "You know what that does to me!"

"No, tell me! "I tease, grinning broadly.

She whispers the details into my ear and we both feel our level of arousal rising.

When we get to the pub, Charlotte is waiting at the door. She had only been there for a couple of minutes. I introduce her to Nicole and as we walk through the door Charlotte looks at me and mouths the word… 'Nice!' We both smile as Nicole leads us to the bar.

"What are we drinking, ladies?"

"Can I have a vodka and coke please?" Charlotte asks.

"Cider for me, please!"

The bar lady serves us our drinks and tells us to have a good night… oh I plan to… don't worry… a very good night…! We sit at a table and talk. We all have a good laugh together, it is really nice to feel so relaxed out in public with Nicole.

"Your friend is here again" Charlotte says, an hour or so later, nodding towards the brunette.

"She is not my friend, I don't even know who she is!"

"What's this?" Nicole asks.

"She can't keep her eyes off Sam," Charlotte says, "she was like that last week too!"

"I did notice her looking over this way," Nicole says. "I'm going to the bar."

"Charlotte, really, I think you are exaggerating, and actually, Nicole, I'm going to the bar, it's my round, OK?" I say, standing up... I don't know what I am going to say to the woman... what can I say? Oh God... hopefully something will pop into my head... I needn't have worried though, because the second I got to the bar she started talking to me. We stood talking for a few minutes, I could feel Nicole's eyes burning through the back of my head. As I say goodbye and head back to the table with our drinks, she gave me her business card, it's a smart, but plain business card with just her name and number on it.

"If you fancy a drink sometime, just give me a call!"

I slide the card into my jeans pocket, hoping that Nicole didn't notice – is she the jealous type? I don't know... would I be jealous if Nicole had just been given a hot woman's mobile number? Good looking? Do I think she's good looking? Yes... actually she is stunning... but I love Nicole... I'm very happy with Nicole... would I feel jealous? Yes, I bloody would!

I get back to the table with our drinks.

"What was that all about?" Nicole asks... did she see her give me the card? I would never call her... I will throw it away as soon as I get a chance... but did Nicole see? I guess not... or she would have said something.

"You won't believe it," I say.

"Try me?" Nicole says, quite sternly... Charlotte raises her eyebrows at me.

"Well," I say, "Do you remember I told you about the crazy Labrador, Rosie that used to jump up at all the runners along the beach?"

"Yes."

"Well, she is Rosie's owner, Harriet!"

"Right."

"I thought I knew her from somewhere, I just never connected the two. She was just telling me that Rosie ran out in front of a car and was so badly hurt in the accident that she had to be put down. Isn't that sad?"

Thankfully, at this point, Charlotte started talking… telling us about her dog that also had to be put to sleep, and the conversation somehow never got back round to Harriet and Rosie… well not yet…

We enjoyed the rest of the night, although I could tell that Nicole wasn't her normal self. Charlotte went to the toilet and came back very happy. Harriet's friend, Tracey, had asked her out, and they have arranged to go out on Wednesday… really, Charlotte! Of all the women in here and you pick HER friend… why? I see the look on Nicole's face… she could have picked anyone, so why Harriot's friend?

"Our cab will be here in ten minutes," Nicole says, looking at her watch.

Charlotte says goodbye and I tell her that I will text her to arrange another night out.

"It was really nice to meet you, Nicole!" she says.

"You too!" Nicole says, forcing a smile.

Charlotte goes over to the bar area and joins Harriet and Tracey. I go to hold Nicole's hand as we walk out and she says,

"Your friend is waving."

I wave back. The taxi ride back to Nicole's is a very quiet journey.

She opens the front door and we both walk in.

"Nicole," I say. "Have I upset you?"

"Really?" she says. "Tell me Sam, if I had taken another woman's phone number tonight, would you be OK with it?"

Oh… shit… she did see…

"But I never asked her for it… she just gave it to me! Is that what has been bothering you?" I ask, and I then take the card out of my pocket and throw it into the bin.

"Nicole, I would never have called her, I'm with you, and I'm in love with you," I say, walking over to her and cuddling her.

"Nicole, why are you crying?"

"Sam, I thought I was going to lose you, I know this is all new to you, I thought you might… well…"

"Nicole, I love you, I want you and only you, and don't you think I noticed the blonde woman who kept giving you the eye?"

"I didn't take her phone number."

"No, but she was watching you, I actually found that quite hot!"

"Did you?"

"Yes Nicole, it was actually a bit of a turn on, I could see she really liked you, however, I also knew I was the one leaving with you, and I'm the one who is going to spend the night making love with you."

"Sam…"

"Yes?"

"Shut up and get in the bedroom, I will grab us a couple of bottles," we smile at each other, the tension from earlier has gone.

I go into the bedroom and strip down to my Basque. I lie under the quilt as she comes in and passes me a bottle of cider, I ask her to put it on the bedside table and join me in bed. She strips off, climbs in and cuddles me. When she realises what I am wearing, she throws the quilt off.

"Oh my God" she says, looking from my eyes all the way down my body and then back up again. "Have you been wearing that all night? Oh, I really want you, right now!"

Her hand goes straight between my legs,

"You are wet!" she says.

"Really," I say, in a teasing voice.

Before I have time to think or say anything else her mouth is on me, licking me… oh God, that's hot…

"I'm going to cum!" I moan.

She sits up, "Oh we don't want that yet, do we?"

"Yes, actually, we do…" I plead. "Please!"

"Oh 'please', you really do want to cum!" she says, smiling wickedly and getting up off the bed.

"Where are you going?"

"Handcuffs…"

She's going to cuff me… hot… hurry up… touch me… make me cum! She puts the cuffs on, then she walks out of the room…

"Now where are you going?"

"One minute, don't worry!"

Don't worry? I'm cuffed to the bed… in a Basque… and she says don't worry! Thankfully, she quickly returns with a cup in her hand.

"What's in that?"

"Just warm water, don't worry!"

Don't worry! I'm cuffed… and you have hot water! Don't worry!

"What are you planning to do with it? "

"I will show you" she says, taking a mouthful of the water. She kneels between my legs and goes down on me, I can feel the heat, she sits up and takes a mouthful of her cold cider and does the same thing, warm water, cider, warm water, cider. She repeats this process about 4 times, I think.

"Oh wow, that feels amazing!" I moan.

"Good" she says, coming to lay beside me, touching and caressing all of my body.

"Nicole, what are you doing to me?"

"Making you horny, baby!"

"Please make me cum, I want to cum, I need to!"

"Oh you need to, do you? If I make you cum, will you look into my eyes as you do?"

"I will do anything you want, just please, please make me cum!"

"OK, baby!"

"I want to fuck you with your strap-on!" I say.

She moans as her fingers find my clit; we look into each other's eyes as I cum.

"That's so hot!" she pants, as she cuddles into me, my whole body is shaking. After a few minutes, I say,

"Can you undo the cuffs, please?"

We both giggle.

"Sorry I forgot about them."

"My turn!" I say. "Can I use the strap-on?"

"Yes" she says, handing me my bottle, we both have a drink and then she helps me with the strap-on… she made this look easy… what do I do? How? She looks at me, she must be guessing what I'm thinking.

"Don't worry!" she says, and she gets down on all fours.

"Sit behind me, on your knees and touch me," she directs. I do as she tells me… it's not long before we are both moaning, my hands are roaming all over her body, touching her breasts, then going between her thighs, my fingers slide inside her, then touch her clit. I guide the dildo inside her, she really moans as I slowly push it further inside her. I watch as it goes in… so horny… I pull it slowly out, I have to use my hand to guide it back in, this time I push my hips hard against her body holding it inside her. I bend over and play with her clit with my fingers,

"Oh God… I'm going to cum!" she moans.

I pull my fingers away, she moans, and says, "Please don't stop, baby!"

I move my hips, pushing into her and slowly pulling back out, and then watching it disappearing into her. Very slowly, then a bit faster.

"Are you watching it go in?" she pants.

"Yes!"

"Oh that's horny… go faster, baby… fast and hard…!"

I can't watch and do that at the same time, so I sit up a bit straighter and fuck her faster and harder, as she asked. It's not long before she orgasms. She screams with pleasure, and I hold her until the ripples of pleasure have finished. Then I pull out of her but stay on my knees and touch myself.

"Oh, I need to cum now!" I say.

She quickly turns and watches me… I am so wet that my hand is sliding around. I pull the strap-on off.

She puts her hand on mine, and stops me…

"Stand up!" she says.

My legs only just hold me up. She pushes me against the wardrobe and pushes my legs apart, and bites gently up my thighs, and sucks my clit very hard. As I cum, my legs give way. She holds me until I come back down to earth.

We crawl back onto the bed and she pulls the quilt over us, and we lie there together, sated, comfortable and secure together… no words are needed.

Chapter 20

The next two and a half months fly by. Christopher is doing really well and is now walking around on crutches. He and Cassie are still going strong. My feelings for Nicole get stronger every day... I didn't know it was possible to love someone this much... I still haven't told Dad about Nicole and me because he is off to Australia soon, and I don't want him to worry... or is that just my excuse? Is it just me being a coward? However, on the positive side, we have done all his shopping now and he is ready to go. He is really looking forward to it. It is lovely to see him so excited about something. I will miss him so much. Matthew's mum is still ill, and sadly, the future is not looking very good for her.

It is our birthday on Saturday! Just two days away. We have decided to have a joint party. There won't be loads of people there... just our friends and family. We have booked a function room in a hotel where we have stayed a few times. We have decided that we are going to have a joint party there every year.

"And who knows..." she teases "maybe this time next year everyone will know that we are a couple!"

She has been so understanding and never pushed me into 'coming out'... I don't think the time is right yet, what with Dad going away for a year... I'm nearly ready to tell the world... just not quite yet... our friends at the bar where we drink all know, of course, and Jess knows... I think that when Dad goes to Australia I will probably tell my friends... Louise will be surprised… she has had a lesson with Nicole every week and has no idea that we are a couple… Harriet is our friend now, although Nicole has never really taken to her fully since that first meeting. Charlotte is still with Tracey, Harriet's friend, so we often go out all together on a Saturday night. I have been having saxophone lessons, Dad was over the moon when I suggested it, he said,

"Mum would love the fact that you are learning, and using her saxophone."

I'm not very good yet, however, I am making progress.

The next few weeks are going to be very busy, our birthday party is on Saturday. We are both really looking forward to it and then Dad jets off the following Thursday. I start Uni a week after that, but luckily it's local to our house, so I don't need to move away. Dad has left money in an account to cover all the bills, and he has also put a few thousand pounds into my account. I wouldn't have been able to go back to Uni without him, he really is the best dad in the world! He has also bought me all the books I need for my course. I have got a part time job now at our local hospital, inputting data into a computer system, not exciting, but it gives me a bit of money in my pocket.

I'm going to see Nicole tonight, I can't wait… I have not seen her for three nights. Dad is out with Tom tonight, they are going to plan the first leg of their trip. They are not going to map the entire year out as they want to see where the journey takes them once they are out there. They are hiring a camper van and just hitting the road. I'm so pleased for them, they will have such an adventure!

When I get to Nicole's she seems to be a bit down.

"Are you OK, gorgeous?" I ask her.

"I am OK, but my mum isn't very well, I find it very hard when I'm this far away from her, I can't just pop round and see her in Dubai can I?"

"Oh no, that's not good." I say, joining her on the sofa and giving her a hug.

We sit there for a while, just cuddling.

"How are you?" she asks.

"Really good thanks, but it makes me feel sad seeing you so upset."

She looks at me and smiles,

"I am OK now that you're here! Shall we go and cook something nice for dinner?"

"Yes please, I'm starving!"

We go into the kitchen and look at what is in the cupboards and the fridge, and decide on Shepherd's Pie.

"I love cooking with you!" she says.

"Good, because I love cooking with you!"

The Shepherd's Pie is in the oven, and we have 40 mins to wait, so I start the washing up. She comes up behind me and starts kissing and gently biting the back of my neck, one of her hands slides up inside my blouse and undoes my bra strap, her hand is now cupping my breast,

"Excuse me…!" I say, feigning indignity.

"Shh, concentrate on your washing up, please!" she laughs, as her other hand slides down the front of my jeans and into my knickers,

"Oh, so you have knickers on today!" she says.

I can tell she is smiling. Her fingers start playing with my clit, her other hand is still cupping my breast, her fingers expertly find my nipple and squeeze it very gently… she is making me very aroused… I can't wash up… I can't concentrate… oh my… in a matter of minutes she makes me cum… I can hardly stand up. I put my head back so that it is resting on her shoulder.

"I love washing up here!" I say.

We both giggle. I turn around to face her.

211

"You're very bad! Very good… but very bad!" I say, "How long is the Shepherd's Pie in the oven for?"

"Why?"

"I want to take you into the bedroom and remind you of the alphabet."

She has her jeans off before I finish my sentence, she lies down on the floor and says.

"Don't waste time, show me here!"

I don't need to be asked twice… I start by gently biting her neck… that always sends her wild… I pull her blouse up and I nibble her nipple whilst my hand is pulling the crotch of her knickers to one side so that my tongue can get in to play with her clit and it does play. She is writhing around on the floor. I think I only get as far as "k" before she starts moaning,

"Oh, I am going to cum!" I hear her say very quietly, her body starts shaking then goes limp. She pulls me up to her,

"You are amazing!" she says.

"I'm shocked at how easily you drop your jeans… I trust you don't do that for just any woman!" I joke, and we both laugh.

We go into the living room, Nicole puts Ed Sheeran's Divide CD on. 'How would you feel?' is playing.

"Our song…" I say smiling at her.

"I know, dance with me baby?"

"What?" I laugh, letting go of my necklace.

"Dance with me, please?" she repeats, pulling me up off of the sofa.

We have a lovely dance and a kiss, I look her in the eye and say,

"I've never really thought about it before, but I don't think that I have ever done a slow dance with anyone."

"Well, I'm the lucky one then" she says, holding me tighter. "It's such a shame that we won't be able to dance like this on Saturday night at our party."

"I will ask them to play this song," I say, "and when they do, we will both know that I'm thinking about this exact moment, and about this lovely dance that we are sharing!"

"That's lovely, and just to let you know… I have booked a room at the hotel for us for that night… as a birthday treat for us both!" she smiles.

Dad won't think that's funny… he knows we are friends… he knows I stay here some nights… I will just tell him that some of the girls are staying overnight and meeting up for breakfast… I kiss her.

"Thank you!" I say.

The oven timer starts beeping and we sit at the table enjoying our delicious dinner, chatting and putting the world to rights.

"What are you wearing on Saturday, Sam?"

"I can't divulge information like that!" I laugh.

"Mm, how is work going? You have done quite a few shifts recently."

"Really well thanks, and what else is a girl meant to do when her sexy girlfriend is at work all day?"

"Sexy, eh?"

"Oh you are definitely that, but I will have to go soon, I need to spend some time with Dad."

"What, and leave me all alone to do the washing up? I helped you!" she smiles, with a twinkle in her eye.

"Oh yes, you really helped me, but not really with the washing up!" I stand up and help her to clear the table.

"You get off, then," she says. "I'm really looking forward to Saturday night, babe."

"Me too" I say, as I kiss her goodbye.

I drive home thinking about how lucky I am to be with Nicole. She has transformed my life! I smile contentedly to myself.

Friday morning comes… it's early and I'm running along the beach… the sun is shining… all is well in the world… tomorrow is my birthday… our birthday… party and a night in the hotel… I would settle for just the night in the hotel…

"Morning… yes it is a lovely day!"

I haven't thought about Rosie and Harriet until now…poor Rosie…

"Morning!"

Oh this is so nice… I love a bit of sunshine on my face!

"Hi!"

And also, I definitely need to run more often… I am finding it very hard-going this morning.

When I get home, Dad asks if I would like to join him for a cooked breakfast,

"Yes please, I'm just going to have a quick shower first!"

"OK, fried or scrambled?"

"Scrambled, please"

- *Morning, I have just been for a run and Dad is cooking my breakfast x x x*

- *All right for some!! Love you baby x o x*

"Sam it's ready!"

"Thanks Dad," I say, sitting up at the table.

"All set for your party?"

"Yes, I think so, and a group of us girls are going to stay at the hotel that night."

"Good plan!"

"Are you all set for Australia?"

214

"I think so… I'm starting to feel a bit nervous now! It's less than a week away!"

"You will have a great time, and please take loads of pictures, we will all really enjoy seeing them. You do remember how to share them on your iPad, don't you?"

"Of course I do, but, erm… you could show me just once more if you like, but remember Sam, Tom is an I.T. teacher, so I'm sure he can help!"

"He will have you making little slide shows with your pictures in no time!" I laugh.

"Now you are being silly, Sam!" and we both laugh.

"I'm going out with Jess today to buy an outfit for tomorrow night, would you like to join us, Dad?"

"You don't want me tagging along… do you?"

"Of course we do! We could get you a new shirt for the party too!"

"OK, I would love to join you, thanks!"

We have a really fun time shopping. It was really nice for the three of us to spend time together. We talk in him to buying a very nice pink stripy shirt which really looks good on him.

Dad drives us to the party. I get the key for the room from Reception and put my overnight case in there. The DJ is setting up and I see Nicole talking to him. Wow! She looks amazing… stunning… beautiful… she has a little tight skirt on… and a new blouse that I have not seen before… she comes over and says hello… breathe, Sam… remember your dad is standing next to you… act normal… stay calm…

"Hi Sam, Hi Mr…"

"Nicole!"

"Sorry, 'Harry', how are you both?"

"Good!" Dad and I say at the same time.

"Happy birthday Nicole! Now, will you excuse me ladies, I need to go and give Jess a hand" he says seeing her enter the hall with the boys and some bags, "I will catch up with you both later, I'm sure."

"Nicole, my darling, you look absolutely gorgeous!" I whisper.

"I do?"

"Sam, go and look in a mirror! You are lucky that I'm not ripping that little black dress off you here and now!"

"Later…" I smile.

"Please tell me you have knickers on, Sam."

"No I don't, and that's not all!"

"What do you mean?"

"I will show you later… we should go and say hi to our guests now… look who has just come in!"

"Sam, you can't just say something like that and then not tell me…"

"Oh, I can, and I am!" I say, walking away and smiling broadly.

Charlotte, Tracey and Harriet walk into the room, Nicole looks at me and smiles,

"I have you, she doesn't!" she says, in a very low voice.

We go and mingle with our friends, people are turning up now… there is Christopher and Cassie. Wow…! Christopher is walking with just one stick now, he has worked really hard at his physio exercises… they never did catch the bastard that knocked him over, the coward!

Nicole is talking to Louise, I need a drink… it's my birthday… 25 today! What would my mum think of me now… all grown up… in a relationship… I realise that I am fiddling with my necklace… it always gives me strength, and makes me feel close to my mum. Nicole calls me over to where she is talking to a group of people, she introduces me to her driving instructor friends from the 'Curry Night' group, and they all wish me a very happy birthday.

"They all seem very friendly!" I say, as we walk away.

"Fancy a dance?"

"Why not! It's a fast dance and lots of people are dancing."

"Wow, you can sing, you can dance, are there no ends to your talents, Sam? Why don't you dance on a Saturday night?"

"Because I would rather spend time with you, that's why!"

"Next Saturday we should dance, Harriett's tongue would be on the floor just like it is now, look at her!"

Jess joins us.

"Happy birthday ladies, are you enjoy yourselves?"

"Yes!" we both say, smiling at her, and then at each other.

"Ah… you two are just so sweet together!" she says.

"Jess!" I say looking around.

"No one heard, don't worry!" she says, raising her eyebrows at Nicole, they both smile.

"I'm getting a drink!" I announce, but right at that moment, Matthew walks over with two bottles of cider and gives one to me and the other to Nicole.

"Happy birthday, girls!"

"Where is mine, then?" Jess asks and we all laugh.

Later on in the evening, I ask the DJ to play, "How would you feel," by Ed.

"I have actually already been asked to play this song with the simple message 'You had me at hello!' I'm told the person it is intended for will understand," says the DJ.

Nicole moves closer so that she is standing beside me,

"Thanks baby, I remember!" she whispers.

I make sure no one is looking and then gently take her hand and brush it along the top of my leg,

"Are you wearing suspenders?" she asks.

"Maybe!" I say, walking away and smiling broadly. I look back and I recognise that look on her face, take me to bed, its pleading... and I will later... I am so looking forward to that...

"Hi Sam!"

"Oh, hi Harriett, how are you?"

"Really good thanks, and guess what? I have a new puppy, it's another Lab!"

"Oh that's lovely, what have you called it?"

"Coco"

"I take it that it's a chocolate lab?" That or it's a clown... "I look forward to seeing you both down at the beach!" I say, making a getaway. As I stand beside the bar, I feel someone's hand brush the top of my leg exactly where my suspender clips are,

"You are so bad!" I say to Nicole.

"I want to be bad with you, Sam!" she whispers gently into my ear.

Just then I hear my dad's voice, he is talking over the microphone and starts giving an embarrassing speech about me and some of the amusing things that I did when I was younger.

"Ah... he loves you and he is saying some very interesting things!" Nicole jokes. I look at her and wonder how she feels about my dad saying these things about me. I know that she has never known her dad, or shared this type of close relationship in her life, and that makes me feel a bit sad for her.

The party continues and everyone seems to have a good time. By around midnight, people start leaving. Jess and Dad have already gone home, and pretty soon everyone has left, and then there is just Nicole, Charlotte, Tracey, Harriet and me left in the function room.

"What's your song?" Tracey asks Nicole.

"'How would you feel?' by Ed Sheeran," Nicole answers, before I get the chance. Tracey gets her phone out of her bag and starts playing our song on her phone.

"You two can dance now…" she says.

"Shall we?" Nicole asks.

"If you and Charlotte do, then I will too" I say.

Harriet had just gone to the toilet, so the four of us start to dance, it was wonderful being able to be close to her at long last. My body has been aching to be close to hers. What a lovely idea of Tracey to play music on her phone for us! Nicole ran her hands up and down my thighs touching the suspenders,

"You can't do that here!" I whisper.

"Yes, I can!" she says, as she starts kissing my neck and ear.

"No, Nicole, not here!"

She kisses me and all of a sudden I don't care where we are.

"Take me to bed!" I say, urgently.

Harriet comes back into the room, and we all finally say our goodbyes, tidy up the last few chairs and tables and then arrange to meet up again next Saturday night.

A few minutes later, in the lift, going up to our room, Nicole can't keep her hands off me.

"Well… if you are going to look that hot, wear that perfume, have no knickers on… AND then tease me half the night with your suspenders… what do you expect?"

"There is probably a camera in here!" I say, looking around in the lift for one.

"I don't care… I want you and I want you now! Anyway, I know you find being naughty outside a real turn on."

"Maybe, but we are not actually outside!"

Saved by the bell, the lift bell, the door opens, and luckily our room is close by.

"Be honest!" Nicole says, "You do find it a turn on being naughty outside or somewhere we might get caught, don't you?"

I look into her eyes, say nothing and smile bashfully.

We fall in through the door of our room, she pins me against the inside of the door and runs her hands up my thighs, and then inside my dress, and then she plays with the top of my suspenders, moaning.

"God, Sam, I have been waiting all night to do this!"

She pulls me close to her, kisses me passionately and then turns me around so that my back is against her chest. She kisses my neck whilst her hands seek out my breasts. She is frustrated, she can't get to my breasts because my dress does not allow it, but I find it very horny that she's getting frustrated, she really wants me. She pushes me forward a bit and pulls at the zip, and before I know it, my dress is on the floor and my back is against her chest again.

"Oh yes," she moans, putting a hand inside my bra, she just leaves it there, her other hand goes down to the top of my legs, she moans almost like she had forgotten I was wearing them when she touches the top of my suspenders, she pushes my upper back gently so that I have to bend over, her hands roaming all over my suspenders.

"I have been waiting all night to fuck you, baby!" she says, so quietly that it's almost like she is talking to herself. I moan softly and that seems to snap her back into reality, her fingers push inside me, her other hand finds its way around my hip and onto my clit.

"Oh Nicole, you are fucking me!" I moan.

She is fingering me, it feels really nice.

"How many fingers have you got inside me?" I pant.

"3… is it too many or do you want more?"

"More! Please!" I say, surprising myself with my response.

She stands up and guides me to the bed. I lie on the bed as she rubs some baby oil onto her hand. She goes down on me, licking me hard with her tongue, sucking my clit, and as she is licking me her fingers start sliding inside me,

"Just relax, I won't hurt you!"

"Fuck me with your fingers again!"

She starts slowly, sliding her fingers in and out whilst still sucking me, oh God I'm going to cum! She stops sucking me as if she knew that I was about to cum and wanted to delay it... she is still fucking me, though.

"Oh my God, what are you doing? That feels amazing, but different! Do it slowly, don't stop but do it slowly... Oh my God... How many fingers?"

"My fist, baby."

She sucks my clit again, my head is going to explode... then she slides her fist out of me.

"I was just going to cum," I say urgently.

"I know, that's why I stopped... can we carry on outside on the balcony?"

"What? What if people see us?"

"Sam, it's after midnight and we are on the top floor, no one will see!"

She hands me a dressing gown and leads me to the balcony. She is right, it's positioned in such a way that it is very private.

"I'm standing here in my bra and suspenders and you are still fully dressed, Nicole, how did that happen?" I ask, as I start undoing her blouse, it falls to the floor followed by her skirt and underwear. Now she is naked!

"You are so beautiful!" I say, touching every inch of her body.

There is a bottle of champagne on the table next to us, I look at it, slightly confused.

"I had the staff put it in our room at 11p.m." she says, smiling. She opens it and pours us each a glass, then she hands one to me and clinks her glass with mine.

"Have you had a good birthday baby? I love you!"

"Oh yes! I think it has been the best birthday ever! What about you?" I say, tipping a small amount of my champagne just above one of her nipples. It trickles down her nipple and carries on south... I follow the path of the champagne with my tongue.

"Oh yes, go down on me baby, I love it when you do that!"

I am on my knees in front of her, sucking her clit. She falls forward a little bit and grabs the railing on the balcony to steady herself. I carry on sucking and licking her, my tongue slides inside her.

"Oh yes, fuck me with your tongue!"

I let my tongue play, darting in and out of her, she grabs my hair.

"Suck me again, baby, suck me now, hard!"

She falls against the railing as she cums; I look around, no one can see, no one else even seems to be awake, just us and the stars. I stand up next to her.

"Sam, you are fucking amazing, that felt so good! But you are getting cold, let's go inside, now."

We take our drinks and the bottle with us and lie down on the bed, drinking the ice-cold champagne.

"Shower?" I suggest.

"Oh yes!" she replies, smiling.

We spend almost an hour in the bathroom, in the bath, in the shower, on the floor.

"Are you going to be this good every birthday?" I ask her, after my fourth orgasm.

"I plan to be, if you'll let me."

I have three fingers inside her, fucking her gently. Then I slide my very wet fingers along to her clit, and this time I ask her to look into my eyes as she cums.

"Oh, that's too hot, I have never looked into some one's eyes when I cum... and oh... I like it a lot!"

222

"I love it!" I say.

"Shall we go back into the bedroom and finish our drinks?" she asks.

Wow… the clock is saying 3a.m…. is it wrong? It must be wrong… no, it's right… we get into bed, both naked in each other's arms, and we finish our drinks,

"I nearly forgot…!" she says, handing me a beautifully wrapped present. "I didn't want to give it to you earlier, because it is very personal."

"And your present is in my case, for exactly the same reason!" I say, jumping out of bed to get it.

We both open our gifts. She has bought me a lovely watch which she'd had inscribed. It says, 'I love you more with every minute'. I gave her a necklace with a gold heart pendant. I'd had it inscribed with the words 'How would you feel?'

"I love it!" we both say, at the same time.

"Will you put it on for me, Sam? I'm never going to take it off"

"Of course I will!" I say. As she turns her back to me, I kiss her neck and back as I fasten the necklace around her neck.

I smile and fiddle with my own necklace… isn't it funny, I think… we both had our presents inscribed… we lie in each other's' arms… hang on… her hand is in between my legs again… touching me…

"More?" I say.

"Yes, please!" she says, pushing my legs open… oh God… what is she doing to me…? I'm not sure I can cum again… hold that thought… I think… maybe… OK, I was wrong… I'm cumming… my whole body is shaking…

"Nicole, are you trying to kill me?" I say eventually, when my breathing has returned to normal.

"No, baby." she chuckles and snuggles closer to me. I can feel her getting heavier on my chest, her breathing is getting deeper and deeper… within a minute or two she's sound asleep.

"Night, night, gorgeous! I love you!" I whisper, as I kiss her forehead with a huge sleepy grin on my face.

Chapter 21

For a change, Nicole wakes before me. I awake to see her lying beside me, she must have been watching me sleep. She smiles, and I smile back.

"Do we have to get up already?" I ask.

"No, just cuddle in to me, baby, there's no rush today."

We lie there for ages cuddling, it's really nice, but eventually, I say,

"I should go soon, my darling. Dad is leaving this week and I would really like to spend a bit of time with him. We are going to Jess's this evening for dinner, which will be very nice."

"It's not a problem, baby, we have forever, and you need to spend as much time as you can with your dad before he goes on his travels," she says, smiling at me.

"Thanks, gorgeous, I should probably have a shower before I go, if you're interested?" I do love showers with Nicole... it's weird but when I shower alone now I always imagine her there with me... it has made showers much more interesting... but for now, I have the real thing... Nicole gets a puff ball and lathers it up, she washes every part of my body, so softly, so gently, and so sensually. She's so tender and loving with me... we don't make love... we don't even kiss... we just wash each other including our hair. I love washing her lovely blonde hair, and I love it when she washes mine. We get out of the shower and dry each other. As I stand in front of her, looking at her amazing body, the mirror catches my eye, I stare at her back, she has an absolutely perfect body, I think to myself.

"What you doing?" she asks.

"Admiring your gorgeous body; also I'm remembering the time you used the dildo on me and I watched in the mirror, I can still remember watching the expression on your face."

"Oh no…" she says, looking slightly embarrassed.

"Why oh no? It's a lovely memory, I have so many lovely memories of things you have done to me."

"With you, baby," she laughs, "it takes two, you know, we've done everything together and I also have many good memories and plan on making many more."

"Oh good! Something to look forward to, then." I say, my mind wandering off.

When I get home, Dad is checking and re-checking his list, bless him, makes me think of Santa Claus! I think he has checked it a hundred times already. I smile at him,

"You can never be too sure! Did you have a good night?"

"Very good thanks, not long until you go now… how are you feeling about it all?"

"Nervous, it's so different from anything that I've ever done before!"

"It will be amazing, Dad, just make sure you enjoy every minute!"

We get to Jess's house later that day, and find that Matty isn't there; he's at the hospital visiting his mum.

"They don't think she has got long to live, now." Jess tells us, very quietly so that the boys can't hear her.

"You should go and be with him!" Dad says.

"I want us all to have dinner together, Dad!"

"Why don't you go after dinner?" I suggest "We can stay with the boys, can't we Dad?"

"Of course we can, I will drop you at the hospital and come back and sit with Sam and the boys." he offers.

"That's really kind, but you must have lots to do though?"

"No, we were planning to stay and spend time with you all anyway, so please don't give it a second thought!"

"Thanks, Dad! Thanks, Sam!"

"No problem at all!" I say, letting go of my necklace.

We all sit down and enjoy a roast; Jess really does cook the best roast!

"How is everyone, Sam? The party went well, we had such a good evening! Christopher looked really good!"

"He's doing so well, and is working really hard at his physio. Charlotte and Tracey seem to be getting on really well together."

"And how is Nicole?" she asks

"She's OK, I think," I say, not looking up from my plate, "But her mum is not very well, which is really hard for her as she lives in Dubai."

"Oh that's not good, she didn't mention that in her e-mail!"

"She e-mails you?" I ask, a bit too quickly.

"Oh, it was just some pictures from the party last night."

"Can we have a look at them later, please?" Dad asks.

"Me too!" little Harry pipes up.

My mind is doing summersaults... I must ask later... how long have they been e-mailing... or am I thinking too much of it? It's just some pictures... but is it strange that Nicole has never mentioned it...?

Sitting around the table after dinner, we all look through the photos. There's a really nice picture of Nicole and me, I must get Jess to send that one to me later.

Jess gets up and starts to clear the table.

"No, Jess, you get off to the hospital, the boys and I can sort this out" I say.

Jess explains to the boys that she's going to see Nan at the hospital and that Dad and I are going to stay with them. Just before they leave, I ask her to give Matty and his mum my love.

I wash the dishes; John dries and little Harry puts them away. Then they beat me at Mario Cart... yet again! You would think that they'd get bored of beating me; however, they don't seem to! I guess it is an important role of an Auntie to be beaten at every computer game!

Dad comes back and then we all play a couple of board games.

"I told Jess not to rush home, I hope that's OK with you? I could always drop you off and..."

"Dad, it's..." I nearly said 'fine'. "It's OK," I say, fiddling with my necklace.

Matthew and Jess get home at ten. We had bathed the boys and got them into bed and finally to sleep, after two stories. Dad tells Matthew that he has decided to put Australia off for a while so that he can be here. Matthew wouldn't hear any of it.

On the way home, Dad and I discuss whether he should stay for Matthew's sake. I told him that I agreed with Matthew, there is nothing he can do and that Matthew was very adamant that he should still go.

Dad, Jess and I take the boys to the country park on Monday. It was Mum's favourite place to take us. We all had a good day and did lots of reminiscing. We took a picnic with us, just like Mum used to make.

I think Dad's arms were about to drop off pushing little Harry on the swing. We all had a really good time in the park, it was lovely seeing them having so much fun. Whilst they were playing on the slide, we told Dad that we understood how much he loved Mum, but that if he happened to meet someone whilst away, we would understand. He actually did have a brief relationship a few years ago but it never really went anywhere. He told us he had no plans to meet anyone special.

"We know, but if you do, please just remember that it's OK with us."

It was a very emotional day for Dad, Jess and me. Throughout the day I was aware that I spent a lot of time touching my necklace.

Another run on Tuesday morning... the weather is gorgeous... so many thoughts running through my head...

"Morning!"

Matthew's mum... dad... Nicole... always Nicole... she's always on my mind... she sent me a lovely text this morning...

"Morning!"

"Morning Harriet!" Harriet and Coco... Coco is much calmer than Rosie... still a Lab but much calmer... poor Rosie.

Harriet said, "Hi Sam, it was a great party, thank you!"

"Yes! It was a brilliant night! Glad you enjoyed it too! Really sorry, but I can't stop!" I say, as I wave and carry on running... was the party really only three days ago? It feels like weeks ago... I'm seeing Nicole on Thursday night... I can't wait... I have work tonight... I'm really enjoying this job, which surprises me... I think I will ask her if she wants to stay at mine for a change... Dad leaves on Thursday morning... and the plan is that Jess and I will take him to the airport... Matthew will be there for the boys... Dad has to be at the airport at 5a.m.

I spend the rest of the day with Dad, he has only checked his list about three times today.

"I do need to get some sun tan lotion," he says. "Fancy coming shopping?"

"Yes, let's do that!" I say, excitedly.

"We could have dinner out?" he suggests.

I could tell that Dad was getting more nervous as his departure date was getting closer, which is understandable.

It's the day before Dad's big adventure! Jess and I spend it with Dad and the boys. We take them to a park. They give Dad a card that they had made for him. It's fantastic; it's made of photos of us all that they had cut out and made into a collage. He promised them that he would keep the card safe in his suitcase, all the way around Australia.

That evening, Jess came around on her own and the three of us ate spaghetti bolognese together. My last little treat for Dad. We have to leave for the airport at 2a.m. so we had already decided that it would be best for Jess to stay over with us.

Dad was really excited, but kept checking that we were still OK with it, I told him again that we want him to go and enjoy himself. We had a very emotional evening, I sat deep in thought, fiddling with my necklace. Should I tell him… tell him about Nicole… tell him about me… tell him about us… no…it's too late… he goes in a few hours… I can't drop that bombshell on him just before he leaves the country for a year.

- *Night, night, gorgeous, I'm really looking forward to seeing you tomorrow, I need a cuddle x x x*

- *Me too baby, drive safely in the morning please x o x*

- *I will, I will text you when I get back home x x x*

- *Why don't you come here for a cuddle straight from the airport? x o x*

- *It will be about 6am, is that OK? x x x*

- *No problem, see you about 6 then, I can't wait x o x*

- *Thanks, I love you x x x*

- I love you too baby, drive safely x o x

We all go to bed and try to get a couple of hours of sleep. Well, I say all, I'm not actually sure that Dad did. At two o'clock in the morning, we put his case in the car. He only has one case and a piece of hand luggage, Jess and I laugh and say how impressed we are.

"I would have had to take about four cases!" Jess laughs.

"Jess, I'm travelling round for an entire year… I can't take too much!"

"I know, I'm just teasing you," she laughs.

"Do you think I have everything I need?" he asks, clearly panicking slightly.

"I'm sure you have!" I say, remembering how many times I saw him checking his list over the past few weeks. Santa! "And remember that they will actually have shops over there….it is not all deserts and spiders, you know!" We all giggle.

Dad tells Jess that he will fly home if Matthew's mum does pass away while he is away.

"Dad, Matthew doesn't want you to, honestly… We can deal with it. He said that he will be upset if you come home, you need to go and enjoy yourself!"

At the airport, we say a very emotional goodbye. We make him promise to Skype us often and to send lots of pictures. We will also send him pictures of the boys. We stand with Tom's family and wave them both off through the passport control gate. Jess asks if I would like to go back with her to her house. I tell her that I am going to Nicole's, and she was happy about that.

"I'm so glad that you two are happy, but I'm still a bit sad that you never felt able to tell Dad."

"I know, I did nearly tell him a few times this week. I just felt that it was too late; how could I tell him just before he left?"

231

"I know, it's just a shame he doesn't know how happy you are."

"I am happy, Jess, I'm really happy. I love her, I really do!"

"I know, Sam, and it will all be OK!"

I drop Jess off and then drive to Nicole's.

I use my own key to let myself in. I creep into the bedroom, get undressed and slide gently into bed beside her. I snuggle into her and she cuddles me without even waking. I wake up again just after 9a.m. but Nicole isn't there. I look at her pillow and there is a note on it.

I have a lesson 9–10 then I have a two hour gap, keep the bed warm for me x o x

I can't believe that I didn't hear her get up and get ready for work. I must have fallen back to sleep again, though, because suddenly she is cuddling me again. We start kissing, my hands roam all over her body, I place my hand between her legs, I realise that she's wearing the strap-on! Excitement rushes through my body. I straddle her, I pin her arms down with my hands, then run my hands down her arms and then across to her nipples. She moans, and that makes me even more excited. I carry on playing with her nipples. As I sit up and slowly lower myself back down onto the dildo. I feel it entering me. She starts playing with my nipples, they are very erect... she gently pinches them... oh God! I am going to explode... but she holds my hips and stops me rising again. I look at her, confused.

"Go down on me, please!" she moans.

I willingly oblige, unfastening the dildo to allow my tongue to play, ensuring that she cums almost instantly. Once the orgasm has passed, she puts the dildo back on and asks me to stand up. Again, I willingly oblige. She stands behind me and her hands are everywhere, all over my body, touching my breasts, running down my body. She turns me around and lifts me on to the dressing table. She kisses me and slides the dildo inside me, I am very wet. She walks to the wall carrying me, the dildo still inside me. She fucks me strong and hard up against the wall. My legs are around her waist. Finally, we both cum. It was just amazing… Incredible… we both end up in a panting heap on the floor.

"Fucking hell, Nicole! You are so hot!"

"You liked that, then?" she smiles.

"Oh baby, I like everything you do to me!"

"What about what I do to me?" she asks me, as her hand finds its way down between her own legs.

"Fuck, you are one horny bitch!" I say, as I watch her bring herself to orgasm again.

Afterwards, we smile at each other.

"Somehow, I need to get back to work now!" she says, getting up, taking my hand and leading me through to the shower.

Chapter 22

"I'm guessing your dad got off OK then, babe?" Nicole asks, later on, once we have both showered.

"Yes, he did and it was really nice that Jess and I were both able to be there, it was hard watching him disappear through Passport Control, it was very emotional."

"I bet it was, but at least you can still have contact with him."

"Yeah, I just wish now that I had told him about us."

"Well," Nicole says, "maybe we can both go and visit him in Australia and tell him together?"

I suppose we could do that... I will give that some thought... but not right now...

"How long have you got before you have to go?" I ask her.

"Not long now, babe, just time for some of your lovely eggy bread!" she smiles.

"OK," I say, getting dressed, I notice that she's watching me.

Just as we walk into the kitchen, my mobile phone rings, it's back in the bedroom, so I run through to answer it.

"It's Jess!" I shout back to Nicole, before I pick it up.

Nicole walks back in to the bedroom to see me sitting on the bed telling Jess how sorry I am, and asking what I can do to help.

"Could you pick the boys up after school, please?"

"Of course I can, do you want me to… to… to… tell them? OK, I will collect them and then take them out… if you need anything else please just call me… and please give Matthew my love."

Nicole gives me a hug,

"Matthew's mum?" she asks, knowingly.

"Yes, oh poor Matthew and Jess… Dad is still in the air. He will want to fly back, it will be so hard for Jess not having him here to support her. Jess and Matthew are adamant that they don't want him to come back. They want to tell the boys tonight about what has happened. I'm very glad about that. I would have told them if Jess had wanted me to, but it's much better coming from their mum and Dad, I think."

"Come and sit down a minute," Nicole says, patting the bed.

"Poor Matthew and Jess," I repeat. "Right, I need to call work and ask to change my shift… I am supposed to be working tonight."

"OK, you go call your work and I will cook breakfast." Nicole says, giving me another hug.

I call my manager, Lesley, and she says that it's OK to change my shift, I can work tomorrow night instead and also she wants to have a word with me!

"Nicole, why do you think she wants to see me? Do you think they are going to sack me?"

"For changing one night, Sam, I don't think so, don't worry about it!"

Don't worry? How can I not worry? I'm worried… very worried now!

"Sam, are you listening to me?"

"Sorry, I was miles away, what did you say?"

"I was asking what time you have to pick the boys up."

"Twenty past three from the school Reception. Jess will call the school and let them know it will be me picking them up, they know me, so it will be… fine… I have often picked the boys up, why?"

"Well, I finish at four today, so I was thinking… if you want… we could take them for something to eat and to the cinema or something…?"

"You are so lovely, Nicole! That sounds like a good plan! I will text Jess and just check that it is OK as it's a school night."

"Sam, I'm going to have to eat breakfast and run. I'm really sorry, I have to go, but you don't have to rush, you are welcome to stay here as long as you like."

"Mm, OK, why do you think my manager wants to see me?"

Nicole walks over to me and gives me a cuddle and says,

"Babe, try not to think about it, don't worry, you will find out tomorrow!" she gives me a kiss and apologises again for having to leave.

"Text me and let me know what Jess says, darling!"

"I will do, I love you!"

"I love you too, baby, and I will see you later!"

Jess agrees with our plan for the evening as it's not a normal night. Their Nan has just died, after all. She said they are in for a hard few weeks so it would be nice for them to have a treat.

I clear the dishes away, tidy up the kitchen and then just sit at the table for a while, lost in thought. Before I know it, it's 1 o'clock! Wow… Where did the morning go?

- *Are you OK, baby? Have you heard anything from Jess? x o x*

- Sorry, I am OK and Jess is cool with it, I don't even know what is on at the cinema, shall we meet there just after four and go from there? x x x

- OK, I will see you there, I hope you are OK, I love you x o x

- I will be and I love you too x x x

We watched a film that the boys wanted to see and then we went next door to Nando's for dinner. The boys thought it was brilliant going out on a school night. I just kept thinking about how their bubble would burst once they got home, and heard the sad news.

"God, I remember the last time I was at this cinema!" I whisper to Nicole.

She looked at me, not understanding, then I saw in her eyes as the penny dropped. She also remembered, smiled, and said,

"Oh yes, the night that Jess found out!"

We take the boys home in my car. When we get to Jess's, it is very apparent that she has been crying.

"Come in!" she says, opening the door.

"I think we will leave you to it," I say, "if that's OK with you?" I can only imagine how hard it will be for them to tell the boys about their Nan.

"OK, thank you so much for tonight, Sam, thank you Nicole! What do you say, boys?"

They both run back out to the front door and give us big hugs,

"Thank you!"

"You have both been really well behaved tonight, thank you boys." Nicole says.

I give them both a kiss and try not to cry. I hug Jess and then Nicole says,

"Jess, if you need anything at all, please just call! We will help in any way that we can."

"Thanks Nicole, and Sam! I will call Dad in the morning and then call you."

She can see I'm struggling to hold back the tears and she goes quickly inside, and closes the door.

We walk to the car and my tears begin to flow. Nicole takes my car keys out of my hand and opens the passenger door for me to get in. I look at her,

"I'm insured to drive any car, so don't worry," she says, as she gets into the driver seat.

"I wasn't thinking that, I was thinking how lucky I was that Dad picked you! He could have picked any driving school in this entire area… but yet he picked you!"

She smiled at me and said,

"Oh, so it's all your dad's fault then… I'm glad he picked me and even more glad that you picked me baby! Do you want to come back to my house tonight?"

"Is that OK?"

"Of course it is, do you really need to ask?"

It has been a long stressful day. We get in and go straight to bed. I am in tears again, Nicole cuddles me.

"Baby, you've had a rough couple of days, just let it all out!" she says, kissing away my tears.

"I love you!" I say, in between sobs.

"Good, because I definitely love you!" she says, cuddling me in tighter.

"It's awful for Matthew, Jess and the boys" I say, "The boys are too young to understand any of this!"

"I know," she says. "However, they have their mum, dad and two Aunties now!"

"Two Aunties, I like that!" I say, snuggling into her.

I kiss her and say, "Thanks for being you, night, night."

She kisses me back and says "Night, night baby, sleep well."

I feel safe… I feel loved… I lie in her arms wondering what my manager wants to see me about… what does she want? I hope my dad has arrived safely… I hope that Matty, Jess and the boys are OK… I am sure that Matty is devastated. But he has Jess with him to help him through this awful time. I let go of my necklace just as I fall asleep.

Chapter 23

We wake early and share a sensual shower. Nicole's first lesson begins at eight.

"How is Louise getting on with her driving?" I ask, as we are getting dressed.

I really must give them a call… we've not been in touch for a while… we are registering at Uni this week… I am in on Thursday… I'm not sure what day their registration is… maybe we could all meet for lunch?

"Yeah, she is doing OK!" Nicole giggles.

I look at her in a confused way,

"Sorry, I was just thinking that I don't look forward to her lessons anything like as much as I used to look forward to yours!"

"Nicole! You are so bad!" I giggle. "But I'm very glad that her lessons are not as exciting as mine!"

"Oh… exciting, were they?"

I smile "Oh yes… very exciting, I couldn't wait for you to pick me up so that I could find out what I was going to learn!"

"Do you think I could put that on the advertising leaflets?" she asks, with a glint in her eye, walking over to me and giving me a kiss. "Is it still exciting?"

"Oh yes, very exciting and that was a nice kiss," I say, letting go of my necklace.

"Are you happy, baby?"

"So happy Nicole, you make me very happy, are you happy too?"

"Happier than I have ever been before" she says, giving me another kiss, "But I do need to get going or I will be late! Will you let me know how things go with your manager and if Jess needs anything please?"

Oh God… my meeting… with my manager… what does she want? I forgot about that… how could I forget?

"I will," I say and give her a kiss goodbye.

"Don't worry about it Sam, text me later, babe!"

Don't worry…!

"Hold on," I say, "I need to drop you off at the cinema to pick your car up"

"Oh I forgot about that! Thanks babe."

After dropping Nicole off, I drive home. It's really strange here without Dad, no little notes on the fridge and no-one to ask how my day has been. I call Jess and there is no answer… I wonder where she is… it's not like her to not be in… I leave a message after the tone… I hate leaving messages…

"Hi guys, it's only me, just calling to see how you are and whether I can do anything, call me when you get…"

"Hi Sam, I'm here, I'm here, I have just got back from taking the boys to school."

We have a long chat, she said the boys were upset when she explained what was happening, but that is to be expected. She said that Matthew is being very quiet, which is also understandable. She also said that Dad got there safely, he knows the news and has accepted that Matthew does not want him to fly back. I gave her Nicole's love and asked if there was anything we could do; she thanked me but said there isn't anything to be done yet and explained that they are waiting to collect the death certificate before they can arrange the funeral. I ask how she is and she said that it hasn't really sunk in yet. I

241

guess she hasn't had much time to think about it what with worrying for Matthew and the boys.

"You are last in line when you are a mum," she admits. I told her to call me if she needs anything. I told her about the meeting with my manager this morning.

"Oh, that's exciting!" she said.

I think it's terrifying… what does she want? What is she going to say to me? I guess I will find out soon…

"Don't worry about it, Sam, you haven't done anything wrong… have you?"

"No… well, I don't think I have!"

"Don't over think it, I know what you are like… just let me know how it goes, please!"

"You have quite enough to worry about!" I say to her.

"Sam, just go and find out what it's all about and then let me know."

"Thanks, I love you and I wish I could do more to help!"

"Knowing that you are there is helping me, little sis, and I might need your help over the next few weeks with the boys."

"Anytime, you know that." I think she was trying to make me feel needed, however, she knows that I will do anything for her, Matthew and the boys.

The meeting with my manager lasted for forty minutes. When I came out afterwards, I sat in a coffee shop for ages cuddling a cup of hot chocolate… what should I do? I don't know… I sit there on my own… trying to decide… Ed Sheeran is playing, oh no….no, it's not on the radio, it's my phone, it's Nicole!

"Hi babe, are you OK? Have you had your meeting?"

"Yes, sorry, I forgot to text you, I have been sitting here trying to decide what to do."

"That's OK, why? What happened? Is it OK? Are you OK?"

"Yes, she said she wanted me to go full time!"

"Oh I see… but what about Uni?"

"Well, that's what I'm trying to work out. I was thinking that maybe I could defer my entry for a year and just see how the job goes…what do you think?"

"Will it be doing what you are doing now?"

"Yes, and much more… she also said I would have the opportunity of promotion if I wanted it!"

"And she offered you the job there and then?"

"Well, she said there would have to be interviews, however I would stand a really good chance as I am successfully carrying out parts of the work already and they like the way I work."

"Oh, lots to think about then, when's the closing date?"

"Next Friday, a week today."

"Would you like to meet up tonight and discuss it?"

"Yes please!"

"How are Jess and Matthew?"

"Well… they are as good as can be expected under the circumstances, I gave her your love and best wishes"

"OK, listen babe, I have got to go… do you want to come around about seven?"

"Why don't you come to me, I will cook us some dinner… oh, and bring your toothbrush!"

"Oh, I see… Are you assuming that I want to stay with you?" she giggled.

"Don't you?"

"Of course I do, see you at seven, babe, I love you!"

I look round the coffee shop to see if anyone is listening, and then I reply quietly,

"I love you too!"

Seven o'clock comes and goes and still no sign of Nicole, I try calling her mobile but it's constantly engaged.

- *Running late… sorry… will explain when I get there… which should be about eight x o x*

It's lucky that I cooked Shepherd's Pie for tonight… I can just leave it in the oven on very low… it's not like her to be late… she has never been late… I wonder what has happened… I hope she's OK.

I take the opportunity to call Cassie. Everything is good with them and Christopher is doing really well with his recovery. I tell her that I'm considering deferring Uni for a year, and all about the job. She said that it sounds like a good idea.

"Nothing to lose!" were her actual words.

I also give Jess a call, and she says pretty much the same thing. She said that the boys were very upset and full of questions about dying and what happens to the body etc. all questions that only children ask.

Nicole finally turns up at eight-thirty, looking very flustered, she walks into the kitchen and I hand her a cider, and ask her,

"Are you OK?"

"No," she replies, bursting into tears.

I hold her close to me and she tries to tell me what's wrong but I can't work out what she is trying to say through all her sobs.

"It's OK," I tell her, "take your time, you're scaring me… what has happened?" I guide her into the living room, and we sit on the sofa… is she going to dump me? Is it all over? Are we over?

"Is it me?" I whisper.

"No, Sam, it's… it's my mum!"

"Take your time, breathe." I say… thank God it's not me… we are not over… oh God… her mum… what's happened? I hope she hasn't died… Nicole gathers herself a bit.

"That's why I'm late."

"Nicole, that's not an issue, please tell me what has happened?"

"My mum's friend called me a while ago and said that Mum isn't in a very good way, I need to fly out there. Her dementia is getting worse and she keeps putting herself into dangerous situations. She set a tea towel alight on her gas hob yesterday and only just got out of the house in time. She inhaled a lot of smoke but the firemen were able to get the fire out very quickly, so there was not too much structural damage… just smoke damage."

"So you need to go out to Dubai?" I ask.

She just looks at me,

"Sorry, silly question, she lives in Dubai, so obviously that's where you need to go."

She sighs, "It's OK, I know it's a lot to take in, I wasn't expecting it either."

"How long for?" I ask.

"I don't know Sam, it could be for a few weeks!"

"So, have you been arranging your travel? Do you need any help? What can I do for you, darling?"

"I have just booked an outward flight, I have spoken to the driving school and they are going to get another instructor to cover my lessons while I'm gone. I can't book a return flight yet as I don't know when it will be."

"Oh, my darling," I say, giving her a big hug. "When do you fly?"

"Ten o'clock."

"Tonight?" I gasp.

"No, tomorrow night. I would really still like to spend the night with you, if that's OK?"

"Of course it is," I say, and we sit there holding each other for a while, trying to come to terms with the news.

"What smells nice?" she asks.

"Oh shit, it's the Shepherd's Pie," I say, running into the kitchen. "Would you like some or do you want to wait for a while?" I shout back towards the living room.

"I would love some, I'm starving, I haven't eaten all day. Mum's friend called me at around 3p.m. and I haven't stopped since, I didn't realise how hungry I was until I smelt that… it smells delicious!" she says, joining me in the kitchen.

I start dishing it up, and ask Nicole to grab us both another cider from the fridge.

"Why didn't you call me? I could have helped you!"

"You've had enough going on recently, and, to be honest, I haven't had time to think, this is the first time I have sat down, I'm sorry I came in in such a state."

"Don't be silly, I totally understand!" I say, giving her a huge bear hug.

We eat dinner and pretty much go to bed straight afterwards, we don't get much sleep… we just cuddle and talk for hours.

"I have decided that I'm going to go for the job, if I don't like it I can always go back to Uni next year." I announce in the middle of the night.

"Oh Sam, I'm sorry, we were meant to be discussing that, I totally forgot, that sounds like a good plan though!"

"Hey, don't worry, you have had quite enough to deal with today!"

"I'm sorry I won't be here to support you with that and with Jess and Matthew," she says.

"Nicole, you need to go and look after your mum, don't worry, I'm not going anywhere."

"Thank you, baby, for being so understanding!"

We make love much later, well into the early hours of the morning, slowly and gently, with no toys or gadgets, just tender, sensuous love.

Dad... Matthew's mum... Nicole's mum... the job... Uni... I can't believe how much has happened in the last week... at least I can drive and I have a car... thanks Dad! That will help... oh, that makes me think...

"Do you want me to take you to the airport?" I ask Nicole.

"Oh, would you Sam? I hadn't even given that a thought, thank you!"

I text Charlotte and explain what is going on and tell her that we will not be going out tonight as Nicole has to go to Dubai. She tells me to give Nicole her love. We drive round to Nicole's house, and I help her to pack.

"I'm really going to miss you, baby," she says.

"Not as much as I'm going to miss you," I say, giving her a cuddle.

Before we know it it's time to leave for the airport.

"At least you are not going for a year!" I say, thinking about Dad and playing with my necklace... It was an emotional goodbye with Dad... just days ago... was that really just days ago? It feels so much longer... but it really is just days...

I drive into the drop off section at the airport, I don't think I can go into the airport with her. The security guard tries moving us on before Nicole is even out of my car. We have to say a rushed goodbye, we hug, and I make her promise to Skype me. She walks away.

"I hope your mum is OK!" I shout after her.

She runs back and kisses me.

"I love you baby!" she says, and then she walks away without looking back.

I don't care if anyone saw her kiss me. The security guard is rushing me, I let go of my necklace and drive out of the airport with tears rolling down my face.

No Dad... No Nicole... I don't want to be alone... I haven't even had the chance to tell Jess what is happening yet... I pull into the garage and fill the car up with petrol. I text Jess to see if she is around.

- *Yes, what's up? X*

- *Can I pop round? X*

- *Yes of course you can little Sis, are you OK? X*

- *Yes, I will explain when I get there x*

When I get to Jess's house, Matthew is just going to bed, he looked absolutely shattered, but he has had a rough few days, bless him.

"I am so sorry to hear about your mum!" I say, giving him a hug,

"I should go," I say, looking at Jess.

"Thank you, Sam, and please don't go on my behalf" Matthew says, "I will be asleep the second my head hits the pillow."

After Matthew walks upstairs, Jess turns to me and asks,

"What's up?"

"I just didn't want to be alone tonight," I say.

"Cider?" she asks.

"I can't, I'm driving!"

"Crash on the sofa, Sam, and then we can have a drink and a catch up."

I smile at her, we spend the next two hours discussing the past week, Dad, Matthew, his mum, the boys, Nicole going to Dubai, and all about the job versus Uni. We drink a bit too much and put the world to rights. I decide that I am definitely going to apply for the job. My manager has told me how to apply, it's all done online now. I will do that over the weekend. We get some sleep but not much, it's a good thing Jess doesn't have to get up for the school run. Jess ended up falling asleep with me, downstairs on the other sofa.

I drive home in the morning, have a shower and then go back to bed for a few hours. When I wake up I go for a run, none of the usual people I see are on the beach as I am much later than normal. Thoughts... I have so many thoughts running through my head... it really helped talking to Jess last night... she is a good sister... she knows me so well... it's really good that she knows about Nicole... about us... about how I feel... I can be myself with her... I can tell her anything...

"Morning!"

Why haven't I heard anything from Nicole...? I hope she got there safely... I hope she's OK...

When I get back home there is a voicemail from her on my mobile. She's safely there with her mum. I can relax a little now. But I miss her so much already. I complete the job application, my finger lingers over the send button... shall I... oh, why not? I hit the button. I also send an e-mail to Uni asking to defer my course for a year. Oh, maybe I should have waited to make sure that I do actually get the job... oh God... I really should have thought of that before sending that last e-mail!

Chapter 24

Thankfully, I did get the job. I've been in post for three weeks now and I'm really enjoying it. Matthew's mum received a really nice send off. Her funeral was attended by lots of her friends and family. The boys didn't attend. Jess and Matty gave them the choice to attend the funeral, or not and explained to them that it wasn't really a place for children. They both agreed that they didn't want to go. But, the day after the funeral, Jess, Matty and I took the boys to the park that our mum used to take us to. We all released balloons with personal messages written on them into the sky for Matthew's mum to catch. I also added a message to my mum, and I stood holding my necklace as we watched the balloons soar high up into the sky.

Nicole? Well… Nicole has been gone for six weeks and six days. She e-mails and skypes me every day but I miss her terribly; I just want to cuddle her, kiss her, touch her, make love to her. We still have no idea when she will be back. It's breaking my heart. Dad is happy and having great adventures in Australia, which is good. He Skypes when he can and sends us a postcard every week telling us what he has been up to which is lovely… but… Nicole… oh God, I miss her.

E-Mail:

Hi Jess,

How is Sam?

There's still no change with my mum; I'm now her full-

time carer, which of course I want to do for her, but I
miss Sam so much, I can't even put that into words.
I am glad the funeral went well and that you are OK.
I am missing home and Sam most of all.
X Nicole X

E-Mail:

Hi Nicole,
Sam is at least enjoying her job; she misses you terribly
and just stays in most nights which is extra hard for her
as Dad isn't even there to keep her company. I am sorry
to hear that your mum continues to need your support,
this must be very hard for you. Make sure that you take
care of yourself as well as her.
Matthew is getting there and the boys are OK, children
tend to bounce back quite quickly, don't they!
Love to you and your mum
Jess X

I phone Jess to see how they all are, and she invites me over
to theirs for dinner.

"I don't mind if I do, thank you very much."

What she didn't say was that football is on the TV and the
three men in the house are all watching it.

"Have you heard from Nicole?" she asks me.

"Yes, we Skype as often as we can but it's not the same,
Jess, I miss her so much!"

"I know you do, but she wouldn't want you sitting in alone
every night, you know? You need to go out with your friends
and let your hair down a bit. When was the last time you saw
Charlotte and that group?"

"The week before Nicole left. I'm not sure that I want to go there without her, though. It would just make it even harder for me to come home to an empty house, afterwards."

"You meet the ladies on a Saturday night, don't you?"

"Yes, why?"

"Would you like me to come with you tomorrow then? Matthew can look after the boys."

"I'm not sure…" I say.

"How about we go out just for one drink. If you are OK we will stay a bit longer, if not we can come back here and have a drink?"

"Mm…" but before I can say anything, she adds,

"You would be doing me a favour to be honest, I can't remember the last time I went out… oh yes, I can… it was your birthday party"

Oh I don't know… it's…. it's where I go with Nicole… I don't know if it would feel a bit strange… she looks at me with those puppy dog eyes and I cave in.

"OK, but if I feel uncomfortable we leave? Deal?"

"Yes, Sam."

Louise, Christopher and Cassie have all started back at Uni. Cassie told me that Louise is having second thoughts about teaching… inwardly, I laugh… out of all of us she was the one who was 100% convinced she wanted to teach… she wouldn't entertain even looking at different options… I hope she works out what she wants to do…

- *Hi Charlotte, are you out tomorrow night? X*

- *Yes, are you joining us? Is Nicole back? X*

- *Sadly she isn't, but Jess and I are planning to pop in for a drink X*

- Lovely, I hope to see you both tomorrow night then X

Matthew was happy to look after the boys.

"Yes, boy time!! We can connect the X-box up to the television in the sitting room with no nagging!" he laughs and all three of them giggle. Little Harry announces,

"I prefer playing the X-Box with Aunty Sam!"

This makes us all laugh because we all know that he only prefers playing the game with me because I am the only one he can beat! Matthew insists that he and the boys will drop us off at the pub and also give us £20 for a taxi home.

"Have a drink, have some fun! You both deserve it!" he says, "Have you got a new perfume on, Sam? It smells nice."

"As opposed to my normal horrible smell?" I laugh.

"No, I didn't mean that at all" he laughs, slightly embarrassed, and I laugh with him.

"No it's not new, just new for tonight and I am very impressed with your powers of observation!"

Jess looks at me, realizing immediately why I have a different perfume on tonight,

"Was it Nicole's favourite?" Jess asks me when Matthew is out of ear shot.

"Was it?" I say, looking at her sternly.

"Is it, I meant," she says, quickly correcting herself.

"Yes, my normal one is Chanel No. 5, but tonight I am wearing Burberry."

Jess gives me a hug.

We walk into the bar and Charlotte waves to get our attention. Our group of friends are all standing near the dance floor. We indicate that we are going up to the bar to get a drink, and the bar lady comments that she hasn't seen me for a while. I just smile. Drink in hand, I take a deep breath and we join Charlotte and the others. Jess knows Charlotte, but no-one else, so Charlotte does all the introductions which I am glad about as there a few newcomers to the group that I don't know, either.

Once I have a few drinks inside me, I begin to relax, and on our fourth trip to the bar, Jess asks me who the stunning brunette is that can't keep her eyes off me.

"Come to think of it half the women in here can't take their eyes off you!" she says smiling.

I say, "That's Harriet, she's just a friend!"

Jess raises her eyebrows at me and then heads off to the toilet. I turn around and Harriet is right behind me.

"Hi Sam!"

"Hi Harriet, how are you?"

"I'm good thanks, is there any news on when Nicole will be back? She has been gone a while now, hasn't she?"

"Seven weeks today," I say. "Not that I'm counting. How's Coco?"

"Really good, thanks!"

Jess comes back, and I introduce her to Harriett. Jess has an amused look on her face,

"What have you done?" I ask, raising my eyebrows.

"Well, I went into the Ladies and was chatted up! A lady was trying her hardest to get me to go on a date with her!"

"Do you want to go?" I asked her, laughing,

"No I don't, I'm flattered though! I can't remember the last time I was chatted up or asked out on date"

"Matty, I hope," I say, and we all laugh.

Ed Sheeran comes on, and loads of people are dancing,

"Our song!" I say to Jess.

She just smiles and holds my hand,

"God, I miss her, Jess."

"I know, Sam, I know."

Harriet says her goodbyes as she has an early start tomorrow. She is running a 10k race... I respect her for that... I wonder why I have never seen her running... every time I see her when I am out running she is just walking... with her dog... strange... very strange...

"So," Jess says, as she watches Harriet walk out of the door. "How many seconds after I left you did it take for Harriet to corner you?"

"We are just friends, I would never cheat on Nicole... and I mean that... I love her!"

We announce to the group that it's time to order our taxi. Charlotte insists that she'll take us home, she hasn't been drinking tonight as she is on antibiotics. Jess says that it's OK as long as we give her some petrol money. However, Charlotte wouldn't take any money.

"You live on my way home, I drive past your house! Come on... get in!"

All four of us get into Charlotte's car. Tracey has been very quiet all night... I must text Charlotte tomorrow and find out why... I wonder if they are not getting on very well... at least they are in the same country... that's a start!

It's nearly midnight before we get home. We try to work out what time it is where Dad is, this takes us a little while as we are both quite tipsy, and we just can't stop giggling!

"It's 10a.m., I think" I say, eventually, working it out.

"Let's try then..." Jess says, getting her iPad out.

We skype Dad and he answers straight away,

"That was strange, I had just picked my iPad up to e-mail you and it started ringing," Dad said. "How are you both?"

We giggle!

"Hi Sam, Hi Jess... have you both been drinking, by any chance?" he asks, laughing.

"Maybe just a little!" Jess says, trying to act sober. It doesn't work; we tell him what's going on, which isn't actually very much our end. He tells us what he and Tom have been doing – it comes to something when your sixty-year-old Dad is having much more fun than you are. He looked so well and so tanned already, although it's only springtime there. I'm so pleased that he's enjoying his travels, it was really lovely to see him so happy!

"Give the boys a kiss from me!" he says, just before saying goodbye.

"Bless him, he always says that!" Jess says, as she staggers up the stairs to bed, falling up about every third step.

"Sleep well!" she says. I get the quilt out of the cupboard and snuggle up on the sofa… what a good night… such a shame that Nicole wasn't there… then it would have been a perfect night… I fall asleep thinking about Nicole and how much I'm missing her. I sometimes think that I am going to wear my necklace away by touching it so much.

I drive myself home in the morning, I have got lots of housework to do. Working full time and running a house is hard work… it makes me appreciate more how Dad managed all that as well as raising two of us… he really is an amazing man.

"What are you doing, Jess?"

"Just emailing Nicole, Matthew, I won't be long."

"Be careful! I don't think Sam would like it if she knew you two emailed each other!"

"It's not very often, I think I have only emailed her three times, and only because we both love Sam and want to make sure that she is OK."

E-Mail:

Hi Nicole,

I actually managed to get Sam out for a drink last night, we had a good time and a woman even tried chatting me up in the toilets, that was a first!

Half the bar were looking at Sam and she didn't even notice, she loves you so much.

I hope your mum is OK.

Love Jess X

I spend most of the day doing housework and ironing. Now that I work in an office I have to dress smartly, so everything has to be ironed. Oh, I miss my jeans, but at least I don't have Dad's shirts to iron now… although… I wouldn't mind ironing them… it would mean that he was here with me… no Dad… no Nicole… but I am starting to make friends at work now… which is nice.

E-Mail

Hi Jess,

I am glad you got Sam to go out, I miss her so much and love her even more.

I don't think it is fair to ask her to wait for me… because I have no idea how long I will be here, there is still no change with Mum… the doctors have said that it could possibly be years.

Jess… sit down while you read this… I have put a lot of thought into what I am about to tell you, in fact, I have thought about little else. I know she won't listen if I tell her not to wait for me, but I have a little plan that I think may work.

She won't like it and neither do I very much, but I can't sit back when I know she has put her life on hold and is just sitting there waiting for me… that's not fair… and I have no idea how long that wait will be.

I have to ask you to please NEVER to tell her about this email. I urge you to understand how much I love Sam, but she will have no problem meeting someone else… you said it yourself, half of the bar were looking at her. She is absolutely stunning and has a personality and a heart to match her looks. I know that you will be there to help her, and support her to move on, but please never forget how much I love and care for her, please take care of her and make sure she has a happy life.

I'm sending my love to you all.

Heartbroken in Dubai,

    X Nicole X

- Sam I need to Skype you tonight, will you be around at 6pm your time? x o x

- Yes, I can't wait to see you and hear your sexy voice, I love you! x x x

Work is very busy today which is good as it makes the day go much more quickly… only a few hours until I get to talk to Nicole… I can't wait… I was going to try and get my haircut tonight… it will have to wait until tomorrow night now!

6p.m. comes at last. I sit at the table with my iPad open and my drink next to me… come on Nicole! Call me! I have been looking forward to this all day… I wait and wait, it's nearly 6.20… why hasn't she called? I will leave it another ten minutes and then text her… Oh, no need, she is ringing, at last.

"Hi," I say, with excitement running through my body… how can she still make me feel this way? She looks terrible.

"Are you OK, have you been crying? Is your mum OK?"

"Sam, I have to tell you something and I'm afraid that you're not going to like it."

Not going to like it… what does that mean… oh no, is she staying out there even longer? How much longer? This is so difficult… I love her… I just want to be with her…

"Sam, listen to me please, this is really hard for me to say."

I don't like the sound of this… is she never coming back?

"You know how special you are to me and what an amazing time we've had."

"Nicole, you're scaring me!"

"I'm really sorry, Sam, and there is no easy way to say this... but... we need to end our relationship."

"What? No! Why? We can get through this... I will wait for you, however long it takes!"

"Sam! Listen! I don't want you to wait, I am selling my apartment and I am going to stay here, in Dubai."

"I will move out there with you, whatever it takes... I need to be with you!"

"It won't work, Sam."

Why is she saying this... I clutch my necklace... I don't understand... why?

"Why... have you met someone else?"

The silence went on forever.

"Nicole?"

"I'm so sorry, Sam, yes I have!"

And she was gone... just like that... gone...

She has left me.

She has found someone else.

She has gone.

I go to bed, my clothes still on.

I put Ed on replay... at full volume...

I can't believe it.

I can't even cry.

What do I do now?

Who am I?

What next?